Praise for *On Two Feet and Wings*

'Abbas Kazerooni's predicament is set firmly in the real world...Abbas is cheated and treated harshly at times but his belief in people's kindness and truth as the way to freedom is uplifting.' *The Australian*

'As absorbing as anything Dickens might have written...Immerse yourself in this plucky character's story, and educate yourself about what it is like for a child in a world of dispossessed people.' *Reading Time*, Australia

'*On Two Feet and Wings* is written simply and often deals with mundane challenges...But Abbas's tale is so absorbing it reads like a stomach-clenching thriller.' *The Times of India*

'A story that is deeply moving, its piquancy enhanced by the sombre thought that all the episodes of survival against such odds are based on the truth.' *The Telegraph*, India

'It's an astonishing story that makes you want to hug decent people such as Ahmed the taxi driver and Murat the hotelier who helped Kazerooni without taking too much advantage.' *Independent on Sunday*, UK

'A riveting read. With the pace and tension of a good novel, this makes for an engrossing read.' *The School Librarian*, UK

Other books by **Abbas Kazerooni**

On Two Feet and Wings

THE BOY WITH TWO LIVES

ABBAS KAZEROONI

ALLEN&UNWIN
SYDNEY · MELBOURNE · AUCKLAND · LONDON

This book is based on real events that happened to me a long time ago when I was a child. To write it for you I have simplified some events and changed some details. ABBAS KAZEROONI

First published by Allen & Unwin in 2015

Copyright © Abbas Kazerooni 2015

The moral right of Abbas Kazerooni to be identified as the author
of this work has been asserted by him in accordance with the United Kingdom's
Copyright, Designs and Patents Act 1988.

Allen & Unwin – Australia
83 Alexander Street, Crows Nest NSW 2065, Australia
Phone: (61 2) 8425 0100
Email: info@allenandunwin.com
Web: www.allenandunwin.com

Allen & Unwin – UK
c/o Murdoch Books, Erico House, 93-99 Upper Richmond Road, London SW15 2TG, UK
Phone: (44 20) 8785 5995
Email: info@murdochbooks.co.uk
Web: www.allenandunwin.com
Murdoch Books is a wholly owned division of Allen & Unwin Pty Ltd

A Cataloguing-in-Publication entry is available from
the National Library of Australia www.trove.nla.gov.au
A catalogue record for this book is available from the British Library

ISBN (AUS) 978 1 74331 483 8
ISBN (UK) 978 1 74336 689 9

Cover design by Sandra Nobes
Cover photos: boy © Adrian Pope / Getty Images; road © Claudio Divizia / Shutterstock;
pattern © daniana / Shutterstock
Set in 11/14.5 pt Sabon MT by Sandra Nobes
Poem on page 15 is John Keats' 'Ode to a Nightingale' from *Annals of the Fine Arts*,
1820 (written in 1819)
Poem on page 125 is 'If I Should Die' by Thomas Gray (1716–1771)
Printed in Australia in July 2015 by McPherson's Printing Group

10 9 8 7 6 5 4 3 2 1

*This book is a continuation of my last and,
as such, it is again dedicated in loving memory
to my mother, Marzieh.*

*However, I would also like to dedicate
this book to Fereydoun, Nadine and Fiz –
the ending is only the way it is because of you.*

ONE

I was woken from a deep sleep by the echoing clang of the morning bell, followed almost at once by the thud of children's feet on the old floorboards of the dormitory. I could smell the floor polish, and hear the boards squeaking as they had for decades. I opened one eye and saw the others were changing out of their pyjamas and into their uniforms as if their lives depended on it. I peered at my watch – it was 5.55 a.m. I was not happy.

Why was everyone in such a hurry? I was not used to getting up so early, but I struggled out of bed.

It seemed like I had travelled back in history and was part of a ritual that thousands of children had observed before me. I could not get over how old and immaculate everything was – the school and its traditions were impressive.

'Abbas,' Murphy called from the other side of the dormitory, 'get up.' He gestured to me to hurry. 'Get up now.' I noticed that he and the other children were dressing in only their vests, shorts, socks and sandals; their shirts, ties and jumpers still lay on their beds. They would then grab their handtowels and flannels and rush out of the dormitory.

Murphy kindly and patiently waited for me as I dressed, then gestured for me to follow him. I could see that he was desperate to leave, but he took his duty as my 'uncle' very seriously; it was his responsibility to look after me.

Murphy led me at a brisk walk to the communal washroom. Ten feet away the smell of bleach hit me, and the bright walls shone in the thin dawn light. Everyone was hurriedly brushing their teeth and washing their faces and armpits with their flannels. I had never washed my armpits with a flannel before; I did not understand why they didn't just take a shower. As strange as it seemed to me, I did as the other boys did, although they took no more than three minutes to wash themselves. Once again Murphy had long finished by the time I was done. He said something to me, which I did not understand, so he gestured for me to follow him.

He led me back upstairs to the dormitory where everyone else was busy putting on the rest of their uniforms at an alarming pace. I had never seen people change so quickly. I was doing up my shirt buttons when I noticed the tricks the other children were using to dress faster. They had all left their shirts buttoned the night before and pulled them off over their heads; their belts were still in their shorts and their clothes were laid out in a way that allowed them to dress as quickly as possible. This whole process was a science. I knew I had to catch up fast.

As soon as they finished dressing, they pulled back their sheets, blankets and duvets, then stood to attention at the foot of their beds in silence, awaiting instruction from the head of dormitory, which in this case was Alan. Alan was in the fifth form and would be transferring to a high school the following year. He was also a prefect. Only the previous day I had seen him embarrass Smith and Haynes by making them stand up before Mr Griffiths had come in for tea.

I was the last to be ready. Alan looked at me and then at his watch. He murmured something, and although I did not understand the words, I understood that I would have to be quicker in the future.

'Lead on, Humphries,' Alan said in a disciplined way. Humphries was in the year ahead of me. Goofy-looking, with a slip-in crown for one of his front teeth and an uncoordinated way of walking, he was sloppy to look at, sloppy in his movements and seemed like an easy target. But I sensed he was a good kid.

I was third in line as we headed back downstairs. I had no idea what was coming and I was too tired to care much. Alan brought up the rear as our dormitory headed towards the ground floor. A lanky geek shouted something as we passed, and Humphries turned and started shouting back at him. Alan immediately shouted at both boys. I could not understand what was going on, but it was obvious that there was no love lost between Humphries and the other kid.

Murphy turned to me and subtly indicated the lanky boy. 'That's Crookshank.' He looked grim. 'Stay away from him … he's not very nice.' I thought I understood and realised quickly that, like anywhere else, this place had its politics and its power struggles.

I put my head down and tried to forget how tired I was as I followed Murphy downstairs. Soon we were in the assembly room, where I assumed we would wait for breakfast. Alan took charge of the room and I took my place at the bottom of my year, as I'd been instructed to do last night when I'd first arrived at the school. I hated being last and planned to change that as soon as possible.

Crookshank and Humphries both tried to sit in their respective places but Alan brought them to their feet with a shout. A few others were caught talking and they were also made to stand. After about five minutes the headmaster, Mr Griffiths, walked in. He was wearing his tweed suit, with a pipe in his mouth and a book in his right hand. He took his position at the top of the room and reached for a board covered in neat columns of ticks and crosses. Mr Griffiths looked at each of the boys standing and made a note on the board for each individual then told them to sit down. Crookshank and Humphries glared at each other throughout the whole process. You could see that Crookshank was a sneaky character and was looking for easy prey. I immediately disliked him. As goofy as Humphries looked, he had a kind of charm and though I had no idea what the dispute was about, I had already taken the side of Humphries.

I later learnt that this board contained each boy's disciplinary and academic record throughout the term and was displayed for everyone to see. Under the discipline column you could get small 'x's for minor infractions, called Minor Marks, or a big 'X' for a major infraction, called a Major Minor Mark or MMM. If you did something very bad, you would automatically get one MMM, otherwise you needed to get six Minor Marks to make up one MMM. If you behaved well, and depending on whether your teachers believed you were doing well, you could get a tick, for a Plus Mark. Your Plus Marks would be announced every Saturday night after the end of the school week, and the total for each 'Colour' would be calculated and recorded. The school was split into different Colours. I was a Green and would remain so for the rest of my Aymestrey school career. Each Colour had boys from all years in it to make it as diverse and fair as possible.

'Let us pray,' said Mr Griffiths. All the boys leant forward, clasped their hands in front of them and bowed their heads. I had not been brought up in a religious environment and had never really prayed, but I did as everyone else and bowed my head, keeping an eye on Mr Griffiths and my surroundings, just to be sure. Everyone had their eyes closed.

It was not yet 6.30 a.m. and I had already experienced so many firsts. Mr Griffiths opened up the book he was holding and began to read from it. I did not understand a word he said, apart from something about Saint Francis of Assisi. After four or five minutes, everyone murmured 'Amen'. I hurriedly said 'Amen' as well, a little belatedly. I had no idea what I was saying or who I was praying to, but I did not care; fitting in was far more important.

'See you in twenty minutes,' Mr Griffiths said. The entire school suddenly rose and stood to attention, then Alan began to lead off. As soon as everyone left the common area the boys all dispersed. Murphy pointed, directing me upstairs, and made a sleep gesture to indicate the dormitory when I failed to understand what he'd said. All the dormitories were named after birds, and ours was Mallard, although the word meant nothing to me then. I nodded and began to hurry back upstairs. On the way I saw Crookshank gesturing at Humphries again. Humphries was about to turn around when Murphy grabbed him and pulled him upstairs past me.

Back in our dormitory, everyone was already busy making their beds. First we had to pull the underblankets over the mattress and smooth out the creases. When we were confident that we had done a good job we would ask permission from Alan to move to the next step. He would indicate either yes or no, and if no, we would have to do it again. The blanket was easy and everyone passed. The sheets were the next step. Ensuring there were no creases in the sheets was hard, and as I tried to copy the others, I saw Humphries denied twice. Hesitantly Humphries asked for permission to proceed for a third time. Alan looked over at Humphries' bed and suddenly lost his temper. He stomped over, pulled the sheets off and started screaming at him. I could see that Humphries was close to tears.

'For the last time, Humphries,' Alan fumed as he began making the bed, 'I am not going to do it for you again. Just watch. It's not hard.'

Though I was not sure what Alan was saying, I could guess. I felt bad for Humphries, who, as he watched, dragged his left sock up from around his ankles.

'Where the bloody hell is your garter?'

'I lost it; I couldn't find it this morning.'

'Really? This is the third time in a month you've lost a garter. Go and see Matron for another one at lunchtime.' I was picking up odd words like *third* and *month*, but I couldn't keep up with the conversation. The upside for me was that I'd been able to copy Alan's bed-making and, luckily, I was far better at it than Humphries.

When Alan had finished, I cautiously drew his attention to my sheets.

'Yes, see, even Abbas can get it right' – he walked over to me – 'and this is his first morning. You have to step it up, Humphries…you just have to.' I could see tears in Humphries' eyes behind his bulky glasses.

Eventually the beds were made and boys began on their chores. It seemed that everyone had a different chore:

Camozzi walked over to the curtains and pulled them open; he was then dismissed. I would learn later that the ever smiling Camozzi was the youngest in our dorm. The little Italian boy was always up to no good but generally got away with it because of his cheeky temperament. Humphries was on bin duty. There was a sole tissue in it, which Alan just pointed at. Humphries grabbed the bin and disappeared. I would learn that even if there was only one piece of rubbish in the bin, we still had to take it to the cellars and empty it into the main rubbish bins to be taken away each day. I was new so I had no chores to do, but I was watching like a hawk. I knew that my turn would come soon enough.

Back in the assembly room we waited in silence for breakfast, the faint smell of tobacco wafting from Mr Griffiths' pipe. O'Grady sat up straight next to me. It was obvious from his slender build that he was athletic. He had a pleasing smile on his long face as he sat patiently with his hands resting perfectly symmetrically on his grey shorts.

Suddenly Mr Griffiths said, 'Alexander…what does a good schoolboy always have on him?'

I could not understand what Mr Griffiths had said, but I later became familiar with all his routines and sayings, and from what transpired I could hazard a guess at his meaning. Everyone looked straight at Alexander, a sneaky-looking boy with small eyes and curly blond hair. I was still undecided about him, but his demeanour did not sit well with me. Alexander glanced down at the floor and then patted his pockets as if he knew where the conversation was going.

'A handkerchief, sir.'

'And?'

'Erm…a penknife, sir.'

'Precisely, so let's see them, chaps,' he said as he blew out the remainder of his pipe smoke.

All the boys suddenly began to rummage through their pockets.

'Everyone check their neighbour to the left to make sure the essentials are on their person,' Mr Griffiths intoned in his great baritone voice. O'Grady looked towards me and indicated that I should empty my pockets. I had a handkerchief in my left pocket because that was part of the uniform, but I had never owned a penknife and until I saw most of the others pull theirs out, I did not know what I was looking for.

'Don't you have a penknife, Abbas?' O'Grady whispered.

I shrugged, not knowing what O'Grady was asking. He pointed to his penknife, a small hunting knife with 'BOG' beautifully engraved on the wooden handle. I just shook my head. O'Grady reached into his pocket again and to my great surprise pulled out a tiny worn old Swiss Army knife and shoved it into my hand. I could not believe that in England children were expected to carry knives. I would have been punished for this in Iran.

'Everything okay, OG?' Mr Griffiths headed in our direction. My heart started to beat faster and I knew the entire school would shortly be looking directly at us.

'Yes, sir. Just a few language issues.'

'I'm sure. Now let me see.' The sound of those clunky shoes was getting louder and louder. Before I knew it, all six foot two inches of Mr Griffiths towered over me. I did not know what to do, so I stood up and waited to see what would happen. Mr Griffiths smiled at my show of respect.

'So, let's see it, Abbas.'

I could see Murphy in the corner of my eye waving his

handkerchief and penknife at me. I took out my hanky and my newly acquired penknife and showed Mr Griffiths.

'Outstanding,' he roared as he leant over my head to reach the window behind me to empty his pipe against the outside of the wall. 'You may sit down, Abbas.'

'Thank you,' I said softly and continued to stand. I did not know what else to say. Once again Murphy stood up and sat down and gestured at me to do the same. I immediately sat and gave Murphy a grateful nod. There were murmurs and giggles as the rest of the school watched Murphy gesticulating behind Mr Griffiths' back. Mr Griffiths knew what was going on but chose to ignore it, with a knowing smile on his face. The gong suddenly sounded and the entire school stood in unison, ready for their morning meal.

In single file we entered the dining room and walked to our designated tables. I went to sit in the place I'd had the previous day but OG pushed me one seat to the left. I learnt that each day we would rotate one seat clockwise so that a different person would sit next to our head of table. Our head was Mr Goodyear, a tall, well built man with mousy white hair, glasses and a no-nonsense demeanour. He looked at each of us in turn, doing a swift headcount, then looked at me a second time and acknowledged me with the tiniest hint of a smile.

Mr Griffiths bellowed from the top table, 'For what we are about to receive may the Lord make us truly thankful.'

'Amen,' we replied and took our seats.

Mr Goodyear nodded at Auty, a boy from my year, who dashed away to a line that was already forming next to a small table on the far side of the dining room. Mrs Griffiths was at the table, leaning over a giant metal pot. Mr Goodyear began to pour us all tea from a large metal teapot on the table, while OG poured milk into each cup. Then we would hand the cups down to the bottom of the table until everyone had their tea. Auty brought two bowls at a time and put them in front of two of us, again working his way from the bottom of the table to the top. When it came to my turn I peered into the bowl. There was a slimy beige substance in it that I had not seen before. Sneaky Alexander was sitting next to me, and I tapped him on the shoulder and pointed to my food.

'Porridge ... That is called porridge.'

I nodded to show that I'd understood. There was already a small sprinkle of sugar on it. I noticed that no one was eating and so I waited. When Mr Goodyear received his bowl, we looked up and he said, 'You may begin.'

The boys around me were eating at high speed. I tasted the porridge; it was pretty good, especially the part with the sugar on it, but unfortunately there was no more sugar. I did not dare ask for more, and I soon learnt that getting more sugar was not an option anyway.

I reached over to sip my tea, and as much as I enjoyed the warmth in that cold morning room, it would have been nice to taste a little sweetness. I understood that all our food was regulated – they decided the size of the portions, they decided the contents of the food, and it was not possible to add sugar or ask for more.

We were soon done with our porridge and Auty dashed off again. While he was gone we all stacked our bowls and passed them to the top of the table. OG, who had sat next to Mr Goodyear, took the big stacks and walked over to a window at the end of the dining room, where a lady was waiting for the dirty dishes. Auty was coming and going and placing one piece of toast on everyone's side plate with tongs.

When he returned to his seat, Mr Goodyear again nodded for us to start. There was one tub of margarine that was passed around the table clockwise. Each boy took a small amount, showed it to Mr Goodyear and, if he nodded, was permitted to transfer the margarine to his plate. Exactly the same procedure applied for the jam. We ate our toast and finished our tea and we were done. We all stood up and once again Mr Griffiths said prayers, then we filed back to the assembly room.

Mr Griffiths followed us and promptly said, 'Fifth form.' The oldest boys all stood up and filed out, followed by the fourth form, and then it was our turn.

Murphy dutifully led me to the cellars, where there was a row of overalls, each hung below an individual's name. Mine were new, unlike the others, which were worn and paint-spattered. I slid the overalls on over my school clothes, then we changed our shoes for wellington boots, yet another first for me.

Outside, the brisk morning air suddenly hit me in the face – summer was turning to autumn. I had not realised how much countryside and woodland surrounded us, nor had I ever lived in such a remote place before. I was in a different country, a different climate, a different culture and very different environment. The beauty, the crisp cold air and the purity of my environment gave me solace. I knew that I still had to fit in and earn the respect of my classmates and teachers, but I felt that I was going to be all right. The delicate smell of the English countryside was one that I will never forget.

Huge trees edged the wide grassy lawn in front of the school, and I wondered how many children these trees had witnessed over the decades and centuries. I was overwhelmed by the splendour of the oaks and limes, the grand Victorian building, the broad sweep of the surrounding countryside, the forest behind the school and the tradition that seemed to envelop every inch of the place. I had been there only one day, but already I felt part of something very special.

Mr Goodyear appeared from the cellars wearing his own overalls and wellingtons. Following him were about fifteen other children. We were apparently 'wooding'. What that entailed I was soon to learn. Mr Goodyear was carrying an impressive sledgehammer, and had steel wedges protruding from his pockets. Some of the children were carrying sledge-hammers, too, and others held saws and smaller wedges. Whatever we were going to do looked like it would be fun.

We walked towards the forest at the back of the school. Under the trees it was moist and dark, with fungi adding patches of colour to the dark-brown forest floor. The cries of the birds echoed more loudly among the evergreens, and the further we went in, the less we talked to each other. I could hear the squishing of fallen leaves beneath our feet.

A muddy lake appeared ahead of us, spanned by the long trunk of a fallen oak tree that formed a bridge from one side to the other. It was not a large lake, but it was big enough for me to worry about falling into it. Just before we reached the lake, Mr Goodyear suddenly stopped and looked around, then pointed to another fallen tree that was already partially chopped up.

'Okay, fifth form, you're on the sledgehammers and wedges – I want those lengths split. Everyone else, you're on the saws.'

Everyone queued up in an orderly fashion and awaited further instructions. I was paired with Murphy, somewhere in the middle of the tree. Murphy went around to the other side of the tree and I contemplated the saw, which was bigger than the two of us put together. The tree looked monstrously big.

We began to saw, and before I knew it, I was sweating. I looked around and saw that Murphy and OG were also sweating. The air no longer seemed cold. We would stop and wipe away the sweat every five minutes or so, then Mr Goodyear would boom, 'Put your back into it, lads. This will sort the men from the boys.'

As soon as we heard that, we would quickly get back to it. It took over half an hour for Murphy and me to cut all the way through the tree. We waited while OG and his partner finished their cut, then Mr Goodyear called, 'Put that length next to the other logs for tomorrow, chaps.'

OG and I tried to drag it, but it was too heavy. Murphy joined in and the three of us tipped it upright and rolled it to a nearby pile. Next to that was a pile of smaller logs that had been split by the fifth-formers while we had been sawing.

'Everyone carry at least three logs back to the cellars, please,' ordered Mr Goodyear.

On our way back to the cellars, Murphy turned to me and said, 'I can't wait till we can use the hammers. It looks like much more fun.' He could see that I was puzzled, so he used his logs to act out hammering. 'I – like – hammer – more.'

'Oh, yes… hammer… good. Hammer is good,' I replied as I realised what he had been trying to say.

Back in the cellars, Murphy led me to the wood room. It was large, and contained more wood than I could have ever imagined. Murphy threw his logs to the top of the pile, which was over ten feet high. He then indicated that I should do the same.

We returned to the area with the pegs and took off our overalls and wellington boots, then Murphy led me back to the wood room, where he took three logs from the bottom and asked me to do the same. These logs were as dry as bones. I realised that this wood had probably been chopped more than a year ago. We carried the wood to one of the many fireplaces in the main building and put it in an iron cauldron. Later I came to understand that we had to keep the cauldrons full of wood so the older boys could keep the fires alight throughout the day. As Murphy was trying to explain all this to me, the bell echoed around the school.

'Bugger, we're late. We have to get to class. You have Draggo.'

'What?' I called, following Murphy as he ran up the stairs.

We were about to run into the third-form homeroom when Murphy spotted Mrs Griffiths and immediately slowed to a swift walk.

'I saw that, Murphy,' Mrs Griffiths said with a menacing smile.

'Sorry, Mrs G... Won't happen again.'

'If I had a pound for every time I heard that.'

We went into the homeroom and picked up my books, then Murphy hurried me to Mr Driver's classroom.

'Abbas, I have to go to my own class. Good luck. Don't get Draggo mad.'

With that, Murphy dashed off. I walked in sheepishly and immediately saw OG and headed towards him.

At the front of the classroom was Mr Driver. If I hadn't known better, I would have thought he was a homeless man, although he had real presence despite his small stature. His curly hair had clearly not been brushed in a very long time, he had a long beard that was anything but groomed, and he wore baggy tracksuit pants and a white shirt, which was strange because all the other teachers wore suits, shirts and ties. All the kids called him Draggo. On the blackboard behind him, I saw a verse from a poem copied out in small, neat handwriting.

'Read this verse to yourselves,' Draggo said quietly, without looking up from his book.

I started to read.

My heart aches, and a drowsy numbness pains
   My sense, as though of hemlock I had drunk,
Or emptied some dull opiate to the drains
   One minute past, and Lethe-wards had sunk:
'Tis not through envy of thy happy lot,
   But being too happy in thine happiness,—
     That thou, light-winged Dryad of the trees,
      In some melodious plot
Of beechen green, and shadows numberless,
   Singest of summer in full-throated ease.

I had no idea what the words meant, and began to panic. Had I known that I would study this very poem, John Keats' *Ode to a Nightingale*, at university some ten years later, I might have felt a little better.

'Tomkins, talk to me about this stanza,' Draggo said, as he put his own book aside.

'Erm...not really sure, sir.'

'Not really sure, huh? Well, let's start from the beginning. *My heart aches*...You know what that means, don't you?'

'It means my heart hurts, sir.'

'So if you know what some of it means then why are you telling me you are not really sure?' Draggo said as he began pacing around the classroom. 'Apply yourself … you're the top of the class, aren't you? You don't mind posing about your position, so now earn it.'

I was already terrified of Draggo, but I would go on to be more influenced by him, probably, than any other teacher in my academic career. Something about him intrigued me, and his sense of purpose and focus was already apparent.

'I guess he is saying he feels numb and drowsy?' Tomkins asked uncertainly.

'Okay, Alexander, you can take over.'

'Well … um … not really sure what hemlock is, sir.'

'Okay, what have I told you idiots before?' he snapped. 'Alexander, we have been through this a thousand times. If you do not know the meaning of a word, what do you do?' Draggo was pacing faster and faster and his face was beginning to grow red.

'Look it up in the dictionary?' Alexander questioned.

'No, you pray and maybe you'll get the answer that way,' Draggo snarled. 'Of course you look it up in the dictionary. This big huge gigantic massive enormous book at the front of the class is the *Oxford English Dictionary*. I do not put it at the front of the class because I like the look of it, but so that idiots like you can use it.' The angrier Draggo became, the redder his ears grew. He was almost like a cartoon character, but not one that I wanted to confront.

Alexander began to get out of his seat when Draggo snapped, 'Oh, sit down. The idea is that you look it up when you prepare, not when we are meant to be discussing it in class. You're pathetic, absolutely pathetic; everything has to be fed to you like little babies. You want to go back to using simplistic, robotic textbooks? Because we can do that. I am trying to put you ahead of the pack, but it takes work from you, too – all of you. You should be grateful to be given the opportunity to read such rich, lush poetry written by a man who had more talent in his little pinkie than the lot of you put together. I don't want to repeat my rules to you again. This is the last time. So before next class, all of you, and I mean all of you, had better know a new fact about John Keats that you did not know today. And I will test you. Understood?'

'Yes, sir,' everyone said in unison.

'Now for the love of God, Roberts, tell me what this idiot could not,' he said, turning his attention away from a red-cheeked Alexander.

I could not understand much of that double English class, but fortunately for me Draggo did not ask me any questions that day. I did learn a lot about him. He was an intense man with no time for pomp and circumstance; Draggo hated posers and loved to read great literature and, I found out later, to sculpt. Despite his flaws, including an unhealthy temper, Draggo strove to make us better. His disgust at mediocrity and his continuous quest to stretch us as students and as human beings were exactly what Aymestrey stood for. I had been there for a day and I already knew that this school was about discipline, about pushing oneself and never quitting. Draggo was the epitome of these virtues; virtues that I would have to rely on in times ahead.

TWO

Murphy grabbed me after English class and we ran to the homeroom, where he made me dump my books in my desk before double-timing me to the cellars to change once more. He threw a pair of shorts, a blue running vest and some trainers down in front of me.

'Get changed, quick.'

I could see everyone flinging their clothes on at an alarming pace. Every second was accounted for at this institution.

Outside, Draggo sat waiting with a book in his hands. He glanced up, and when he saw a few of us dawdling he shouted, 'Come on, chaps – chop chop – going to start in four minutes.'

I was hopping along trying to slide my shoes on as we jogged onto the beautiful lawn. The day was even colder than earlier, and I could feel its bite on my skin, with only my shorts and running vest for protection. We jogged towards a small stile in the fence that separated the lawn from the next field, where the grass was no longer manicured, and the acres of farmland were dotted with cattle. The smell of cow dung was stronger here, and the wind was picking up.

The other children lined up under a huge oak tree, facing away from the school. Draggo suddenly blew a whistle and everyone began to run. I had never been on a cross-country run before, so I started to sprint as fast as I possibly could. Murphy caught up with me and grabbed my arm.

'Slow down,' he cried, waving a hand up and down. 'You'll never make it at that pace.'

Three minutes into the run I was already tired and I already hated it. Little did I know that this was part of our daily routine and would become one of my favourite activities. Suddenly everyone sped up and I saw Draggo bringing up the rear, shouting, 'Come on, you slobs – take in the air and get into a running pattern. I don't want to see anyone walking.'

I began to run faster but I was struggling. The older boys were way ahead of me, and although I tried to maintain a steady pace, I was in second-to-last place. I hated to feel that I was bad at anything. My feet were wet, and before I knew it I had stepped deep into cow dung. I was absolutely disgusted, and spent more time worrying about the smell and the texture of the cowpat than the run. Never in my life had I been this close to cows, and it made me nervous – I had no idea what they might do.

Murphy was by my side, smiling at me. Clearly he could go faster, but he was hanging back to make sure I was okay. As he ran beside me, demonstrating the pace and rhythm that would get me through the run, I realised what a kind and gentle soul he was, and I suddenly hoped that we would become great friends.

About five minutes into the run we came across the infamous Aymestrey Hill, steep and apparently endless.

Draggo had positioned himself halfway up it and was shouting at everyone.

'Smaller steps and dig right in! I do not want to see anyone stopping. None of you will stop! We have the fittest school in Worcestershire because no one trains like us.'

I was beginning to gasp for breath – I really did not think I could carry on. Murphy slipped behind me and pushed me in the back. 'Just don't stop. Just don't stop.'

There was no way that I was going to start walking or stop in front of Draggo. He was watching Murphy and me like a hawk, and his glare urged me on. I was close to hyperventilating by the time I reached the top of the hill.

'Now open your stride down the hill,' Draggo bellowed.

I just wanted it to be over. There were at least five people behind me now, so I did not feel quite so pathetic, and it was all due to Murphy. We started to go a little faster. Just as I thought that I could go no further, we reached the stile next to the school lawn, where we ended our run. To my dismay I realised that some of the boys were going around again – those in the top year had to do the course twice!

'We have to hit the showers now,' Murphy said, his cheeks red. He was usually so pale, but the run had changed that. I was panting loudly and sweating profusely; I was glad we had run in our vests. I could not possibly jog back to the cellars, so I trailed behind Murphy to the changing room, then a washroom in the cellars.

I was shocked to realise that we were to wash in communal showers. I was not used to being naked in front of anyone. Here we all were, displayed in our full glory to each other. I quickly stripped off my clothes and noticed the mud all the way up my legs. Holding my hands in front of my genitals, I lined up for the shower, trying to blend in. It was humiliating. For the first time I felt the clash of cultures. In Iran this would never have happened, nor would it have been acceptable. But I was standing in a school where boys had been doing this for over a century. I just had to deal with it.

I stood staring at one of the stones in the wall, thinking about how many boys before me had stared at the very same rock. There was a strong smell of damp, which pervaded every area in the cellars. As I drew closer to the showers, the smell changed to shampoo and soap. I edged over to my place in the shower and tried to hide myself as I reached for the shampoo.

'Abbas, get a move on. As cute as you may think you look, no one cares,' Draggo snapped. I did not really understand what he was saying, but his tone was obvious. Suddenly my self-consciousness disappeared; my fear of Draggo's temper snapped me into action and I began to wash myself with a swift determination. I hurried out of the shower and began to change quickly, for once feeling like I actually belonged.

Murphy took me to my next class – Grammar with Mrs Griffiths. As headmistress, she had absolute authority, and she sat at her desk calmly, gazing at us through her dense glasses. She wore a long skirt and a cardigan, which I would learn was her usual outfit. She handed me my exercise book and my task – some handwriting to copy out – and I began to write with my new ballpoint pen.

From the very first day, Mrs Griffiths made no allowance for my almost non-existent English; she believed full immersion was the best way for me to learn, and I was sure she was right. Mrs. Griffiths taught us the small things I had not thought about before, such as copying out handwriting: she would critique the way I joined letters and show me how she liked each letter to look. Handwriting was very important to the teachers at Aymestrey, and my first Grammar classes were purely based on this. The classes later went on to concentrate on vocabulary and grammar, with our textbook exercises showing us the best words to use in different contexts and the correct use of punctuation.

I noticed Tomkins' fountain pen gliding across his page. I had never seen a fountain pen up close before, and my love of them began from that moment. Tomkins used an old steel Parker with a refillable cartridge. It had an aged, faded look about it that made it even more attractive to me. I looked around and saw that almost everyone had a fountain pen. I continued to work with my cheap ballpoint, yearning for a fountain pen.

Harper, a blond kid in the back row, caught me looking at him and gestured to ask if I needed anything. I smiled and gestured no. I had not really interacted with him yet, but he seemed nice enough. He had been near the front in the cross-country run; he was thin and tall and perfectly built for running. He continued to watch me and gestured at me again, indicating that he wanted to see me after class. I returned to my work – it was actually quite simple, and came to me a lot more easily than to my newly made friends because I was learning the writing fresh rather than having to let go of preconceived notions of what I'd believed was correct and relearn it like the others.

The time passed quickly. Suddenly the bell rang, and everyone hurriedly began to pack up. Every time the bell sounded, it felt as if there was a stampede through the school. The noise of all those children desperate to make their next class or appointment underlined the importance of punctuality in this school. As I stepped outside the classroom Murphy was already waiting for me. The smell of polish on the floorboards was stronger now that the maids had finished their polishing. Murphy and I were about to head off when I felt a tap on my shoulder.

'I saw you looking at everyone's pens,' Harper said with a shy smile.

I looked at Harper inquisitively, not fully understanding him. After an awkward silence, Harper realised and pretended to write in the air to explain what he meant.

'Yes … yes … very nice,' I said, remembering his pen. 'Thank you.'

Murphy and I set off, but Harper stopped us again and put a hand in his pocket.

'It's not much, but I thought you may want to—'

I saw that Harper was offering me his spare fountain pen. It was a cheap plastic one, but I felt ashamed that he was offering it to me. I cut him off. 'No, no, I—'

'I insist,' he said, interrupting me.

'Thank you. But I … ' I stopped, because I did not know how to express myself. I didn't want to be treated as a charity case. Unfortunately, I would be forced to become accustomed to it, but I didn't know that yet.

Murphy looked at me, smiling. 'You should take it, Abbas,' he said in a matter-of-fact voice. 'Mr Griffiths says all good schoolboys must have fountain pens.'

'Come on, Abbas, it's my second spare and I never use it anyway. I got it in my Christmas stocking last year. At least it would get some use if you took it.' Though I could not really understand him, Harper went on, 'I have loads of cartridges for it – blue and black.'

'Thank you … very much.'

'No probs, mate,' Harper said as he walked off.

It was a very kind gesture, and sharp of him to have even noticed I didn't have my own pen; I just did not like the way it made me feel.

Back in the assembly room, waiting for lunch, I sat in silence next to OG and watched Alan take control of the room. Soon enough we were lined up before Mr Griffiths as the gong echoed through the corridors. I was astounded at the small portions we received for lunch. The smell of shepherd's pie filled the dining room, and it was clearly homemade and delicious. Mr Goodyear put my measly portion on my plate with a spoonful of cabbage and I watched as it was handed down the table to me. It was literally two bites. As soon as everyone was served, we gobbled down our tiny portions. Then we had the pudding – my favourite English pudding, in all its glory – apple crumble and custard. Again the portion was ridiculously small, but I have never forgotten the taste of that apple crumble. It had been a long time since I had tasted such a delicious meal; I just wished there was more.

After lunch Murphy escorted me to the dormitory for our afternoon siesta. We all took off our shoes and lay on our beds in silence. We could either read or sleep. I certainly could not sleep. This first day had been such an overwhelming experience that I was glad of an opportunity to try to digest it.

'Humphries, what are you reading?' Alan snapped.

'Erm…*Superman*.'

'That is a comic, is it not?'

'Well—'

'Answer the question,' Alan interrupted.

'Yes.'

'Okay, then it's confiscated.' Alan gestured for Humphries

to bring him the comic. 'And make sure you report yourself to Mrs Griffiths for this.'

I gleaned enough from this exchange to understand that our reading material was censored; we could clearly not read comics. Humphries lay sulking over the incident. I had been at the school less than twenty-four hours and so much drama had already centred around him.

The bell sounded, and once again the stampede began. Like a sheep I fell into step and hurried along with everyone else, not knowing where I was going. Murphy grabbed me by the arm and pushed me ahead of him.

'Go to the changing room.' He mimed undressing.

I knew what that meant and also knew the way. I rushed down the stairs to the cellars, and we were soon next to my peg in the changing area. Murphy handed me my shorts and a white rugby shirt and pair of football boots. I thought we were going to play football until I saw Draggo in his worn-out tracksuit spinning a rugby ball in his hands. I changed quickly, intrigued, and waited for instructions. This time I was one of the first to be changed and very proud of the fact. As I stood waiting, Draggo threw the ball at me. I caught it instinctively. Draggo gestured for me to pass it back. I did not really know how, but I did the best I could.

'You can come with me today, Abbas.' He smiled. 'You seem to have a natural ability.'

Murphy put his thumbs up to show that what Draggo had said was good.

'Thank you, sir,' I said, smiling. I was not quite sure why I was smiling, but I felt very pleased with myself.

Murphy crept up and whispered in my ear, 'Good.' He patted me on the shoulder. 'You are going with the seniors, with Draggo...that is very good. I'm only in the junior practice, so I can't come with you.'

'What?'

'Never mind...you'll see.'

Draggo suddenly grabbed my shirt to pull me along with him. He started to jog, so I followed suit. I suddenly realised that I was jogging to the rugby field with Alan and all the boys in the top two years. All my other friends were going with Mr Griffiths to a smaller field.

We stood on the sidelines of the rugby field, and I stared at the rugby posts wondering how this mysterious game worked. Draggo pulled out a piece of paper and started shouting names and positions; seniors walked to either his left or his right in response. I was the last to be called, and I went to his left when he gestured. We on Draggo's left were the white team; those on his right were the coloured team, and they changed into spare coloured shirts they appeared to have brought along just for this purpose; I made a note to do the same next time.

'Abbas, just go with the game and see if you can pick it up,' he said, tapping me on the back of the head. 'Just do not pass forward, and tackle anyone with the ball.'

'Thank you, sir.' I had no idea what he'd just said.

'This will be good,' Draggo said sarcastically.

The colours kicked off, and Barnes, a chubby boy in the top year, caught the ball and began to run. He had some physical presence but it was obvious Draggo did not think much of him. Barnes was tackled and then a bunch of children started to pile on top and push.

'Abbas, get in there and push,' Draggo shouted over the noise, indicating that I should push hard.

It was clear what I had to do, so I did as I was told, without the faintest idea why.

'Good work, mate,' Barnes shouted, 'keep pushing.'

The ball came loose and everyone started to chase it. Gurney, a largish muscular boy on the coloured team, got it. He was very fast and started to charge at us, coming directly at me.

'Tackle him! Tackle him!' The cry rose up from almost everyone.

I was unsure what I could legally do. I had seen others make tackles, but I was not sure when I could do this, so I decided to shoulder-barge Gurney, because it was neither tackling nor getting out of the way. Gurney bounced off me and onto the ground.

'Oooh…that was nice, Abbas,' Barnes commented. It became apparent that Barnes never stopped talking. Suddenly Draggo blew the whistle.

'Abbas, come here,' he barked. 'That was okay, but you have to tackle. Put your arms around him as you hit him.' Draggo threw the ball to Gurney again. 'When he has the ball, you hit him,' he ordered as he punched one hand into the other, trying to indicate a tackle.

'Thank you, sir…yes, sir.'

'You sure you got that, Abbas?'

'Yes, sir…thank you, sir.'

'Okay,' he said hesitantly, 'scrum down, white ball.'

We got back to it and the game went on for a few minutes until Allen, a long-legged boy from the other team, got the ball and began to gallop towards me like a thoroughbred horse. I remembered Draggo's demonstration, ran at Allen, jumped in the air and punched him square in the jaw. Allen hit the deck and my knuckles pulsed with pain. The shock of my act stopped the game – there was no need for a whistle.

'What the bloody hell do you think you are doing, Abbas?'

Draggo shouted as he paced over to me, gesticulating furiously. I knew I was in trouble. He stood there with his hands on his hips waiting for a response. So I repeated his earlier gesture.

'He has ball,' I said, 'and…' I gestured a punch as he had shown me.

The penny suddenly dropped: I realised I had taken his instructions too literally, my English too poor for me to understand what he had actually meant. There was a slight smile on Draggo's face as Allen scrambled to his feet, holding his face and grumbling.

'Oh, do stop your moaning, Allen. You sound like a little girl. That wouldn't even qualify for a love tap.'

Barnes laughed so loudly that he snorted.

'Shut up, Barnes, you lump of lard,' Draggo snapped. Barnes immediately shut up and stood to attention. Draggo then took the time to explain to me what I'd done wrong before the game continued, demonstrating actions in more detail than he'd done earlier. I sensed that Draggo actually liked me, so I was not as concerned about the mistake I'd made as I would have been with another teacher. Allen came up to me at the end of practice and shook my hand.

'Don't worry about it, mate,' he said, smiling. 'It didn't hurt that much anyway.'

'Thank you,' I responded awkwardly. 'I am very sorry.'

'It's okay, mate.'

Once again I found myself in the communal showers washing mud off my legs. Surprisingly, I already felt more comfortable, no longer like such a stranger, because all the boys were now talking to me and making me feel like one of them. It was odd how one game of rugby changed my status within the school.

In the assembly room waiting for the tea gong I realised that I was the topic of conversation; the other boys were whispering to each other, glancing over at me as they did so. It seemed the punch I'd given Allen had caused a stir. I spotted Murphy out of the corner of my eye; he was smiling, holding his thumb up at me, and I knew that the gossip was good.

As we stood up for grace, I looked around me and saw that there were really very few fat children at our school. I was very hungry and hoped that teatime would mean a little more food than at dinner earlier that day. I was disappointed: half a slice of cheese on toast was followed by half a slice of bread and the same routine with the margarine and jam as last time with Mr Goodyear. Clearly our food was rationed. After all that rugby, the white tea really went down well, and the taste was growing on me.

After that we had one hour of free time. Murphy took me upstairs to where a large snooker table stood next to a smaller one.

'You want to play?'

'Yes,' I said as I walked over to the big table.

'We can't play on that one – only fifth-formers are allowed to play on that one.'

So we went over to the smaller table and Murphy proceeded to show me how to play snooker. It was fun learning to play these very English games. At every moment I was learning new words, sports and traditions.

I stood there on the squeaky floorboards with a cue in my hand while I waited for Murphy to take his shot, staring at the old paintings of sailing ships on the walls. Those paintings must have been there for over a hundred years. The play area overlooked the top of the grand staircase that wound its way to the ground floor. Its mahogany banisters shone with splendour. To the right of the snooker tables was an old table-tennis table. Around the room lay old tuckboxes with children's names printed on them.

The bell sounded for us to gather downstairs in the main hallway of the school. We lined up in our years, standing before the staff, each of us holding a small book, while Mr Griffiths led the evening prayers. After he read a passage from the Bible, which lasted for about ten minutes, he announced a number and everyone began to flip to a page. OG helped me find my way. Before I knew it the entire school was singing a hymn. I did not really sing, just tried to follow the words in my book. After the hymn, Mr Griffiths read from his prayer book, to a united 'Amen' at the end of the prayer.

After the evening prayers, we had thirty minutes of spare time before bed. I went to my homeroom and sat at my desk to ponder the events of the day. I could not help but think of my mother, wondering what she was doing and whether she was thinking of me. I missed her so very much.

When it was time for bed, I wasn't tired, despite the activities of the day. Cries of 'goodnight' and '*bonne nuit*' echoed in the corridors. The loud clunky sounds of Mr Griffiths' shoes faded into the distance. It was almost time for lights out. I was about to spend my second night at the school. It was not so bad, I reflected; in fact, I was beginning to enjoy it. I lay there hoping that I would fall asleep soon. The heavy weight of missing my mother was bothering me. Aymestrey's many activities kept my mind off things for most of the day, but when it was bedtime, my mother was all I thought about. I craved the dark nothingness that sleep would bring.

THREE

Two weeks passed with no news from my parents, my guardian Mehdi, his girlfriend Kate, or the rest of my family. The other children would go down after breakfast each day and pick up letters and cards from their loved ones from the old oak table outside the dining room, next to the gong. I would always go, too, though deep in my gut I knew I would receive nothing. Still, I hoped for a surprise.

Murphy's time as my 'uncle' was over, so I was now left to my own devices at school, responsible for my own actions. Luckily I had become good friends with Murphy, though, and we saw each other often between classes. I had become accustomed to the school's daily routines – each day was very similar to the days that had gone before.

I was now running the full cross-country course without needing to stop, and I was finishing in the top six within my age range. That meant that if we had a cross-country event against other schools, I would be in the team. There had been no rugby fixtures yet, but it seemed inevitable that I would make that team also.

I was enjoying school. I was being given opportunities

that I had never even deemed a possibility before. One example of this was Aymestrey's obstacle course, which we tackled on the weekends. I loved it. I could not believe the school had a real flying fox, and that we were allowed to go on it every week. There were balancing beams, rope swings over small lakes, and so much more.

There was not a moment when I had time to think about anything other than the tasks given to me. I was always occupied. Nevertheless, thoughts of my mother would still creep in and overcome me. It was so hard trying to hide my homesickness – although I did not so much miss my home as my mother. I missed the way she nurtured me; I missed the way she fussed over me; I missed the way she loved me. It was hard to miss my father as much, since it was because of his decisions that I found myself in this position.

It was three and a half months since I had seen my parents. At night I would lie in bed and wonder if my mother was any closer to getting out of Iran. Why had they not contacted me since I'd arrived in England? It was difficult not knowing what they were doing; it was even more difficult not knowing whether I was even missed. But I could not let my feelings get the better of me. No one knew how I felt. I just had to get on with life, but each day was privately a struggle because of this.

The previous Sunday, we had been instructed to write a letter home. We were instructed to tell our parents that we had an exeat the following weekend – meaning everyone would be picked up by their parents on Saturday morning, stay at home overnight, and return at six the following evening – and Mrs Griffiths had added to me that she'd like me to write my letter in English. So I wrote a letter to Mehdi and Kate rather than my parents. Mrs Griffiths helped me with the letter to make sure that the instructions were clear. It was approved and sent off, so I was anticipating seeing Mehdi and Kate the following Saturday.

Saturday morning came with no reply, however. I checked the mail table after breakfast, but I could see that I'd still received no mail. I took a deep breath and headed to the assembly room to await further instructions. All the children were looking forward to seeing their parents. Everyone was talking about the chocolates and the treats they would eat as soon as they got home. Mrs Griffiths arrived, and everyone stopped their whispering and sat up straight.

'I don't want any of you scallywags overeating while you're away. If any of you come back sick tomorrow night, I will not be entertained. Understood?'

'Yes, madam,' came the response in unison. I could see the little smirks on the other children's faces.

'Is that funny, Barnes?' Mrs Griffiths asked, half joking.

'No, madam,' Barnes responded, quickly sobering up.

Before I knew it, parents started arriving. The joy on the faces of the other children was evident. The way they ran to their parents and hugged them, one would have thought we had been in a prison camp. On the whole, life was good at school, but a lot of the children moaned about how hard it was for them. The main complaints were about the lack of food and the cross-country – which I had quickly realised was not worth trying to skip, as the only reason accepted was illness, and then you would be quarantined in the sanatorium with only bread and water for no less than a week!

Murphy's mother arrived, and he came up to me with his ever present smile to say goodbye to me before he went to her. 'Is anyone coming for you, mate?'

'I think so,' I said, trying to sound confident.

'Well, have fun, Abbas, and remember, Mars Bars are the ones you should get.'

I smiled at him and said goodbye, then peered through the window and watched him get into a Volvo and point me out to his mother. She looked over to me with a huge grin and began waving. The Murphy smile was contagious – it was impossible not to smile and wave back at them. I watched until the car had driven away.

The other boys were disappearing swiftly one by one. Soon only Humphries and I were left. Humphries cradled his head in his hands. I was not sure what to do – he looked as if he was almost in tears – so I put my hand on his shoulder and said, 'Okay, mate? Okay? They come soon.'

'They're always late. They know how much I hate it here,' he whimpered.

'Yes, mate … they come.'

'You don't know that—'

An old BMW pulled into the driveway, and a smile transformed Humphries' face. He did not even say goodbye.

I watched him run across the gravel in his characteristically sloppy style, his socks around his ankles, his shorts at half-mast and his shirt flapping in the wind. He flung himself into his mother's arms and wept helplessly. After about thirty seconds, Humphries' mother helped him into the car and closed the door behind him. His teary face turned towards me at the window then. I smiled a slow, encouraging smile and he waved. I watched until their car disappeared, then turned away from the window.

After a few minutes of total silence, I clicked my tongue against the roof of my mouth. The sound echoed slightly in the empty space. I tested the echo with other small noises –

there was nothing else to do – then I peered outside again, to see if Mehdi or Kate was approaching.

About thirty minutes later Mr Griffiths appeared, his gait more casual than usual. He looked alarmed to see me.

'Abbas, I didn't expect to see you here.'

'Hello, sir.'

'Have you not been picked up?' he asked slowly, knowing that I still did not understand everything.

'Guardian not here, sir,' I responded shyly.

'Oh dear, oh dear.' He smiled. 'Well, young fellow, what are we going to do about that?'

I felt slightly anxious, unsure if I was in trouble or not. Mrs Griffiths showed up and seemed as taken aback by my presence as her husband.

'Oh dear, Abbas,' she said, 'let me make a quick call.' She mimicked a telephone conversation, then she and Mr Griffiths left.

I was alone again. The feeling of uncertainty made me feel very uncomfortable. I waited in silence, wondering what was to become of me. I was not sure how long this arrangement with Mehdi – him funding my place at the school, while he awaited the money my father had promised him but not sent – could be maintained; the future already looked bleak.

I returned to the window, kneeling on a bench and gazing through the glass, waiting for something to happen. It felt shameful that no one had come for me yet. Hope that somebody would come was all that I had; somehow, if someone showed up, I felt as if my shame would go away.

'It seems you have been forgotten, my boy,' Mrs Griffiths said as she walked briskly back to me.

'Sorry, madam,' I responded. 'I write last Sunday.'

'I know, Abbas,' she said calmly. 'It isn't your fault.'

'Thank you.'

As formal as Mrs Griffiths was, she had a way of being maternal just at the right time. Fleetingly she stroked my hair before she turned to go, and the human contact and kindness made me smile. How little it took.

'Mr Griffiths will come and see you shortly, Abbas,' she said, turning at the door. 'Please wait in the assembly room.' With a quick smile she was gone.

I had suspected all along that no one would come for me, and yet I had dared to hope.

Mr Griffiths ambled into the assembly room soon after, throwing something at me. I caught it instinctively and discovered that he had brought me a packet of Cherry Drops. It was incredible how quickly a bag of boiled sweets could put a smile on my face.

'The others are stuffing their faces by now. It's only fair that you eat something yummy, too.'

'Thank you, sir.'

'Follow me.' Mr Griffiths led me to the large snooker table with the old oak cue rack by its side.

'This is a privilege, my boy,' Mr Griffiths mumbled with his pipe in his mouth, 'but I think on this occasion you deserve to enjoy this fine table.'

'Thank you, sir,' I replied, not knowing precisely what he had said.

'Have fun. I'll see you in a little bit.'

With that I was left alone to do as I wished with the large snooker table. Murphy had already taught me how to play, so I racked up and began. Though it was fun playing on the large table, it was considerably less enjoyable playing alone. I leant over to take a shot and a small tear rolled down my cheek and onto the green baize. I was in England; I was at a boarding school; and I was very much alone.

The feeling I had experienced in my hotel room when I'd been alone in Istanbul, trying to get to England, had returned. For two whole weeks at this school I'd not had time to truly reflect on my situation, but as soon as the pace of school life slowed, reality flooded back.

The irony of the situation was that I did not even want to be with Mehdi – yet something within me badly wanted to be picked up by someone, anyone; it almost did not matter who. I had not talked to my parents for some time, and loneliness was overtaking me. The feeling of isolation gave me butterflies in my stomach.

I tried to keep playing snooker, but my anxiety and distress made it hard. I slowly put the balls away and scuffed back to my homeroom to sit at my desk, staring out the window. The greenery was spectacular – just the way I had imagined England to be – yet there was something missing.

Soon Mrs Griffiths came up to find me in the homeroom. 'Come on, we have to walk the dogs now.'

I had eyed Mr and Mrs Griffiths' two springer spaniels longingly anytime I'd caught a glimpse of them since arriving; as a new boy, I'd never had the opportunity to interact with them. So it was a real privilege to be able to walk them and play with them now. Mrs Griffiths always knew exactly what to do or what to say to make me feel better. Most of the time, like all the boys, I was scared of her commanding figure, but everyone experienced her nurturing side too at some point during their time at Aymestrey.

Following a brisk walk with Mrs Griffiths and the dogs, she left me to play with the two springer spaniels for almost three hours on the front lawns. Too soon, I noticed

Mr Griffiths standing between the large oak doors at the front of the school. Time had passed so quickly, and in those three hours I had fallen in love with those dogs. All they required of me was my attention and my willingness to play with them, and in return they gave me their affection. Mr Griffiths was smiling at the three of us, so happily occupying ourselves for such a long time.

'Put them away and come and see me,' he shouted, his pipe still in his mouth. I led the dogs to their large open-air compound then headed back to the front of the school. Mr Griffiths was waiting for me in the enclosed porch area.

'When was the last time you spoke to your mother, Abbas?'

'Erm…' I said hesitantly as I tried to understand the question. 'I think… three weeks, sir.'

'When was the last time you saw your mother?' Mr Griffiths pointed to his eyes to explain what he was asking.

'Three… maybe nearly four months, sir.'

'Here.' Mr Griffiths pointed to an old telephone with a rotary dial. 'You have five minutes.'

'Thank you, sir,' I said slowly. 'I call mother?'

'I think you mean, *I can call my mother?*'

'Yes… sorry, sir… I can call my mother?'

'Yes,' he said with a smile, 'but no longer than five minutes; it will be expensive.'

Just to hear my mother's voice would be such a treat. I missed her so much. I hoped fervently that she was at home. I picked up the receiver with such care and began to dial my home number, which I knew by heart. After a long pause, the phone at the other end of the line started to ring.

'Pick up… pick up… pick up,' I murmured to myself in Farsi.

The phone continued to ring for what seemed like an eternity. I was about to hang up when I heard a voice.

'Hello?'

'Maman?'

'Abbas? Is that you?'

'Yes,' I said, with the biggest smile on my face, 'it's me. I don't have long…I only have five minutes.'

'Oh my God, oh my God, how are you? Where are you? Are you okay?'

'Yes, yes, I am fine,' I said softly. 'I made it to England. I am at a boarding school. We are not usually allowed to call people, but they made an exception for me today.'

'Boarding school?' she asked, distressed. 'Are they good to you?'

'Yes, it is really good here. I have friends – I like it.'

'Is Mehdi looking after you?' she asked.

'Yes,' I said after a slight pause, 'he is fine.' My eyes were welling up and I was getting that feeling in my throat that made it hard to speak. 'All is fine. How are you getting on with trying to get a visa, Maman?'

'Well…' she said, 'we are trying our hardest.'

'You don't even have your passport back yet, do you?'

The air felt dead as silence answered my question. I felt tears roll down my cheeks and hit the polished floorboards beneath my feet. I really did not want my mother to know that I was crying, so I tried to hide it when I spoke.

'I know you are trying,' I whispered. 'Maybe soon.'

'Yes, soon, my darling,' she said. She could not stop herself from sniffling. I knew how upset she was, and I did not want to make it worse, but my tears were flowing faster and faster.

'Well, I had better go, Maman,' I said sadly. 'I called the first chance I got.'

'I know, my sweetheart,' she said, crying openly now. 'I love you so much. I am so proud of you. You take good care of yourself, okay?'

'I will … Say hi to Baba.'

'I will.'

'Bye, Maman,' I said, trying ever so hard to muffle the sound of my crying.

I put down the phone and knelt next to it, breathing deeply, my tears flowing. After maybe thirty seconds I pulled myself together before going to report to Mr Griffiths.

The rest of the day was pretty uneventful. I had tea with Mr and Mrs Griffiths and played a little more snooker until bedtime – I was allowed to stay up till eight p.m. before being sent to my dormitory.

The thought of being with my family back in Iran inevitably ran through my mind. Recalling my short conversation with my mother earlier in the day brought fresh tears to my eyes. Sleeping was the last thing I could think of. My new friends had all hoped to eat as many sweets as possible during their weekend away, but I would have gladly gone without sweets for a year just to be able to see my mother for a day.

After staring out of the window at the stars for a few hours, I climbed back into bed and lay awake in the big dormitory in that vast mansion, all alone.

———

Another four weeks of school passed without real incident. My English was improving at what I later realised was a staggering pace. Without my really noticing it, conversations with my friends had started to take far less effort, and I could understand most things.

This transformation amazed me. I enjoyed school; the competitive environment that I found myself in and the discipline that came with it suited me. I gave myself up to the system and was soon completely integrated into the life of the school. Immersing myself in everything made me forget how much was missing from my life, and the constant distractions were a relief. For me, school was a source of enjoyment, something most other children probably never experienced. And as I found my place, my true character began to reappear. My friends became my family, and Aymestrey became my home.

Soon it was time for another exeat. The previous Sunday, at Mrs Griffiths' suggestion, I had written my weekly letter to Kate's parents, Brian and Nancy Bradford. I hadn't met them yet, but when I'd arrived in England Kate had told me that they were looking forward to meeting me and that they had asked her to pass along their contact details to me. So Mrs Griffiths had suggested I write and tell them about my upcoming exeat, and just see what happened.

To my great surprise, Nancy had written back to me – my first English letter, which I received on the Saturday when we were all meant to leave for the night. I experienced such delight at the sight of a letter actually written to me. For close to seven weeks I had visited the mail table, watching my friends receive cards, letters and all kinds of goodies in the mail. At last, I had a handwritten letter of my own.

I took Nancy's letter with me to read as I watched the other boys' parents arriving. The first few cars pulled up, and some of the children began to leave. I was a little hesitant, because I did not know Nancy and Brian very well, but I opened the letter with great excitement regardless.

Dear Abbas,

Thank you for your letter. Kate has spoken very highly of you, so it was a lovely surprise. Brian and I are very glad that you are enjoying school. I am amazed at how well your letter was written. Good job!

Brian will come and pick you up, and I will be excitedly waiting for the two of you to arrive. I am not sure if Mehdi and Kate will be here, but you are welcome to stay with us for the weekend either way.

Since I will see you in a few days, I will not write too much. We will see you on Saturday, and both look forward very much to meeting you.

Yours,

Nancy and Brian

As I reread the letter I couldn't help smiling. They really did want to meet me! I brushed down my blazer with my hands to make sure I would be as presentable as possible when Brian arrived. As I was inspecting my reflection in the window, I felt a tap on my shoulder.

'Hey, Abbas,' Murphy chirped, his face alight with the excitement of the weekend, 'my mum said that if you get left here, you can come to our house for the weekend.'

'Thanks, Spud,' I replied in a low tone. I knew that Murphy was just being kind to me, but it was hard not to feel like a charity case, receiving such an offer. 'Your mum is already here, though – she won't want to wait around.'

'She said to tell Mr Griffiths that we can come back and get you. We live close by.'

'Thanks,' I said, feeling happy despite my misgivings. 'I

think someone is coming this time. But if not, that would be cool; I don't want to be here alone again.'

'Okay, Abs, see you soon.'

'Bye.'

Almost as soon as Murphy's car had disappeared, a man pulled into the driveway and waved to me, so I knew it must be Brian. I jumped up, inspected myself once more, and hurried out to the car. I walked fast so that Brian did not have to get out, so I could make his life as easy as possible. As I passed Mr Griffiths he waved at me with his pipe and gave me a knowing smile.

I opened the front passenger door.

'Hello, Brian,' I said politely. 'It's very nice to meet you. How are you?'

'I'm well.' Brian chuckled. 'Nice to meet you, too. And look at you. Your English is so good – no accent or anything.'

'Thank you.'

'Get in.'

I got into the car and Brian started the fifteen-minute journey to Layton Avenue in Malvern Link.

'So, how's school, young man?' he asked, smiling over at me as he drove.

'School is going very well, thank you. I have made friends, made the rugby team and I am sure I will be in the top three ranked students in the class next term.'

'You made the rugby team?'

'Yes.'

'I'm not sure which is more impressive – your English or the fact that you are on the rugby team!'

I just smiled and bowed my head, embarrassed by such praise.

'I'm not sure if Mehdi and Kate will make it today.'

'They won't come?'

'They've gone to Gloucester and I'm not confident that they will make it.'

'Oh, okay. Thank you for having me for the weekend,' I said. On the one hand I was delighted that Mehdi would not be there and on the other hand I felt like a burden on people who did not even know me.

'You're welcome,' he said, smiling. 'It's nice for us to have a visitor once in a while.'

We soon pulled up in the driveway of Brian and Nancy's home. The front lawn was mown in neat lines and looked immaculate, surrounded by beautiful rose bushes, with an oak tree in the centre. Before we reached the door Nancy opened it to welcome us and a scruffy dog rushed past her and leapt up at me, dancing around my feet and whimpering with joy.

'Hello, Abbas, how are you?' she said with a warm, genuine smile. 'It's so nice to meet you. I see Polly has introduced herself!'

'I am well, thank you,' I replied, patting the dog. 'I'm pleased to meet you, too. How are you?'

'Oh, I'm just fine, thank you,' she said. 'Well, come in … don't stand on the doorstep.'

'Thank you.'

'I'm so impressed at how well you are coming along with your English, Abbas,' Nancy said as she led me to the living room. 'You don't even have an accent.'

'That's what I said,' Brian chipped in, 'and you haven't even heard about the rugby team yet.' His grin showed me how excited he was about that; he was glowing with pride, as if I were his own son. It was so strange to me to see such kindness, especially from people who had only just met me and were associated with me only remotely, through their daughter.

'Get started on these, boys.' Nancy pointed to some sandwiches and crisps and a jug of orange squash. Brian and I started to dig into the food. Nancy came back a few minutes later with a simple jam-filled sponge cake she had just baked. The smell of freshly baked cake filled the entire living room and kitchen.

'So have you heard from Mehdi since you started school?' Nancy said.

'No,' I replied shyly, taking a small bite out of my sandwich.

'What would've happened if Brian hadn't come to get you today?'

'I am not sure. Maybe I'd have stayed at school again ... or maybe if Mr and Mrs Griffiths allowed, I could have gone with Murphy,' I said uncertainly.

'Again?' Nancy said in a slightly harsher tone. 'What do you mean, *again*?'

'Erm ... well ...'

'Go on, Abbas, you're okay, you're not in trouble,' Brian interjected.

'You are definitely not in trouble, Abbas,' Nancy said.

'Well,' I said uncomfortably as I sat up a little, 'four weeks ago we had an exeat and I had to stay at school.'

'Why?'

'No one came for me,' I said softly, looking down at my plate.

'Were Mehdi and Kate meant to come for you?' Brian asked, concerned.

'Well, I had written to them telling them about the exeat,' I said, quickly trying to tell the whole story.

'So how many people stayed at school over the exeat?' Nancy asked.

'Erm … I was the only person.'

'Why does that not bloody surprise me?' Brian snapped. 'Give Mehdi half a chance and—'

'Brian,' Nancy said sternly, 'not now.' She tilted her head in my direction.

'This is why I don't like him,' Brian whispered to his wife, but I heard it quite clearly.

'Brian, not now, dear.'

'Abbas, from now on, if you have any exeats, you be sure to write to us,' Brian said, ignoring his wife. I could tell he was not a huge fan of Mehdi.

'Quite right,' Nancy added. 'You are welcome anytime you want; in fact, every time you have an exeat, you write to us. If Mehdi and Kate happen to be here, then great; if not, it will be the three of us. How does that sound?'

'Great, thank you.'

We continued to eat Nancy's cake, then settled down to watch some television. After some time, Nancy turned down the television during a commercial break, and looked over at me.

'When was the last time you spoke to your parents, Abbas?'

'Erm … Mr Griffiths let me call them for five minutes last exeat.' It was clear that this had only been because Mr Griffiths had felt sorry for me, but I didn't want to say that. 'I was able to speak to my mum.'

'What about your dad?' Brian asked.

'No, he was not home.'

'Would you like to call them now?' Nancy asked.

'Well, it is expensive …' I said, not wanting to be a bother.

'It's okay, Abbas. You should call them,' Brian said, springing up out of his chair. 'Follow me.'

He led me into the hallway, where their main home telephone was located. Nancy followed, smiling.

'You know the number, don't you?' Nancy asked.

'Yes, thank you.'

'Okay, go for it.' Nancy seemed almost as excited as I was.

I picked up the phone, and as I did, both Nancy and Brian returned to the living room. I appreciated the privacy, even though they would not have understood what I was saying to my parents anyway. After about three rings, my father picked up.

'Hello?'

'Hi Baba, it's me, Abbas.'

'Hi, son,' he said excitedly. 'How are you?'

'I'm well. How is everything?'

'Oh, you know,' he said, his voice growing softer, as if he was about to lie, 'things are good.'

'Where is Maman?'

'She's not here. She'll be so upset to know she missed your call.' He sighed. 'She's visiting your grandfather and won't be back till later.'

'Oh.' Not being able to speak to my mother on this rare chance was a real blow for me. To hear her voice would have really cheered me up.

'Sorry, Abbas,' he said. 'Where are you?'

'I am at Mehdi's girlfriend's parents' house.'

'Where?' he asked, sounding confused.

'I am with some very nice people Mehdi knows.'

'Oh, so where is Mehdi?'

'I am not really sure, but I think he is working.'

'Well, is he looking after you?' he asked, sounding concerned.

'Oh yeah, he is,' I said, almost too confidently. I really wanted to tell my father the truth about what kind of a man Mehdi was, but I felt as if I could not, as I feared the consequences if my father talked to him. I also felt guilty: as a family we had gone through so much for me to be in England, and there was a huge responsibility on my shoulders to make this situation work.

'So how is school?'

'Going really well. I am almost fluent in English already,' I said proudly. 'I just need to increase my vocabulary.'

'Well done,' he said. I could almost see him smiling. 'Why don't you call more often?'

'At school we are not allowed to use the phone, and I rarely get to leave.'

'I see,' he replied. 'Then make sure you continue to study hard, okay?'

'Okay, Baba.' I paused. 'Baba?'

'Yes?'

'Is Maman going to be able to come soon?'

There was a very long pause before my father spoke again. 'We are working on it, son,' he said diplomatically.

'Is it going to be long, do you think?' I asked.

'I don't know, Abbas…I don't know.'

It was obvious from the tone of his voice that my father was getting impatient with me, so I decided not to inquire further.

'Well, I have to go, Baba. Will you say hi to Maman for me?'

'Sure I will,' he said a little more calmly. 'Look after yourself.'

'I will. Bye.'

I felt so deflated as I walked back to the living room.

'Did you get to speak to them?' Nancy asked.

'I did,' I said quietly, 'to my dad. Mum wasn't in.'

'That's a shame,' Nancy said sympathetically.

'Well, at least you spoke to your dad.' Brian was trying to see the good in the situation.

Though I pretended I was happy, the conversation with my father had actually dampened my mood. I was not terribly optimistic about the progress my parents were making to get my mother out of Iran. I wished I had been able to speak to her; I missed my mother more and more as time passed. It was she who gave me hope; thinking of her encouraged me to be strong.

That evening we watched television until I excused myself for bed at nine p.m. Nancy handed me a towel and showed me the bathroom upstairs, then took me to the room where I was to sleep. I thanked her and turned to get ready for bed, but Nancy stood in the doorway and looked at me.

'I know you miss your mum, Abbas,' she said kindly, 'and I know no one will ever replace her, but I am here if you need me. You will always be welcome here, irrespective of where Mehdi is or what happens.'

'Thank you so much,' I said. 'Thank you.'

She leant in and kissed me on the head and stroked my hair.

'Goodnight, Abbas.'

'Goodnight.'

With that I closed the door behind her and sat on the bed. I did not know whether it was because I missed my mother so much or because of Nancy's warmth and kindness, but I sat there and cried silently.

When at last I could compose myself, I went to the bathroom.

Nancy was waiting for me when I returned.

'Do some of the children at school have soft toys for the dormitory?'

'Soft toys?' I asked, puzzled.

'You know, teddy bears...'

'Oh, yes, everyone has one.'

'Well, that's good to know.'

She gave me a smile and a knowing look, and I knew she was up to something. I never really stopped feeling shy around Nancy and Brian – I always felt as if I was imposing – but I liked and trusted them.

'Goodnight, Nancy,' I said as I headed for bed.

I knew the future would be hard, but at least Brian and Nancy cared about me.

FOUR

First term passed incredibly swiftly, and by the end of it, without noticing, I had become fluent in the English language. My vocabulary was a little limited still, but I was soaking up information like a sponge soaks up water. I had done extremely well in my classes, and knew that next term I would reach third in the class standings – a long and rapid climb from my beginnings at the bottom of the class. Strangely, I received my best mark for Grammar. Mrs Griffiths told me my English was better than my classmates' because I had learnt it the correct way.

The exit hall resonated with the energy and excitement of end of term, and the other children were all eager to go home for the Christmas break. I was actually feeling depressed. I did not want to see Mehdi or be an imposition on Brian and Nancy. I felt safe and comfortable at Aymestrey, and I loved being treated like everyone else. Instead of feeling like a burden, I could excel, and behave like other boys my own age. What's more, I never had time to think about my other problems.

I did not know who was going to pick me up. I had not

seen Mehdi since I'd started school, but I had stayed with Brian and Nancy twice now, and gone once to Murphy's house after I'd written to Kate and Mehdi rather than Brian and Nancy (on Mrs Griffiths' insistence) and been forgotten again. Now I was too anxious to sit still, so I started to help the other children out with their bags and trunks when their parents came.

To my astonishment, almost every mother in the school seemed to know who I was, and almost all of them offered me a place to stay if I needed it. Obviously a lot of children must have told their parents that I was sometimes left behind. All the offers seemed genuine; they really did seem to care. I felt that I might be able to take them up on their offers for exeats, but that there was no way I could impose myself on any of them for almost four weeks. Even so, it made me happy to know I was well liked.

I noticed Mr Griffiths smiling at me from afar as he puffed on his pipe. He walked over to me and patted me on the back.

'Good lad, Abby.' This was his new pet name for me. 'Makes the time go quicker, eh?'

'Yes, sir.'

'I see your stock has gone up around here, young man.'

'Sorry, sir?' I said, not really understanding.

'Life has a way of rewarding you if you persevere, young man. If you act like a gentleman even when things are not going well for you, ultimately you will see a reward.'

'I guess, sir.'

'You see how many new friends you have?'

'Yes, sir.'

'People do not open their homes to just anyone.' He puffed again. 'You must be doing something right. You had a great term. I don't expect anything less next term.'

'Thank you, sir. Absolutely, sir.'

He began to tap his pipe against the wall, smiling at me as I turned to help someone else. Mr Griffiths was not one to pay a lot of compliments and this little exchange made me feel good about myself. It was so long since I had talked to my parents that Mr and Mrs Griffiths' good opinion was really the only thing that I cared about now.

Once again I sat alone after everyone had left, but this time, it being the end of term, I knew that someone had to come for me because the school was going to close for the holidays. I knelt on the wooden bench and stared out of the window, wondering who would come.

I heard Mrs Griffiths striding towards me. 'Abbas, last one here?' she said. I just stared at her, not knowing what to say. 'Go on, you can play snooker on the big table if you'd like. I will make a few calls.'

'Thank you.'

I walked upstairs, but realised I was not in the mood to play snooker, so I went to my homeroom and sat at my empty desk. I rested my face on my hands and stared out the window. A few hours later I felt a tap on my shoulder, waking me from a deep sleep.

'Mehdi is here to pick you up, Abbas,' Mrs Griffiths said gently in my ear.

'Yes, madam.'

'Go and wash your face then go downstairs.'

'Thank you, madam.'

My heart started to beat at a thousand miles per hour. I was afraid of Mehdi's moods, and of what might happen. I went to wash my face, trying to prepare myself for the inevitable unpleasantness.

As I walked slowly downstairs I glanced through a window and saw Mehdi standing next to his Saab looking impatient. In the exit hall I picked up one end of my trunk and began to drag it outside, where Mehdi watched me haul it through the gravel. Mrs Griffiths came outside and hurried towards me, and I knew I had to reach the car before she reached me, or Mehdi would be mad at me for making him look bad. I pulled on the trunk with all my might and jogged it to the car before Mrs Griffiths could catch up. I was panting as I bent my knees and tried to lift the trunk into the boot. Mehdi watched me struggle, his face impassive. We had not even said hello to each other when he bent down and whispered, 'Watch the paint.'

'Yes, sir,' I groaned as I lifted the trunk. Somehow I managed to get it into the boot of the car. Mrs Griffiths gave Mehdi a look of sharp disapproval – a look I knew only too well. She was far too smart to say anything, though.

I climbed into the front passenger seat and watched Mehdi and Mrs Griffiths exchange a few words. Then Mehdi flopped into the car and drove off erratically, crunching the gears. I did not dare speak.

'You happy with yourself?' he shouted.

'No.' I was not sure what he was talking about.

'Do you know how much I owe the school for next term?' he cried loudly. 'Who the hell is going to pay that?'

'I'm sorry,' I said softly, keeping my head down.

'Sorry is not going to pay your bills, Abbas,' he screamed. 'You think I'm made of money?'

'No.'

'Well, it doesn't grow on trees.'

'Perhaps I could call my dad…'

'Your dad? What a joke. Are you serious? Your loser

father is going to be able to find that kind of money in under four weeks?'

I was boiling inside. Why did he have to insult my father?

'He is not a loser,' I said quietly, and Mehdi clipped me hard around the back of the head. My heart started to beat even faster.

'Not a loser?' he shouted in fury. 'Shut the hell up. When I want your bloody opinion I will ask you. Do we understand each other?'

I sat in shocked silence.

'I asked if we understood each other.'

'Yes, sir. Yes, sir,' I responded swiftly.

'You calling me sir is not going to help you.'

'I'm sorry,' I said. 'I will do anything to help.'

'You're going to have to work like the rest of us.'

'I can do that.'

'We are going to my work in Malvern. Abbey International College. I'm head cook.'

'Okay.'

'In the holidays they have kids come from abroad, to learn English in the morning and go and see churches and stuff in the afternoons,' he muttered. 'They need packed lunches.'

'Okay,' I responded, not knowing where he was going with this yet.

'I have to pay someone four pounds an hour to make those lunches, so you are going to make them instead.'

'I can do that.'

'Well, you don't have a choice. And you can't come and go as you please.'

'I don't understand.'

'You're going to have to make the packed lunches at night so that no one sees you.'

'Why?'

'Because you are underage, Abbas,' he shouted. 'You cannot let anyone see you or we are going to have problems, big problems.'

'Of course.'

'If you don't want to get deported, then don't get seen. Keep your head low and make sure you're done by five a.m., before the milkman does his deliveries – understand? The only reason you're still in this country is because of me – okay?'

'Okay,' I replied, still not understanding exactly what I would have to do.

'I told Kate, Brian and Nancy that you're doing one of the college's holiday camps and that you'll be staying there.'

'Okay.' I hesitated. 'Where will I be staying?'

'There's a spare room next to the kitchen with a bed in it. You'll spend the holidays there.'

Twenty-five minutes after leaving Aymestrey, we arrived at Abbey International College. It was set deep in the Malvern Hills, in stunningly beautiful surroundings, but I could not help feeling scared as I dragged my trunk behind Mehdi towards some buildings.

'The kitchen is to the right' – Mehdi pointed it out to me – 'but that small building is where you're going to stay.'

The building was right next to the kitchen and the size of a shed. There was a small sofa, one side table and a sink inside.

'The sofa is a pull-out,' Mehdi said impatiently. 'Drop off your things and I'll show you the kitchen.'

I dumped my trunk and took one more look at my small, dark room. As we walked outside, Mehdi showed me an even smaller building.

'That's your toilet.'

'An outside toilet?'

'I'm sorry I didn't book the Hilton for you, you spoilt little brat.'

'I was just asking,' I said quietly.

I followed Mehdi to the kitchen in silence, glancing back at my room and the outside toilet. I was wondering how I would shower, because Mehdi had made no mention of a shower or bath, but I was too scared to ask him.

We went through a door and walked past a messy room on our left, which Mehdi proudly announced was his office. There was a paper-covered desk with a chair either side of the desk. The corridor continued on to a large kitchen.

'You have to make five hundred and sixty-seven packed lunches every night for at least the next two weeks. After that the numbers may change.'

'Okay.'

'There are brown lunch bags in the pantry,' he said, opening the door, 'and the bread is here, too.'

'All white bread?'

'All white,' he responded. 'I want you to make half with cheese and ham and half with just cheese.'

'Okay, but five hundred and sixty-seven is an odd number,' I said.

'You always have to be a smart-arse, don't you,' he snapped.

'I don't mean to be. I just—'

'Just shut up and listen, will you?'

'Yes, sir,' I said. There was no pleasing this man.

'Just make two hundred and eighty cheese and ham, and the rest cheese. Make the cheese ones with pickle, and throw in a sachet of mayo and mustard with the cheese and ham.'

As he talked, he pointed out the ingredients.

'You'll butter all the bread first, then add the ingredients and wrap the sandwiches up in cling wrap. Put a bag of crisps and a bottle of water in every bag, and that's it.'

'Okay.'

'If you have time, put a slice of tomato and pickle in with the cheese and ham, but if you're running out of time make that your last priority.'

'I can do that.'

'You make sure you're done before five a.m. – let's say by 4.30 to be safe – because you must not be seen, you understand?'

'Yes, I will be done.'

'Here's the key for the back door,' he said, handing me a fat brown key. 'I'll be out of here at seven at the latest every night after we've washed up the dishes.'

'I will come and start at 7.15 then.'

'Okay, but make sure you wash up after yourself so the breakfast crew doesn't get wind of you.'

'What shall I do with the bags when I'm finished?'

'Pack them in these boxes and leave them in my office.'

'I will,' I said. 'I will label the boxes with the type of sandwiches they contain, too.'

'Whatever. Now go get some rest because you'll be up all night.'

'Yes, sir.'

'And if you get caught, I swear…'

'I won't, I promise.'

With that I walked out. First I went to my room and pulled out the sofa to inspect the bed, and realised that there were no pillows or bedding and the mattress was worn and stained. The room was damp, with a pungent smell, and mould stained the corners where the walls met the ceiling. The tap over the sink was dripping and there were brown stains all over the white bowl. The old stained curtains kept out the light, and I decided to keep them closed for now.

I needed to investigate my surroundings before I did anything else. The college campus was set amid lush green hills, its buildings surrounded by tall evergreens scattered over the slope. At the bottom of the hill was a large outdoor swimming pool, with three outdoor showers nearby. I made a mental note of the showers and walked back up the hill to see what else I could find. There was a tuckshop next to the student lounge selling all kinds of chocolates, soft drinks and crisps. The chocolates looked very tempting, but I did not have a penny to my name.

Back in my room I sat down on the bed and opened the top drawer of the side table. There was a key inside it, which fitted the door. I felt a little better knowing that I could lock the door behind me. Mehdi had scared me with his talk about my being deported, and I did not want anyone to know I was there. I lay down on the bed and wondered how I would spend the rest of the day.

I just wanted to be back at Aymestrey; I hated being away from school. I wondered whether my life would always be like this. What was the purpose of coming to England if I was going to be treated so badly? But then I thought of school and remembered my friends. At school I was treated like everyone else, and because I did well, I was often rewarded.

Eventually I fell asleep and woke up at around 5.30 p.m. I'd had nothing to eat or drink all day, and felt hungry and headachy. I got up and washed my face with cold water in the sink, then sat on the edge of the bed staring at my watch, waiting for it to reach 7.15 p.m.

After a while I opened my trunk, took out some paper and a pencil and began doodling. Then I decided to use the time to write a letter to my mother, which I hadn't been able to do from school since I did not have access to airmail stamps. In Istanbul it had been liberating to be in control of my money and able to choose when to write my mother a letter. Although at Aymestrey I was kept so busy that I had little time to reflect on the fact that I had not communicated with Maman.

I took out a fresh piece of paper and realised that I did not know what to write. I could not tell her what was happening now because it would upset her, so I decided that I would keep it short and tell her as much of the truth as I could.

Dear Maman,

I hope that you and Baba are well. I have not heard from you in a long time so I wanted to just send you a letter saying hi! I am well. You will be glad to know that I am doing really well at school. I will be second or third in my class next term. I am also in the rugby team. Who would have guessed that I would one day play rugby! They don't play football at my school but that's okay because I really like rugby. Not next term but the one after we will play cricket. That is another English sport. It is meant to be fun.

Mehdi is well. He says hi.

Well, I'd better go because I have some homework that I have to do. I just wanted you to know that I am okay.

*It is strange how this letter will get to you –
how it can leave one country and get to another
country without any issues, but when it comes to
us humans we have to go through all this trouble
and be separated like this. At least you will know
that I touched this piece of paper, and you will be
connected to me through that touch. I guess for
now I will take what I can get. I really hope you
can leave soon.*

I love you.

Abbas

xxxx

I folded the piece of paper, put it in an envelope and wrote the address on the front, then in bold capital letters I added VIA AIR MAIL. Only then did I realise that I did not have any stamps, nor any money to buy them. So I put the letter away in the drawer until I could get hold of some stamps.

I was still wearing my school uniform and I knew I could not go to work dressed like that. I took off my clothes, folded them neatly as we had been taught to do at school, and put them back in my trunk. I took out my tracksuit, trainers and T-shirt and dressed for work. After a quick trip to the toilet, I locked my door and walked to the back door of the kitchen.

I could hear a lot of people at the front of the school near the tuckshop and the lounge, but around the back everything was quiet. I put my ear to the door to make sure no one was inside the kitchen, then slowly and carefully unlocked the back door and crept inside. I locked the door behind me and put the key in my tracksuit pants pocket, zipping it closed. There was no soap in my room, so I went to the sink and washed thoroughly to prepare myself for the night's work.

The kitchen was rectangular, with work counters on each of its two long sides. The back door was at one end, a serving area at the other, and in between sat a central workstation, which was fitted out with industrial kitchen equipment.

I picked up two loaves of bread and set out the slices in two rows along one of the work counters, then spread margarine on each piece. I then laid one piece of bread on top of the other to create a sandwich without any filling, piled the empty sandwiches up into stacks of ten, and put them on the other counter. I repeated the process until the other counter was full of empty sandwiches and I had no more room.

I decided to make the cheese sandwiches first, so I took out the pickle and added it to the ten open sandwiches I had just buttered. I then came back around with slices of cheese and finished them up. Each time I finished a stack of ten cheese sandwiches, I'd bag them and swap them for an empty stack from the other workbench.

When I had made about one hundred cheese-and-pickle sandwiches I decided to eat one. I was very hungry and I did not know what else I could eat. I did not know if I was allowed to eat college food, but I hoped that no one would notice if one sandwich went missing.

I spotted a radio in the far corner, turned it on and lowered the volume. It was a nice change to have a little music in the background while I worked, to break the monotony of making sandwiches.

After several hours my sandwiches were mounting up, but it was harder work than I had anticipated. Midnight had passed and I was only about halfway through my work.

I was sweating and tired. I took a small bottle of milk out of the gigantic fridge, feeling slightly guilty, and slid down the wall onto the floor to drink it. It tasted so good and I felt my energy levels rise.

I wondered whether I could possibly earn enough money to pay for school if I worked every day of the holidays. Mehdi had said he'd had to pay someone four pounds an hour, so I did the maths and soon realised that Mehdi would actually save quite a lot of money by having me here. Hopefully it would be enough.

At just before four a.m. I finished making the last sandwich. I boxed the bags of lunches nicely and left them in Mehdi's office, after labelling each box with its contents.

There was still a little time left before I had to leave, so I went into the pantry and took a few bags of crisps and a bar of soap. I took the two additional sandwiches I had made for myself for tomorrow, a few bottles of water, an apple and another bottle of milk. I put all of my goodies into a plastic bag to take back to my room. Then I checked the kitchen one last time – I had cleaned all the counters and put the utensils back in their places so that the place was spotless.

I switched off the radio and the lights and turned to leave, hesitating outside Mehdi's office. Perhaps he would have some stamps. I began to look through the mess on his desk and inside the drawers, but I could find nothing.

Outside, the cold air was a shock on my sweaty skin; the kitchen had been warm but my dank room was chilly. I took out the bottle of milk and drank it down, wiped my mouth and lay on my bed. My back was sore, and there were no bedcovers or pillows, but I was too exhausted to care. Within seconds I passed out into a deep sleep.

FIVE

I woke up after one p.m., my back stiff and sore from sleeping in sweaty clothes in a cold room. I felt groggy and unwell. Suddenly I sneezed and noticed that my nose was congested. I felt like staying curled up in bed but I needed to go to the toilet, so I got up and hurried there, being careful to stay hidden.

Back in my room I felt hot and miserable; my nose ran and my head ached, but there was no way I could get out of work on my second day. I was too frightened to go to the kitchen and speak to Mehdi. I would just have to rest and try to get through another night. The work had been harder than I had anticipated, and I worried that I might not be able to manage if I felt so ill.

I took out a sandwich, but after two bites I wrapped it up again and put it back in the plastic bag. I drank half a bottle of water and tried to sleep, but I kept drifting in and out of wakefulness. I really wanted to have a shower but I couldn't go down to the pool in the middle of the day without being seen. I stripped off my clothes and washed myself in the sink as best I could, using the soap

I'd brought back from the kitchen. It felt good to be clean.

My loneliness reminded me of Istanbul: I was in a room with nothing to do; I was feeling unwell; there was no one to help me or look after me; and I still had to go to work. I tried to occupy myself by washing my underwear and hanging it over the end of the bed to dry, but then there was nothing more to do but lie on the bed and wait for seven o'clock.

At 7.15 I put on my tracksuit again and grudgingly headed back to the kitchen. As soon as I walked in I noticed a sign on Mehdi's office door: *567 again*. There were leftovers in the fridge, but as much as I wanted to eat a slice of pizza, I knew I could not have kept it down. So, on an empty stomach, I began to make sandwiches once more, using the system I had perfected the night before.

After a couple of hours I began to feel extremely nauseous, and I clearly had a fever. I was getting hotter and hotter and I had almost no energy. I could only just keep down liquids, but I needed energy to keep working. I had seen Mrs Griffiths give children Marmite dissolved in boiling water as a soup when they were sick, and had heard her say that it had a lot of good 'stuff' in it and would keep them alive. I began to rummage through the massive kitchen pantry and eventually I found a large pot of Marmite. I boiled the kettle and mixed in two spoonfuls of Marmite, then slid to the floor for a rest with my cup of Marmite soup.

I was dripping with sweat and shivering at the same time. My bones were aching and my teeth were chattering. For a few minutes I became a helpless child again and began to weep, giving way to my feelings of vulnerability, loneliness and weakness.

The radio hummed quietly in the background, and like a sign from God, 'Eye of the Tiger' began to play, the theme song from *Rocky III*. It brought back memories of when I was small and I would fall over and cry. My father would always ask me, 'Would Rocky cry?' Almost without exception that would make me stop crying, because I idolised Rocky. Now, the song brought a small smile to my face in the midst of my tears. I really believed that it was a sign. I stood up and began working again. Although I was still technically a child, I felt like a man. The misery, nausea and shivering were now bearable.

My work was sloppier than the night before, but I was struggling to meet my deadline. All I wanted to do was get back to bed. By 4.30 a.m. I had managed to finish everything. I could barely walk.

I took some water crackers and fruit for the following day, and made my way back to my room. I longed to sleep but I thought I should shower first. I found my towel and hobbled down the hill. As I walked I could not control the nausea anymore and I began to vomit, although my stomach was almost empty. I fell to my knees, shuddering, retching and trying to breathe in the crisp morning air.

At the showers, the moon was reflected in the swimming pool. At any other time I would have appreciated the beauty and serenity of my surroundings, but I just wanted to get washed and crawl back to bed. I took off my clothes and turned on the water. It was ice-cold and showed no signs of warming up. I realised that I had forgotten my soap, so I just rinsed off the sweat and got out. I dried myself, dressed and walked back up the hill as fast as I could.

Back in my room, I dried my hair and lay on the bed. I thought I would fall asleep immediately, but to my dismay I didn't. The shivering fits were keeping me awake, and my teeth were chattering hard. I curled into the foetal position, trying to keep warm. After a while I pulled all the clothes out of my trunk and put on as many layers as possible, then spread the rest over myself. Eventually fatigue overcame me and I drifted into a long, deep sleep.

I woke up sweating profusely, stripped off some layers, drank some water and went back to sleep. My only thought was that I would need to be well enough to work the following night. I had not seen Mehdi in two days and I was unsure how to contact him without going into the kitchen during the day or leaving him a cryptic message. But contacting Mehdi about my fever was not an option anyway; I was just too scared of him.

It must have been past five o'clock when I woke next – only two hours before I had to be at work. I felt just as miserable, but I realised that I was a tiny bit better than the day before. I finished off the food I had left over. The fact that I had slept through an entire day had obviously helped, but I knew it would take all my willpower to work through another night. I had not come to England for a life like this, I thought. Fortunately I had no idea then of what still lay ahead of me.

And so I began what was to become my holiday routine. Once more I crept into the kitchen at night and began to make sandwiches to the murmur of the radio in the background. The shivering slowly faded, but I still felt poorly and needed rest.

Just before midnight I decided to take a break. I was sitting on the floor drinking my Marmite soup when I heard someone fiddling with the lock on the kitchen door. My heart lurched. Quietly I put down the cup and crawled into the pantry. I was absolutely terrified. I left a slight crack in the door so that I could see what was going on.

The noises grew louder and I could tell that someone was rummaging through the papers in Mehdi's office. My only thought was of being caught and deported. After about five minutes I saw a shadow appear in the main work area. As it drew nearer I realised that it was Mehdi, lurching about. He did not look normal; he was walking as if he might fall over at any moment.

Slowly I came out of hiding.

'You scared me. I didn't know who it was.'

Mehdi turned around and his bloodshot eyes seemed to stare straight into my soul. The look was terrifying. He did not say a word, but began to walk slowly towards me. I backed away from him, never taking my eyes off his face. I hit the pantry door, and Mehdi closed in on me. He glanced towards the back door, then with sudden ferocity he struck me across the face. The force of the slap knocked me against the wall and I hit my head, stumbled against the work counter and fell to the floor. I wanted to scream with pain, but my instincts told me to lie still. I held my ear and my head and hoped the pain and the ringing would soon pass.

Mehdi leant over me and began to scream with such rage and hate that fear shuddered down my spine.

'What the bloody hell do you think you are doing?'

I remained silent.

'Well? What do you have to say for yourself?'

'What?'

'What? What?' he screamed. He strode to the other end of the kitchen and pulled the plug out of the wall, silencing the radio, then carried it over to me. I lay huddled on the floor, terrified of what he would do next. Mehdi loomed over me and in a low, menacing voice he said, 'What do you think this is?'

'A radio?'

'A radio. Yes, a bloody radio.'

Suddenly he raised his arm and smashed the radio against the floor beside my head, where it exploded, the splinters ricocheting off my head and body. My heart pounded and I felt utterly terrified. The last time I had felt like this was when I'd been pinned against a wall in Istanbul by a complete stranger with a knife at my throat.

'This is your idea of being careful? Well? Is it?'

'No one could hear. I tested it. I had it on super low ... I promise,' I murmured in desperation.

'You're such a bloody little know-it-all,' he screamed, like a man possessed. Out of nowhere he kicked me in the side with the toe of his boot. I heard my ribs crack before I actually felt the pain. I yelped, clambered onto all fours and began to cough and cry.

He knelt beside me and I smelt the stench of alcohol as he spoke into my ringing ear.

'Whatever you think you know, I know more. You want this holiday camp to end, you keep this up. The way you're acting, you're already on the plane back to Iran.'

He spoke with such hate. I had no idea why he hated me so much – I had done nothing wrong. My side was pounding with pain and I could barely move. Tears were rolling down my face and wetting the floor beneath me.

'Now clear this crap up and get your work done,' he snapped as he turned away. 'I want you out before the milkman.'

With that, he was gone.

I was in so much pain that it must have taken ten minutes before I could sit up by myself. I was sobbing uncontrollably, tears rolling down my cheeks. What had I done to deserve this? My ear was ringing, and I could feel myself growing hot again. I found two tea towels and tied the ends together. Then I took a bag of frozen peas and bound it to my side with the tea towels, a shriek of pain escaping me as I tightened the knot.

I started work as best I could. Every move I made was painful. I could not lift anything, nor could I stretch for anything. I was so exhausted that the previous night now seemed like a stroll in the park. I kept thinking about what had happened. It was so surreal. What had angered him so much? Had it been the alcohol? Or was it somehow my fault?

The sandwiches seemed to take forever to make, no matter how hard I worked, but the idea of not finishing was simply unthinkable after the night's events. I did not take another break that night.

Finally, just after five a.m., all the sandwiches were finished and I dragged the boxes into Mehdi's office. The pain was almost unbearable. When at last I entered my room I heard the rattling of the milkman's cart. I had missed him by seconds.

I got my towel and soap and began to hobble down the hill, every step making me wince. I felt so miserable. At least in Istanbul I had had my friend Murat, who'd worked at the hotel I'd stayed in, to help me.

The sun had still not risen, and the moon was the only source of light. I followed the narrow path down the hill through the lush morning dew when suddenly I noticed a piece of crinkled paper on the pathway. I could not believe what I was seeing – it was a twenty-pound note. Slowly and painfully I bent over and picked it up. That beating had not been worth twenty pounds, but I was ready to take any good fortune that came my way.

With a dejected smile I continued towards the showers. I

took off my clothes and examined the huge swollen bruise on my side. The cold shower eased the pain, and I just stood there and let the water hit my skin, unable to jiggle and dance as I had previously. Standing naked under that shower gazing at the moon, I wondered what my mother was doing. If she had been there, this might not have happened to me. I knew she was trying to reach me; I just had to hold tight until she arrived.

The next day I woke up feeling so stiff that it took a long time to get out of bed. In my hurry to leave the kitchen the night before, I had not taken any supplies. I still had a little water, which I drank, realising that I was in a lot of pain and that my fever was not letting up either. The good news was that I was hungry and actually felt like eating for the first time in two days.

I took my school cap out of the trunk and put it on, then put my newfound twenty-pound note in my pocket and walked gingerly to the tuckshop. I wandered through the little shop looking at all the tempting chocolate bars, then noticed that they had a small medicine section. I took some flu medicine and some paracetamol, a cup of instant noodles, a Mars Bar and a can of ginger ale. I was shocked by how expensive the medication was. As the teller – a man with a substantial stomach, beard and glasses – rang it up, I saw books of stamps and added one to the pile. That made me the most happy because I knew that I could now send my letter to my mum.

'The noodles for here?' the man asked.

'Can you put the water in them so that I can eat them on the go, please?' I kept my head down. I was terrified of being spotted by Mehdi, who would think I was making a spectacle of myself on the campus.

The man poured boiling water into my noodles for me and I took a plastic fork and spoon, threw it into the plastic bag he'd given me, and began to hobble away.

'You okay, mate?' the man asked.

'Yeah, thank you.'

With that I walked as normally as I could from the tuckshop.

Back in my room I began to eat my noodles and took some medicine. I put stamps on my letter and lay back on the bed. I had noticed a postbox near the tuckshop, and decided to mail the letter before work that night. I half finished the noodles and began to gently roll the icy can of ginger ale on my side to soothe the pain. I hoped that the paracetamol would make it go away altogether. I lay down and fell into a deep sleep once more.

When I woke, it was still early, and I felt particularly miserable. I looked at the money on the small side table. There were two one-pound coins and a fifty-pence coin among the pennies, plus a five-pound note. It gave me an idea. I walked up the hill to the campus entrance, where I had noticed a telephone box on the opposite side of the road. I pushed the coins into the phone and began dialling home. It was working – the phone started to ring.

'Hello?' My mother's voice echoed down the faulty line, but I was so happy to hear her.

'Maman? Hi. It's—'

'Abbas?' she interrupted. 'Is that you?'

I was watching my credit tick away at an alarming rate. I knew I did not have long.

'Maman, I have hardly any time to chat. My credit is running down super fast; I have a minute at best. I just wanted to say hi and hear your voice.'

'I know, my darling. It is okay. I'm so happy to hear your voice. Are you okay?'

'Yes …' I paused.

'What's wrong?'

'Nothing. Everything is great, Maman,' I said, trying to sound convincing. 'It's just been so long since we spoke.'

'I know … I'm so sorry. I don't know how to get hold of you, that's why.'

'I know,' I said, staring at the credit. 'So how is the stuff with your passport going? When are you going to get out, do you think?'

'I'm not sure, baby. I'm trying so hard. I miss you so much. I think about you all the—'

With that the phone went dead. My credit was all gone. Tears were rolling down my cheeks again. I just stood there in the phone booth and tried to collect myself as I sniffled and wiped away my tears. I was so happy that I had heard Maman's voice and yet so sad to have to go back to that miserable kitchen. I was frightened that Mehdi would get drunk and return. I could not keep working if he injured me again. I was really being stretched as it was, but it seemed I had few options. With trepidation I returned to the kitchen and set to work.

———

I did not see or speak to Mehdi for another three weeks. Each day I showed up to work and did what I had to do. The only communication I had from him was via the notes on his door indicating the number of lunch bags I had to prepare. Generally the number stayed in the mid five-hundreds – sometimes a little more and sometimes a little less.

With the exception of three more trips to the tuckshop to spend my remaining money, I lived in isolation in my room and worked through the nights. I slept during the days and dreaded each night's work: I was not resting enough to get better; and when I did eventually recover a little all my energy went into worrying instead that Mehdi might return for another drunken rampage. My side still hurt, too – the swelling had gone down somewhat (although the bruise was still the size of a grown man's foot, slowly changing colour) and I had more mobility, but I still could not lift anything too heavy.

Christmas Day came and went. Then New Year's Eve. I spent both alone. The thought of going back to school was the only thing that kept me going.

I was lying on my bed one morning watching the hands of the clock inch forward when the door suddenly slammed open. It was Mehdi.

'Get your stuff together. We need to leave.'

'Hi. Sure.'

I was scared. Mehdi was clearly in one of his moods.

'You are going back to school today, but Brian and Nancy want to see you first. God knows why.'

'We don't have to,' I said, 'if it's too much trouble…'

'Just shut up, will you?'

I packed up my stuff as quickly as I could and began to drag my trunk out of my room, my side aching with each step. Mehdi was striding away and the trunk was really heavy. When I eventually reached the car, I was scared to lift the trunk, but I was more afraid of asking Mehdi for help. I knelt down and wrestled the trunk into the boot, the pain making my eyes water. I quickly looked away so that Mehdi could not see my suffering.

We got into the car and Mehdi started to drive. Neither of us said anything for at least five minutes.

'You say nothing about what you did the last few weeks, you hear?' he said eventually.

I nodded. He reached over and grabbed me by the hair, tugging my head back.

'I asked you a goddamn question. I said, *Do you understand?*'

'Yes, sir,' I said quickly. 'Yes, sir.'

'You have been learning English here for the last three weeks. Okay?'

'Yes, sir.'

We sat in silence for the rest of the journey. When we arrived at Layton Avenue, the sight of Brian and Nancy's house made me so happy that I let out a huge sigh of relief.

Mehdi ran up the path with a big smile on his face, and when Nancy opened the door, he jumped forward and gave her a hug. It was as if he were a different person. I could not believe that his mood had changed so dramatically in a second.

Nancy obliged Mehdi with an embrace, but I could tell that she didn't enjoy it – the whole time she had her eyes on me, and when he released her, she ran to me with a warm smile and gave me a huge hug.

'Abbas, how are you, my dear?'

'I'm well, thank you, Nancy. How are you?'

'Look at you … you've grown, and your English – wow! Brian, get out here and say hello to Abbas.'

Nancy ran her hands through my hair.

'You need a haircut, young man. Look at this mess,' she joked.

I stood there in silence, not knowing what to say or do.

Brian came out with his bright smile and shook my hand.

'So what have you been up to, Abbas?' he said. 'We've missed you. Especially on Christmas Day.'

'Thank you. I have been learning English.'

'That's what Mehdi said,' Nancy cut in, 'but we thought you were doing just fine. Did you really need to go to holiday classes?'

'Oh, I still need to improve,' I said. 'My vocabulary is bad.'

'It's bloody good if you ask me,' Brian said. 'You need rest too, young man.'

'Yes, indeed,' Nancy continued. 'Besides, you only get to be a child once. You need to have some fun, too.'

I forced out a laugh. I could see Mehdi staring at us.

'Anyway, come in and let's have some lunch. I've made some roast beef with Yorkshire pudding and roast potatoes.'

The meal sounded divine. I had been living on sandwiches and the odd chocolate bar for three weeks.

'We can't stay long,' said Mehdi, hurrying up to us. 'I just brought him so that he could say hi. I have to get back to work.'

'Oh, don't worry about it, Mehdi,' Brian said. 'He needs a haircut anyway. I'll take him to the barber and then back to school myself.'

'There's no need for that, Brian,' Mehdi said. 'We don't want to put you out. I'll take him.'

'Don't be silly, Mehdi,' Nancy said authoritatively, 'the boy needs a good home-cooked meal. We will take him and that's the end of it. You go to work and leave him with us.'

'All right. Thank you. I just didn't want Abbas to feel awkward.'

'Mehdi, just leave it, will you? Abbas is not awkward

around us – are you, Abbas?' Nancy looked straight at me.

'No, not at all.'

Mehdi was giving me a death stare from across the room. 'Okay then, I'll be off.'

'I need my trunk before you go,' I said.

'Go get it and put it in the back of Brian's car,' Mehdi ordered.

'It's open,' Brian said. 'What do you want me to get you to drink while you do that?'

'Water is fine, thank you.'

'You sure you don't want squash?'

'Yes, thank you.'

I went outside and got the trunk from Mehdi's boot, struggling to lift it again. I dropped it on the gravel so that I could open Brian's boot, then heaved the trunk up again and was struggling to slide it into the boot when I heard Nancy and Mehdi come out.

'What the hell is the matter with you? It's four times his size,' Nancy snapped.

'He's fine,' Mehdi said, trying to laugh off the issue.

'Yes, I'm fine,' I groaned as I pushed the trunk into Brian's boot. I really did not want any trouble, because I was scared there would be retribution from Mehdi when he next got me alone.

'See, he's fine,' Mehdi said.

'I really can't understand you sometimes, Mehdi,' Nancy snapped. 'Come on, Abbas, come inside.'

'Bye, Mehdi,' I said.

'Bye,' he replied, and held out his hand. As we shook, he squeezed my hand so hard I winced. 'You make sure you are no trouble for Brian and Nancy.'

'I promise.'

He stared at me, then dropped my hand. 'Good. Make sure you don't talk too much.'

Nancy was not impressed. She walked over and took my hand in hers then hurried me inside.

'Are you okay, Abbas?'

'Of course. Yes, thank you.'

'Are you sure?'

'Yes, thank you. I'm looking forward to the roast.'

'That's my boy,' Brian said as he appeared with some orange squash. 'Here, go on, try this. It's good stuff!'

I sat there as both Brian and Nancy attended to me. Their kindness melted my heart. To be mothered by Nancy was such a rare treat in my life that I really did savour every moment. I had come to love them in such a short time – they really cared for me and did so much without expecting anything in return.

I spent a few more hours with them while Brian tried to explain the rules of croquet to me.

As Brian and I were preparing to leave, Nancy approached me in the small front hallway.

'Abbas, wait a moment.'

'Yes?' I said.

Nancy had her hands behind her back. She pulled out an old stuffed toy lion.

'Remember you told me that most of the other children have teddies or soft toys at school?'

'Yes.'

'This was Colin's when he was younger. You haven't met him yet, but he's Kate's brother. I want you to have it. He needs a home.'

I looked at the lion and chuckled. 'It's not necessary, Nancy, really—' But I couldn't help smiling at the funny old lion.

'Don't be silly, Abbas,' she interrupted me. 'You should take him. He needs someone to look after him.'

'Well, if you're sure. Thank you.'

'Colin named him Lion – original, I know, but that's his name.'

'I like it,' I said with a grin. 'Thank you again.'

'You are very welcome, my dear,' she said as she hugged me. 'You take good care of yourself, and I really hope that I'll see you again soon.'

In the car on the way to the barbershop I felt a little embarrassed.

'Brian?'

'Yes?'

'I'm sorry, but I have no money for a haircut.'

Brian chuckled. 'I don't expect you to pay, Abbas,' he said. 'You are my guest and I invited you, remember?'

'I know, but I don't want…'

'What?'

'Nothing. I just don't want Mehdi to have to owe anything on my behalf.'

Brian thought about what I had said for a little bit, then he took a deep breath and sighed.

'Please don't tell him we had this conversation, if that's possible,' I said.

'Listen, Abbas, what you and I do, or what you and Nancy do, is between us. Mehdi will never find out from me. Okay?'

'Thank you.'

Brian took me to the barber shop and we both had our hair cut. He then took me for an ice-cream before he dropped me off at Aymestrey. When we arrived, he got out of the car and helped me with my trunk. Then I walked him back to the car and, as he shook my hand, I felt him slip something into it. It was a twenty-pound note.

'Brian, this is not—'

'Just take it. You never know. Present from me and Nancy.'

'Thank you so much.'

'Our little secret, right?'

'Of course.'

'Good lad,' he said. 'Now go and cause some mayhem, but don't tell Nancy I said that.'

I chuckled and waved to him as he drove away, then I walked inside.

My friends were all telling tales of their holidays. Tomkins had been to Spain with his family. Camozzi had been to the cinema on numerous occasions to see his new favourite, *The Karate Kid III*. Murphy had just relaxed and had fun with his family. The smiles on their faces made it clear they all wanted to be back home doing the things they had been doing for the last three-and-a-half weeks. I sat back, smiling too as I listened to their stories. When at last there was a short silence, Murphy turned to me.

'So how was yours, Abbas?'

I just stared at him, not knowing what to say.

'Abbas?' Murphy said again.

'Oh yeah, it was pretty good, actually – pretty cool.'

'What did you get up to, anything fun?' Auty butted in.

'Not much, really – watched some telly and helped out my guardian.'

It was obvious that I didn't want to continue. The others didn't pay much attention to me, but Camozzi was nosey and kept up the interrogation.

'What does your guardian do?'

'Oh, he runs the catering department at a school,' I said, not really sure where this was going.

'You helped in the kitchens?' Camozzi followed up.

'No, no,' I protested, 'not at all. I just meant that I helped out around the house.'

The others were more interested in Camozzi's exposé of the Karate Kid's latest and greatest moves.

That evening we were in the dorms getting ready for bed when Mrs Griffiths came in to see us. I was in the corner taking off my shirt.

'Evening, chaps,' she said with a big welcoming smile. 'I hope you all had a good holiday.'

'Evening, Mrs G,' we responded in unison.

Mrs Griffiths glanced at me, then away, then back at me quickly. She talked to us about what we'd done over the holidays and what was in store for us for the term. She then said goodnight and moved to the next dormitory.

A little later Mr Griffiths plodded into the dormitory and jested with us in his normal way. It was obvious he was happy to have us back. As he turned to leave he looked over at me.

'Oh, Abby?' he muttered in his rich baritone voice.

'Yes, sir?'

'Mrs G wants a word downstairs. Go and see her, will you?'

'Now, sir?' I asked.

'Yes, please.'

Everyone looked at me as if they were dying to know what this was about. I could not think why I would be in trouble – it was too early in the term for that.

With trepidation I went downstairs and headed towards Mrs G's office opposite the kitchens. The hallways were so silent when all the children were in their dormitories. I steadied myself and knocked on the white office door. I could see Mrs G's reflection through the stained-glass panel. She stepped outside and stood there, towering over me.

'Mrs G, Mr G told me that you wanted to see me,' I said quietly.

'That's right, dear boy.'

She stood there looking me over in silence. I did not know what was happening.

'Abbas?'

'Yes, madam?'

'Lift up your top, please.'

As soon as she said that, I knew what this was all about. I had been particularly careful when getting changed, but Mrs G was nobody's fool. Though she wore glasses, she saw everything. I knew she had caught a glimpse of my bruise. I did not know what to do. I was terrified. If Mehdi found out about this, I would be deported, or perhaps he would just kill me.

'Madam—' I tried to protest.

'It's okay, Abbas,' she interrupted, 'you're not in trouble. I promise you everything is okay.'

I felt so ashamed standing in front of her, and tears began to well up in my eyes. I saw that I had little option. As I lifted my top, the tears began to glide down my cheeks. I held my top up for a few seconds. When I caught a glimpse of Mrs Griffiths' face I could see she was shocked.

'When did this happen?' she asked softly.

'About three weeks ago, madam,' I said, still looking down.

'It's okay, my dear,' she said softly, seeing my tears. 'Don't be upset. This isn't your fault.'

I stood there silently, trying to stop crying. I felt so incredibly uncomfortable. Mrs Griffiths leant forward and touched my side gently with her fingers.

'Does this hurt?'

'Yes, madam,' I said, trying not to flinch, 'but not as much as it did before.'

'Did you go to a doctor?' she asked.

'No, madam. I am getting better now anyway; it should go away soon.'

'We'll see about that, young man. How did this happen?'

'At … at work, madam.'

I proceeded to stare mutely at my feet until Mrs Griffiths said, 'It's okay. Does anyone else know about this?'

'No, madam.'

'Listen, I know this is hard, but I want to tell you that Mr G and I understand. We will keep this between us for now. But you have to let the doctor take a look at you tomorrow. I know that if this gets out – that you worked illegally – you may be deported. I won't let that happen, Abbas. You have my word. But you have to help me help you recover. Okay?'

'Okay.'

'This is serious. God knows what injuries you have. I want to know you are okay, Abbas.'

'Thank you, madam.'

'Are you in a lot of pain?'

'No, madam,' I said, wiping my face, 'it really is a lot better than it was. Thank you.'

The relief was immense. I was so happy that she had agreed to keep this to herself – though those words she'd used, 'for now', worried me a little.

'Does Mehdi know about this, Abbas?'

I glanced at her in alarm. 'Madam—'

'It's okay,' she said after a significant pause. 'I will not say anything.'

I am sure that at that precise moment, she put the picture together. She obviously did not know the details of the work I had been doing, but I was fairly sure she now knew who was responsible for my injuries.

I walked back to bed with a huge weight lifted off my shoulders. I was glad someone would look at my ribs, because despite what I had told Mrs G, the pain was still there and it affected the way I moved.

Back at the dormitory I slipped into bed. Everyone was sitting awake, waiting for me to spill the beans.

'Are you okay, Abbas?' Alan asked.

'Yeah.'

'Are you in trouble?' Tomkins piped up. 'Getting expelled?'

'Shut up, Tomkins,' Alan snapped. 'You're a bloody idiot.' There was a slight pause as everyone took their turn to look at Tomkins in their own disapproving way before Alan turned to me again. 'So everything is okay? Do you want to talk to me about anything?'

'No, I'm fine. I have to go and see the doctor tomorrow and Mrs G just wanted to make sure that I knew I might have to miss class in the morning.'

'You get to miss class? Lucky thing!' Humphries muttered from under his duvet.

'You're a bunch of morons,' Alan snapped. 'Abbas, what's wrong with you?'

'Oh, nothing, it's just my ribs. I had an accident during the holidays and it still hasn't healed.'

'What happened?' Humphries asked inquisitively.

'Okay, enough,' Alan interrupted. 'Everyone shut up. We know he's okay and he's not getting expelled, so settle down.'

The next morning I did miss the first two classes. Mrs Barnett, one of the matrons, took me to the hospital to see the doctor and get X-rays. I had three broken ribs that were apparently healing nicely. The doctor told me I could play rugby within two weeks, but I had to rest and protect my ribs in the meantime. I could still do cross-country, which I was disappointed about, but I could skip wooding in the mornings!

Slowly I did recover, and the term went splendidly. School kept me fully occupied, and I did very well.

I never forgot that Mrs G knew about Mehdi, and the illegal working, but she did not raise the issue with me again. Deep down I knew that she wouldn't turn me in, but still it niggled at me. I made a conscious effort to spend exeats at my friends' houses anytime Nancy and Brian were busy, rather than staying at school. Needless to say, Mehdi never offered to take me, but I was glad about that because, simply put, I was terrified of Mehdi and did not want to see him.

Time flew by me, and I dreaded the end of term because I knew I would find myself back in the kitchen at Abbey International College.

During the last week of term, the energy in the school was electric. Everyone was in a good mood, anticipating being home for Easter. It was just after lunch one day when Mrs G walked into the assembly room. This was a surprise, because Mr G traditionally had this duty. She looked across at my year group and her eyes quickly picked me out. She summoned me with one finger, then took me outside for a private chat.

86

'I need you to stay behind when everyone goes to the dorms, Abbas,' she said with a slight smile.

'Why, madam?'

'Mehdi is coming to see you with some visitors.'

'Mehdi?'

'Yes.'

'Is everything okay, madam?' I asked, immediately concerned.

'Yes, Abbas,' she said with a bigger smile. 'I think some of your family is here to see you.'

'Who?'

'I'm not sure, to be honest; he said it was a surprise.'

'Is it—'

'It isn't your mother,' she said quickly, 'so please don't get your hopes up like that, my dear child.'

'Oh.'

'Okay then, you have permission to stay in the assembly area till they arrive.'

'Thank you, madam.'

At the thought of my mother, I realised that I had not spoken to her in almost four months. I sat in my place and waited. All the children left for their respective dorms. I straightened my tie, pulled up my socks, neatly folded the tops over my garters and made sure I was in tiptop shape. I wondered who it could be if it was not my mother. I was scared about Mehdi visiting, yet I was also excited at the idea of seeing someone I knew. As always, I was hungry and hoped that they would bring me food!

I must have waited for about twenty minutes before I heard a car come up the gravel drive. As it pulled up I walked outside. The first person out of the car was Mahmoud, Mehdi's brother. Mahmoud had lived in Iran when I had lived there, and he and his family had been frequent visitors to my family home, until they had fled to Germany during the war when I was around five. He had three children, and two were with him now. Mike and his younger brother, Masih, tumbled out like little ferrets. I was so excited to see them.

It turned out that Ayeh, their sister, was still back in Germany with their mother, Shohreh, and Mahmoud and the boys were just visiting England. I just could not believe that they were here and had wanted to come and see me. The delight I felt was almost too much to bear. As time had passed, it had felt as if almost no one cared where I was, what I was doing or whether I was okay. The fact that Mahmoud, Mike and Masih had come to see me was so reassuring.

The two boys ran up to me for a hug, and began to talk. It was nice to speak Farsi again. Masih was no more than five years old, and this was the first time I had laid eyes on him. He was a cheeky little monkey who was not unlike me in character, eager to play and to get to know me. Mike and I had always had a close connection, reaching all the way back to Iran, and he was like a brother to me. Seeing him again so overwhelmed me that I had to hold back my tears.

Mahmoud soon approached me, too. He embraced me and kissed me once on each cheek, then held me close. Mehdi followed, but kept his distance.

'Abbas, how much have you grown? How are you?' Mahmoud exclaimed.

'I'm well, thanks,' I said quietly as I observed Mehdi standing behind Mahmoud.

'You look so smart in your uniform,' he said excitedly. 'But you've lost so much weight. You're so thin.'

'I don't suppose you have any food – maybe a chocolate bar – do you?' I asked hopefully.

'No,' Mahmoud said. 'I wish I had known.' He looked back at Mehdi as if Mehdi should have told him. 'I'm so sorry, Abbas, I had no idea.'

'It's okay,' I said with a grin. 'It was worth a try.'

Mahmoud suddenly turned to his brother. 'Mehdi, can you grab Masih?' he said, pointing at his son, who had wandered off and was kicking the school wall. 'He will get us deported back to Germany before we even get a chance to say hi to Abbas.'

He and Mike chuckled, but Mehdi was reluctant. He knew that he couldn't say no, but he did not want to leave me alone with them. As he started to walk over to Masih, Mahmoud drew me further away.

'Abbas, I don't have much time,' Mahmoud said seriously. 'He will be back in a second.'

'Time to do what?'

'To tell you what I have to say,' Mahmoud responded. 'You are unhappy, aren't you?'

I just looked at Mahmoud.

'I'll take that as a yes,' he said dryly. 'I know you hate your life right now and probably feel like you have no one, but you have me … you have all of us. Mike and Ayeh always ask about you, and Masih is clearly mad about you already.'

'Thank you,' I said. My heart was beating faster and faster. Was this going where I thought it was going? Was Mahmoud planning to take me back with him to Germany, to be with him and the kids? Perhaps Mehdi had told him that he did not want me and this conversation was designed to get me to leave school. In my imagination, I was already packing my bags. I could not wait to get away from Mehdi. I loved Aymestrey and my friends, but I hated holidays and Mehdi more.

'It's true, we all love you,' Mahmoud continued. 'We really want you to be with us. It's almost like you are a part of us.'

'Really?'

'Yes, of course,' Mahmoud said with a smile. 'But there is a slight problem. We are leaving for the US in a few weeks.'

'Oh, nice, my school finishes next week.'

'You see,' Mahmoud said in a different tone, 'I already have myself, Shohreh, Ayeh, Mike and Masih, as well as my in-laws, to take with me. I wish I could take you, too, but at this time … I'm sorry … I just can't. I'm already overstretched.'

'Oh, yeah … of course,' I said. 'It would be silly to think differently.' My world suddenly crashed around me. Salvation was so close and yet so far away. I really wanted to cry, but I knew I had to hold it together.

'I just wanted to come here and tell you to your face that we think of you and we love you, and that I'm sorry we can't take you with us.'

I could still hear what Mahmoud was saying, but everything felt like it had slowed down. As I watched his mouth move, I was still just thinking about how not to cry.

'It's fine, really. I completely understand. Besides, all my friends are here now,' I muttered. 'I'm just really happy that you came.'

'You be strong,' Mahmoud said as he hugged me again. 'I know Mehdi is a problem. Just try to stay out of his way.'

'Thanks.'

'Can I get you anything before we leave?'

'No, thank you. You guys had better get going. I have class soon.'

'Yes, of course.'

Before I knew it, I had hugged everyone apart from Mehdi and they had driven off. I was left alone on the lawn outside the school, watching Mehdi's car disappear down the driveway. The disappointment that I felt at that particular moment outweighed my other sorrows and disappointments a thousandfold. Tears rolled down my face as I gazed into the sky, wondering why my hopes had been raised only to be cruelly crushed like that.

I knew Mahmoud had thought he was doing the right thing, and I really did appreciate the fact that he had shown an interest in me – the only person in my large extended family to have done so. But it would have been easier to have thought he didn't care than to have come so close to escaping from Mehdi and then had that chance snatched away from me. I hated my life, and the prospect of having to see Mehdi again in less than a week filled me with horror.

I saw Mrs G staring out at me from her office window. Quickly I collected myself and wiped away my tears, heading back towards the school.

Mrs G always seemed able to read my thoughts, sometimes before I had even thought them. Though she never talked to me about that afternoon, I knew that she understood. Mrs G made me strong.

SIX

Before I knew it I was in the car on my way to Abbey International College for the Easter holidays. I sat in silence as Mehdi drove to Malvern. All I could think about was getting to that small, smelly room and being alone.

'So when are you going to be done with school? You are bleeding me dry.'

I had hoped that we could get through the journey without speaking but clearly he could not help himself.

'I'm sorry, but I am trying to help by working in the holidays.'

'But how much is that worth?' Mehdi barked. 'You really think you know it all, don't you?'

'No, I'm sorry, I really don't ... but I know that the work I do has value. If I didn't do it you'd have to pay someone else, right?'

I saw Mehdi tighten his grip on the steering wheel. Why had I just said that? I was starting to feel very nervous.

Just when I'd thought the moment had passed, Mehdi slammed his fist into the dashboard.

'What the f— would you know about finances, you little shit?'

I sat quietly, determined to say nothing more. Soon we were at the college and I was dragging my trunk behind Mehdi to my smelly little room. He handed me the keys, then put his hand in his pocket and pulled out a five-pound note. He offered it to me, but as I slowly went to take it from him, he pulled it back and stared at me.

'I'll post the numbers on my office door. Be there at 6.30 sharp and make sure you don't f— up this time.'

With that he threw the money on the ground and walked off. I picked up the note and wondered why he had given me anything. It made no sense in the midst of his neglect and irrational rages. Perhaps some guilt lurked in the back of his mind about the way he had treated me. Money meant the chance to talk to my mother, so I stuffed the note deep into my pocket.

I unpacked as best I could and tried to make the shed-like room comfortable, then I ventured out to the tuckshop. French and Italian teenagers were playing pool and table tennis in the hall adjacent to the shop. I wished that I could be there playing games with them, but I envied the kids ahead of me in the queue, who were ordering chocolates and cans of soft drink, even more.

When it was my turn, the shopkeeper looked at me through his glasses and said, 'What can I do you for, young man?'

'Well, sir, I was wondering if you could change my five-pound note?'

'Sir?' he chuckled. 'I haven't heard that in a long time. You can call me Chris,' he continued. 'Now let's see what we can do.'

As Chris turned around, his checked shirt slipped out of his corduroy trousers, which were clearly too large for him. Chris was a messy chap but his heart was in the right place. He was calm and kind, and I trusted him immediately. He turned back with a handful of change and poured it into my hands.

'I presumed you wanted money for the phone box so I gave you a bit of everything.'

'Cheers, thanks so … thank you.'

'You are welcome, young man. Never seen anyone quite so happy about change before!'

'Oh yeah,' I said, turning back, 'I just need to make an important call … sorry!' Realising that I had made a spectacle of myself, I began to feel anxious and shy.

'Well, you come back if you need more.' Chris winked at me. 'By the way, what's your name?'

'Abbas.'

'Nice to meet you, Abbas.'

'You too, sir.'

Chris grinned at my use of 'sir', and I walked briskly towards the phone box until I could not contain myself and began to jog. I closed the door behind me and put in some coins. I dialled the number, which of course I still knew by heart, and waited for the telephone to ring. The sharp smell of urine barely registered – I was desperate to hear my mother's voice.

The telephone kept ringing, and just as I thought no one was going to pick up, I heard Maman say, 'Hello?'

'Maman?'

'Abbas?'

I put in another coin as I continued to speak. 'It's me, yes. How are you?'

My mother broke down and began to sob hysterically, her words incomprehensible.

'I'm so sorry, Maman, I'm sorry it took so long for me to call.'

'It's not your fault, my darling,' she sobbed. 'I know it's so hard for you out there…I just cannot live like this, not knowing if you're okay.'

I didn't know what to say. It was so intense and so hard to listen to my mother crying. My head rested against the metal body of the telephone as I watched my tears hit the ground in silence.

'Are you crying, Abbas?' Maman asked. 'Please don't cry, my darling…I'm so sorry…I'm crying because I'm happy to hear your voice.'

'I'm not crying, Maman. I'm fine.'

'I miss you so much…it hurts so much to be away from you. It makes me sick being away from you.'

'I miss you, too, Maman, I really do. All I think about is you coming here.'

'I'm trying, my baby, I really am. Will you stay strong for me? Will you keep waiting till I get there?'

'Of course I will. I'm strong.'

'I know you are – you're my Abbas.'

I could sense her smile through her tears, the smile that showed how much she loved me and yet told me that she knew what a naughty little monkey I was. The memory of that very knowing smile made me chuckle, and she started to laugh a little, too. We did not have to say anything. We just knew.

I was running out of money, but I didn't care. I put the last one pound fifty into the telephone.

'Maman, I'm not sure how long I will have credit, but if I lose you…'

'I know.' There was a slight pause as Maman realised she had better use the time wisely. 'So how is school?'

'Oh, great. I am almost at the top of the class, and even though I am the only foreign person in my year, I had the highest mark in English!'

'Well done, you clever little rascal,' she said through her dying tears. 'So what else are you up to?'

She had caught me off guard. 'Oh, not a lot. I just study hard and play sports with my friends.'

'I know that, but I mean in the holidays with Mehdi, and his fiancée.'

'You know me, Maman. I'm always trying to make money. I keep to myself, you know.'

'Oh dear Lord, you had better not be embarrassing them. You're not going to the shops asking for work again, are you?'

'Mamaaan!' I laughed. 'No, you can't do that here. It's not Iran!'

'Then how are you trying to make money, smartypants?'

'Maman, I am running out of credit. I have to say goodbye soon—'

'Okay, okay, okay,' she interrupted. 'Just know that I miss you so much. God, I love you, Abbas.'

'I love you, too, Maman. Say hi to Baba for me.'

'I will,' she said. 'He misses you, too. He's out now.'

'I gotta go, Maman. Love you.'

'Love—' and with that my credit was finished.

That was a particularly hard conversation for me, because my mother had not lost control like that since I'd last seen her at the airport months before. She was clearly suffering, and not her normal self. It really hurt me that I was the cause of her distress, and I felt responsible for her pain. The worst of it was that she was the one person in the world I would have done anything to protect. The longer I was away from my mother, the more it became clear to me just how much I loved her. She was my everything.

Slowly I walked back to my room and tried to get some sleep before it was time to work. I lay on the pull-out sofa in that dark, damp and depressing room and cried until I fell asleep.

I woke up around seven p.m. and realised that I was late. I hurriedly washed my face and ran to the kitchen. There was a piece of paper on the door of Mehdi's office that read: *334 sanwichtes*.

I ignored the atrocious spelling and was happy that I did not have to make over five hundred sandwiches. I set to work and found that I was soon in the swing of things. My injured ribs had healed, and it was nice to be able to work without pain. I did not dare to put on the radio, so I worked in silence, going over the conversation with my mother. I kept thinking that I was making money, though Mehdi denied the fact, and paying my own way.

I finished pretty early that first night – I was done by three a.m. I walked down to take my shower by the pool in my usual manner, and then headed back up the hill to the room. Fatigue was setting in.

I thought of Draggo screaming at us as we struggled up muddy hills, passing through cowpat after cowpat, insisting that we did not give up. As much as I hated running in rain, hail and snow, and found his methodology suspect, in that moment I smiled as I realised that if it hadn't been for Draggo, I may not have been strong enough to do this work each night. Although I did everything I could to stay out of his way, Draggo always watched me with great interest. I knew that the way I had climbed tonight's sandwich-making 'hill' – with a bounce – would have made him proud, and knowing that made me feel proud, too. I knew it was of the utmost importance that I kept up my morale by staying positive like this, as it was by controlling the way I'd thought about things that I had been able to endure the loneliness during the last school holidays. The next few days passed without incident as I continued to work at night and hide by day. The college was much quieter than it had been during the previous holidays, so there was not as much work for me. I would usually be done between two and three a.m.

On Easter Sunday I was awakened at nine a.m. by Mehdi banging on the door and demanding that I get up. It was hard to understand what he was saying, because I had woken suddenly out of a deep sleep.

'Get up,' he said when I opened the door.

'Where are we going?'

'Brian and Nancy are insisting on seeing you,' he snapped, sighing in frustration. 'For some reason we cannot have Easter lunch without you.'

'Oh,' I said quietly. I washed my face and started to put my clothes on.

'For some reason everyone thinks you're the golden child,' he said bitterly, 'but they don't see what I see.'

I did not respond.

'When is your stupid father going to take you off my hands? I can't afford this in my life anymore. He said this would be temporary. Seems permanent to me.'

I was now ready and stood waiting at the door for further instructions. Experience had taught me not to engage with Mehdi. Disagreeing with him was not a viable option.

'Now you were here for fun,' he insisted. 'Do we understand each other?'

'Yes.'

'So if they ask what you have been up to, what are you going to tell them?'

'I go to classes in the mornings to improve my English. But I will also say that I get bored because I am too advanced compared to the foreign kids who come here. And that in the afternoons we play sports and go on trips.'

'Good,' Mehdi said with a smile. 'See, lying comes easily to you.'

'I'm just doing what you say, Mehdi.'

'You always have to get lippy, don't you?'

'No, sir.'

He clearly wanted to start with me again but decided against it. 'So, where have you gone on your trips?'

'To Stonehenge, London, Worcester Cathedral and Bath.'

'That was pretty good,' he said, alarmed. 'How did you come up with that so quickly?'

'I look at the order roster for the sandwiches. It says where they are going.'

Mehdi didn't respond right away, but judging by the look on his face, unsurprisingly, I had managed to frustrate him.

'In London, what did you go and see?' he continued to quiz me. 'I know Brian and Nancy will ask you these questions. They are always interested in what you've done and what you've seen. You would think you are related to Kate instead of me.'

'I will say that we went on the Thames and saw the Tower

of London and the crown jewels, Buckingham Palace, Hyde Park and Tower Bridge.'

'Where do you come up with this stuff?'

'History class at school.'

He was satisfied that I could keep up his lie for the day, and so we headed for Layton Avenue in Malvern Link. As we pulled up in the driveway, Nancy hurried out looking very excited. She ran up to the car and opened my door, and as I got out she embraced me in a way that was truly loving. She held me like a mother and gave me a kiss on my cheek.

'Oh, my young man. You are growing. Where have you been? You never come and see me anymore.'

'I'm sorry. I am either at school or holiday camp at Abbey International.'

'I know. No rest for the wicked, as they say. Anyway, you're here now. Guess what I made for you today?'

'Roast?'

'You know I did, with roast spuds and apple crumble just the way you like it.'

'Thanks so much.'

I really was excited about the food, because I had been eating Mehdi's leftovers in the kitchen fridge and I was ready for freshly cooked food.

'You are welcome. Now come to the back garden. Brian has been looking forward to seeing you.'

We walked through to the back, where Kate sat in a outdoor chair and Brian stood in the middle of the garden holding a big piece of wood.

'Hi Kate, hi Brian,' I said, greeting everyone with a shy smile.

'Hi, Abbas.' Kate got up and approached me. 'How are you?'

'I'm well, thanks. You?'

'Good,' she said, then hugged me and gave me a kiss on my cheek.

'Abbas, come over here and take a look at what I've got you,' Brian shouted across the garden. He looked like a child in a sweetshop. I was unsure what he wanted to show me but interested to find out. I approached him and he shook my hand and then held the piece of wood at each end. One end seemed to be a handle and the other, larger half was more rectangular.

'This, Abbas, is a cricket bat. You are going to play this fine English game when you get back to school, and I wanted you to have your own bat.'

'Oh, wow. Thank you so much. My friends told me how expensive these bats are.'

I was shocked that Brian would care enough to spend this much money on me. As he turned the bat over, I read the label – 'Duncan Fearnley 405'. It was a brand named after a famous innings by Graeme Hick, in which he had scored four hundred and five runs. I had heard others talk about this bat, but had not appreciated the talk until now. I turned around to show Kate and saw Mehdi standing in the living room staring at me through the window. His expression took the joy out of the moment.

'What do you think, Abbas?' Brian asked. I turned back around to face him and smiled.

'It's brilliant. Thank you so much, Brian. You should not have done this.'

'It's my pleasure. So what do you say? Want a knock-about?'

'Yeah, sure.'

Nancy suddenly appeared out of nowhere with her hands

on her hips. 'Brian, really? You want to play cricket in this tiny garden? You know what happened to the window last time.'

Brian looked at me and winked. 'Not really, sweetheart – just checking you're switched on, that's all.'

Everyone started laughing as Nancy chased Brian around the garden pretending she was going to spank him.

'Don't you pay any attention to him, Abbas,' Nancy called to me as she ran after him.

It was so good to be with a normal family, where time was spent in silliness and ultimately happiness. Mehdi was the only person who was unhappy, and his eyes never left me the entire day. I could see that Kate was in turn watching Mehdi, and as the day progressed she seemed to become stressed and unhappy.

That evening, after a great meal, Mehdi drove me back to Abbey International. I sat in the car thinking about what a good day it had been with Nancy and Brian. I would have liked to have spent more time with them. I did not know why they were so kind to me, but I really did appreciate it and cared for them deeply. They were good people. Mehdi did not say anything during the journey, just dropped me off and left.

I took out my new cricket bat. Brian had also bought a cover for the bat. I was still not quite sure how to use a bat, but I was very excited to have it. I knew Draggo or Mr G would show me soon enough. I sat on my sofa and took the bat out of its cover. There was a small envelope inside it, with *Abbas* on the front in Nancy's handwriting. I opened it up and there was a twenty-pound note inside it. I could not believe my eyes. In her perfect ladylike script, Nancy had written the following:

Dearest Abbas,
We know you sometimes must get lonely, but
Brian and I are very fond of you. You are always
welcome here. We absolutely love having you. I
know that Kate may seem a little distant, but she
is only twenty-three years old and has never had to
take care of a child before. She does care for you
also; we all do. Brian and I wanted to give you a
little something for sweets or whatever else you
need. Our little secret!
Lots of love,
Brian and Nancy xxx

I was so touched by the card. Brian and Nancy's place was
how I had always imagined life in England. Having grown
up with such wonderful parents, Kate's attachment to
Mehdi was baffling to me. But that was not a puzzle I was
going to try to solve with anyone, and frankly I felt lucky.
Without her serious error of judgement, I would never have
met Nancy and Brian.

The Easter holidays were not particularly long, so I only
had to work for ten more days after Easter before I could
go back to school. I spent a little of the money on a few
Mars Bars from the tuckshop and saved the rest up for more
phone calls. The work was getting easier and easier for me,
and each night I finished a little earlier. Even the loneliness
did not seem as bad.

Draggo had given us homework for the holidays – I had
to read *Puck of Pook's Hill* by Rudyard Kipling and write a
journal entry about it. Everyone had moaned so much about
this homework, but I was actually happy about it because
it gave me something to do during the day. I planned how

many pages I could read per day so that I did not finish it too soon.

Two days before I was due to go back to school, I went to see Chris to get change for a five-pound note so that I could call Maman. In his ever jolly way Chris gave me the change and off I went to the phone box again. I dialled the number, waited, and very quickly my father answered the phone.

'Hello?'

'Baba?'

'Hi, son. How are you?' He sounded a little grumpy, though I was sure he must have been genuinely happy to hear my voice after so long.

'I'm well. Just calling quickly to see how you and Maman are.'

'Mehdi called,' he explained, and my heart immediately dropped. I could barely speak. As Baba continued to talk, all I could think about was how nauseous I felt. 'He was unhappy.'

'With me?'

'With everything.'

'What did he say?' I asked quietly. 'Am I in trouble?'

There was a pause. I felt like I really was in trouble. All of a sudden I felt so tired; I just wanted to go back to my room and sleep.

'He wants money. He says you are costing him too much money.'

'Baba, I promise you I do not ask for anything. I have not even asked for—'

'It's mainly your schooling,' he whispered. 'That is the big burden.'

I kept putting coins into the telephone. 'Why are you whispering?'

'I don't want your mother to hear. She will get upset.'

'Okay, but Baba, I am working. I am trying to pay my own bills.'

'What do you mean you're working?'

I suddenly realised what I had said. I kept quiet and hoped he would move on.

'I asked what you meant by that?'

'Well…' I began, knowing that there was no way out now, 'I work in his kitchen at night. He was paying someone four pounds an hour before I started working for him. If you add up the hours I work, it is way more than he pays for my school tuition. I asked a schoolfriend how much it costs.'

'What… what are you talking about?' he muttered in a tight, angry voice. 'And who is Mrs G?'

I knew he was really upset but was trying to control it. I had seen him speak like this to Maman before.

'Baba, please, promise me. You can't say anything.'

'What are you talking about, Abbas?'

'To Mehdi. You can't tell him I told you. I just wanted you to know that I am already paying for school with my work.'

'You work every day, or you did it once?'

There was a pause as I thought about what I was going to say. I had two extra pound coins in my pocket and I inserted them into the telephone.

'Baba, promise me, please, I am begging you.'

'Okay,' he said reluctantly, 'but if I am not to tell Mehdi, you can't tell your mother, either.'

I had to think about his proposition for a second, but it was the only deal I was going to get, so I agreed. Besides, I did not want to worry Maman either.

'Fine. Yes, I work every night in the holidays when I am not at boarding school. I make packed lunches for the kids who come here to learn English. It varies, but I make anywhere between two hundred and fifty and almost six hundred lunches, depending on how many students they have.'

'And you're there alone?'

'Yeah. It's very safe, but it has to be done at night because kids my age aren't allowed to work in England.'

'Has this just started?'

I could not tell from his tone whether he was angry with me or Mehdi. What I wanted to say but did not dare to was that all of this was outside my control, so I was not sure what else he expected me to do in such a situation.

'I worked the last set of holidays and these holidays, but they are over in a few days.' There was a slight pause; I could tell that he was thinking. 'Baba, can I speak to Maman? I don't have much money left for the phone.'

'Hold on a minute. Is he paying you for the work you do?'

'Baba,' I said, irritated, 'no, he does not pay me. If he did, how could my work be paying for my schooling?'

'Watch your tone.'

'Sorry.' After a slight pause I said, 'Now can I speak to Maman?'

'Not a word of this, okay?'

'And you won't say anything to Mehdi?'

'No, son. I think I get the picture now,' he said in a slightly different tone; it was almost as if he knew everything. 'Marzieh, hurry and get to the phone,' he shouted then. I could hear my mother in the background calling back.

'She's going to pick up the other phone, son,' my father said.

'I'm here,' my mother said almost immediately. I heard my father putting down the phone.

'Hi, Maman, how are you?' I said quickly, trying to change the tone of my voice.

'I'm well, my darling. How are you?'

She had such great sadness in her voice. She was not crying, but I could tell that her melancholy was as strong as it had been the previous time I'd spoken to her.

'I'm well, Maman. Almost time to go back to school.'

'Oh, good. You make sure you study hard, now.' She paused for a second and then continued, 'Are you sure you're okay?'

'Yes, yes, of course. Why do you ask?'

'You know how much I love you, right?' She spoke with such desperation; she really wanted me to know.

'Of course I do, Maman. I love you, too.'

'I know you do. I miss you so much.'

'I miss you, too. I'm fine, I promise. Are you sure *you're* okay?'

I noticed that I had used up all my change and had almost no credit left.

'Yes, I'm okay.'

'Maman, I have to get going. Sorry. My money is almost gone.'

'Before you go ...'

'Yes, Maman? Be quick.'

'Be strong for me, okay? I love you. Know it. Remember it. Never forget it. I love you. I love you. I love you.'

'I will. I promise. I love—'

Again our conversation was cut off due to lack of funds. I put the phone down, and as I did I saw that my hand was shaking.

I was terrified that my father might lose his temper and say something to Mehdi, although he had given me his word – we had a deal – and if my father made a deal, I knew he tended to keep his end of the bargain. I also hated the fact that he knew what had been happening to me in England.

I started to walk back to my room when I suddenly thought of something. When my mother had got onto the telephone, I had not heard a *click* as she'd picked up the phone. Also, she had seemed to get on the phone very quickly. Maybe she had been right next to the phone … but what if she had already been on the line, listening in on my conversation with my father from the other telephone? That would have explained her behaviour. Then again, maybe she just missed me and was very sad.

These thoughts spun around in my head for hours. I felt utterly drained. I could not tell if my father was angry with me, or whether he was angry with Mehdi; whether my mother had heard what was going on; and whether my father would truly not say anything to Mehdi. On top of the work that I'd done the night before, it was all too much for me. Again, I dealt with it by lying on my pull-out bed and crying myself to sleep.

I always felt better when I woke.

SEVEN

The next day passed very slowly – I could not stop thinking about that last conversation with my parents.

The following morning, I was due back at school. I had not seen Mehdi since he'd dropped me off on Easter Sunday, but I'd mentioned to him that I had to be back at school on this very day. I'd been packed and ready since dawn, but there was still no sign of him. Knowing I was already late, I walked to the telephone box with a final few coins I'd saved for emergencies and called Brian and Nancy.

'Hello,' Nancy answered in her chirpy voice.

'Hi, Nancy. It's Abbas.'

'Hello, sweetheart. How are you?'

'I'm well, thank you. I don't suppose you know where Mehdi or Kate are, do you?'

'No. Why? Is everything okay? Are you okay, Abbas?' She sounded genuinely concerned.

'Yes, but unfortunately I don't seem to have a lift so that I can get back to school. I was meant to be back an hour ago.'

'Good God. Will those two ever remember anything? You actually mentioned it at lunch at Easter, didn't you? Where are you, dear?'

'Abbey International.'

'Okay. Brian and I will be there in twenty minutes. We'll take you back, my love.'

'Thank you very much. Sorry to have to disturb you.'

'Don't be silly. We are leaving now. Brian ...' she called as she hung up.

I ran to my room and started to drag my trunk out to the driveway so that Nancy and Brian would not see my smelly room. I did not want to cause trouble for Mehdi and ultimately for myself. They were there early, almost as soon as I'd finished moving my things to the driveway. Nancy and Brian both got out of the car. Brian shook my hand and Nancy hugged me and kissed me as usual, running her fingers through my long hair.

'Why hasn't Mehdi had your hair cut?' she said irritably. 'That man needs to pay better attention to you.'

'Sorry, Nancy. It won't happen again.'

'This is not your responsibility,' she snapped. 'I will be having words with those two when I next see them. They need to get their heads out of their you-know-whats.'

Brian and I both chuckled.

'This is a very beautiful place,' Brian said, to try to change the subject.

'Yes, it is very pretty,' I said.

'So where are the rest of the foreign students?' Nancy asked. The car park was empty; the last of the kids had gone the day before.

'I think they left earlier this morning, Nancy.'

'Shocking! So you were here all by yourself. You could

have at least spent the morning with us, if you were going to be late back to school.'

'Wasn't Mehdi here for breakfast before they left?' Brian asked.

Of course I'd been asleep during breakfast, but Mehdi would not have been here this morning because there would not have been any kids to feed. But I couldn't say that because I would give the game away.

'Yes, he was, but I was saying goodbye to all my Italian friends and I lost track of him.'

'Can we see the dorm you were staying in?' Nancy asked.

'Well, we are very late, Nancy. I'm sorry, but I don't want to get into trouble at school.'

'Quite right,' Brian said. 'We'd better go, but don't worry about getting into trouble. I will speak to Mrs Griffiths myself.'

I was so relieved when Brian said that – I was not even sure where the dorms were.

In the car we chatted about little things and how excited I was about learning to play cricket, but my mind was working away at what Mehdi might be up to and why. My best guess was that he had not paid my school bill.

Twenty-five minutes later we pulled up at the school and I ran towards the door, where Mr G was already waiting for us. He walked over to Brian and Nancy and spoke with them in private, handing them a piece of paper. When they'd finished talking, Mr G came over to me.

'How are you, Abby?'

'Very well, sir. How are you?'

'Splendid, Abby, quite splendid.'

Brian and Nancy came up to say goodbye, and Brian shook my hand again.

'Have a good term, old chap. Let us know anytime you want to come for the weekend.'

'Thanks, Brian. I will.'

Nancy gave me a hug, and I felt her put something into my pocket as she squeezed me tight.

'This is just a little pocket money from Brian and me, in case you need it. Our little secret.'

She pulled away, tapping the side of her nose to indicate the secrecy of the whole affair.

'Thank you so much, Nancy – really.'

'You are welcome, dear boy. Just you be good and take care of yourself.'

I could sense the sadness within Nancy. She ruffled my hair and returned to the car.

I watched as they pulled away and then turned back to see Mr G lighting up his pipe. I had missed the smell of that tobacco. He took a puff and led me into the assembly room.

'I believe these two pests are waiting to help you unpack, so that you can be ready in time for lunch with everyone else,' he said.

I saw Murphy's beaming smile next to Humphries'. Humphries was clearly delighted that Mr G had chosen him to help me. They ran up to help with my trunk and before I knew it I was back in the same old routine. We were in the dormitory putting things away when Smith ran in and scanned the room until he found me.

'Mrs G wants you to report to her office downstairs now.'

'Why?'

'Dunno, mate; she just told me to come and get you,' Smith said. With that he turned and dashed out.

'Oooh, you're in trouble,' Humphries hissed.

'Shut up, Humphries,' Murphy said.

'What could I have done wrong?' I asked. 'I only just got here.'

'You may not have done anything wrong!' said Murphy.

'Oh well, I guess there's one way to find out.'

I walked downstairs, knocked on the door and stepped back in anticipation. Mrs G came to the door with a big smile on her face, and I immediately knew that I was not in trouble. That was not the face that greeted you when you were in trouble with Mrs G.

'Abbas, how are you?'

'Well, madam. How are you?'

'Oh, you know, you rascals have come back already – too soon!' She chuckled and ushered me inside. It was unusual to be invited into the office. Even if we were in trouble, we would usually stay outside. Mrs G indicated a chair on one side of her desk, and I sat down, awaiting further instructions.

'Abbas, this is an unusual conversation to be having with a student. I want this to be purely between us, okay?'

'Yes, madam.'

'Well—' As she began to speak someone darted past the door making a motorbike noise. Mrs G jumped out of her chair, flung open the door, and in a voice full of authority shouted, 'Auty, get back here now.'

A few seconds later Auty appeared at the door looking sheepishly at the floor.

'How many times have I warned you about running in the corridors?'

'Dunno, madam.'

'I think you mean you don't know. Well, I can tell you that it is so often I have lost count. You've been here only a few hours and you're already back to your old tricks. Report yourself to Mr G and tell him to put you down for a Minor Mark. Not a good way to start the term, is it?'

There was no response. Auty stared at the floor.

'Is it?' Mrs G repeated.

'No, madam.'

'Now get out of here before you do something else wrong.'

Mrs G returned to her desk as if nothing had happened.

'Sorry about that, Abbas. Now, where were we? Oh, yes. Now, I understand that Mehdi is having some issues with the school bills. Something tells me you know that already, and I wanted to chat to you because it's completely inappropriate for you to know about this or, even worse, have to worry about it.'

I sat in silence, too shocked to speak. How could she know that Mehdi had yelled at me about money? I had no idea where she'd got her information from, but it was completely accurate. She really did know everything that was going on.

'So I wanted to pull you in here tonight to put an end to this,' she continued. 'Mr G and I think very highly of you. The way that you have taken to the school, your willingness to accept our culture, the way you get stuck into everything that is asked of you, and your integrity and your enthusiasm to learn make you a great student. In fact, they make you one of our best.'

'Thank you, madam.'

'Now we don't always do this, but once in a while we give a bursary or what we call an assisted place to a deserving student. The bursary pays for all your school bills. All you have to do is just keep doing what you have been doing and the bursary will take care of everything.'

'Sorry, madam? You mean I get to go to school for free?' I could barely get the words out, I was so shocked.

'Absolutely. You don't have to pay for anything. I just sent a letter to Mehdi explaining this. All I want you to do is be the best student you can be and not worry about this other nonsense, okay?'

'Yes, madam. Thank you, madam.'

'You deserve it.'

I turned around to leave and then turned back again.

'Madam, thank you very much … really. I am so happy here. I won't let you down.'

'I know you won't, Abbas. Now you had better be top of your class soon, because I know you can be.'

'I will, madam.' I smiled. 'I moved up one place to second last term – but I really want to be number one.'

'That's the spirit. Now go and cause controlled chaos and make sure I do not catch you, or you will be in peril from Mr G with Auty!'

'Yes, madam,' I said with a big grin.

I felt a huge sense of relief, knowing that I would not be so beholden to Mehdi, but it still gnawed at me that Mrs G had somehow known Mehdi had hassled me about my school fees. Could my father have called her? No, he didn't speak English. But he knew a lot of people who did speak English.

I was not sure whether Mr and Mrs G really thought I was a good enough student to be worthy of a scholarship or whether they had just taken pity on me. It would have hurt my pride if I'd found out it was the latter, but either way, it was not an opportunity I was going to turn down. Aymestrey was my happy place, and I wanted to stay there as long as possible.

The English countryside in summer was spectacular, and I was having a good term. I loved rowing among the Canada geese on the school's lake, the long summer days, and the smell of freshly cut grass. I spent almost every exeat at friends' houses. The burden of being beholden to Mehdi had lifted and my life had become much more enjoyable. I was doing extremely well at school, and knew that I had a good chance of being top of the class by the end of the school year. Tomkins had realised he was being challenged and did not like it. I had come a long way from the bottom with poor old OG.

I had learnt the game of cricket and even made the team. I spent every spare second I had on one of two things, and the first was playing cricket – I loved it. The long summer evenings allowed us to spend our spare time outside, and bedtime was now a little later so that we could enjoy being outdoors. None of my friends ever complained about not being able to watch television, because we were always busy.

If I was not playing cricket, my second-favourite activity was following Draggo around like a disciple. Draggo had secretly become my hero – I learnt so much from him. He could play the piano, draw, paint, etch, sculpt, write; he was well versed in almost every aspect of culture; he was extremely well read; and as if that was not enough, he was good at sports. Some of these things he had taught himself, which made him even more impressive to me.

It was not compulsory to do after-school activities with Draggo, but for those who did, it opened up our worlds. We were given opportunities and taught skills that were rare in the contemporary world – from learning about John Keats to designing and building a Roman catapult to see how far it could fling a cricket ball.

Boys were scared of Draggo as a teacher, but I soon learnt that if you applied yourself and tried your hardest, you would earn his respect and his patience would grow exponentially. All I ever did when I was around him was try my best, which built in me a virtue that slowly became second nature – to always do my best.

During my time with Draggo, I also mastered a lifetime's worth of put-downs as he bombarded us with colourful abuse, expressing his deep distaste for ignorance and incompetence and teaching me the traditional English art of sarcastic witticisms. Draggo was always so sharp, and he took every opportunity to exercise his sarcasm on us. He used to credit Oscar Wilde with the saying, 'Sarcasm is the lowest form of wit but the highest form of intelligence.'

A lot of the other children felt intimidated by Draggo. Parents (including Humphries' mother) made numerous complaints about him to Mr G, and he was given very bad press as a sadistic bully by some around the school. Too often he would send me on three-mile runs in hail or snow instead of being able to join the others for dinnertime, for my lack of competence in some area or another, and my friends thought I was crazy to accept this punishment, but I saw it differently. He was certainly a flawed man and a flawed teacher, but despite his wrath and quick temper, I loved spending time with Draggo because I learnt so much as I tried to adhere to his high standards, and because he had a way of entertaining me and keeping me on my toes that helped me to forget anything else that was going on in my life.

That summer, without our knowledge, Draggo entered us into a national competition to create our own book. Everyone in our after-school club was given the task of writing one of the chapters. Then we had to draw an illustration, trace it onto a block of wood and carve the illustration with traditional woodblock tools. When our story was complete Draggo taught us to use a nineteenth-century printing press. We had to lay out every word of every paragraph of every chapter and print the pages the old-fashioned way; each chapter opening was then decorated with one of our woodcut illustrations. I loved every step of the process. Draggo framed one of the copies and had Mrs G hang it in the assembly room. I was very proud to have been part of the team that made that book, which ultimately won a national competition for our age group.

Our following project – a school rose garden – was to be a much longer process. Draggo showed us a plot of overgrown land Mr G was allowing us to use. The first step was to clear away the weeds, which took three weeks of digging and weeding after school. Then we were given the task of designing the garden, and we made plans for a maze, a central sundial, a gigantic chessboard and an elegant arched wooden entranceway to support climbing roses. Next, each of us had to learn about a specific rose that was well suited to the section of the rose garden we had been made personally responsible for. Mine was the Charles Austin rose, suitable for growing into a hedge-like edging to the garden thanks to its bushy growth habit.

Growing the roses that summer would have been premature, and besides, we still had to build the sundial and the gigantic chessboard. Murphy and Alexander were set the task of creating the chess pieces from plaster, and I was given the task of figuring out how to make a sundial. Draggo personally assisted me with this. He taught me how the latitude and longitude of where we were located needed to be accounted for in the angle of the dial in order to keep accurate time. Though this was an extremely arduous process, I really loved going through it because I was aware that most children around the world would not have understood it or been able to do it. After all the upheaval in my life, it was good to feel special. Draggo constantly challenged us with tasks that would generally have been deemed beyond our years, and yet on every occasion we met the challenge.

So, that June of 1989, I was having a great summer. I was concentrating on cricket and the projects Draggo was throwing at me and was completely distracted from the world outside of Aymestrey.

One lunchtime I was messing around with Auty, pinching him and pretending it wasn't me. Every time Auty would look at me I would pretend to be talking to Tomkins. Suddenly I felt a tap on my shoulder. I turned around to see Mrs G towering over me and my heart dropped; she must have seen what I'd been doing. She leant in towards me and whispered in my ear, 'Stay in the assembly room after lunch. Mr G knows that you're staying.'

'Madam … sorry, madam,' I said, a little taken aback. I did not think I had committed a large enough violation to be held back like that. 'Madam, I was just joking.'

'It's not that. Eat up and we'll talk later.'

Mrs G did not seem to be cross with me, and she was not shy about chastising boys in public, so I was very confused by her cryptic message. I had a quiet lunch after that, trying to figure out what the drama might be. After lunch we sat around in the assembly room. Mr G dismissed everyone for afternoon siesta, until I was finally left alone with him.

'Abby?'

'Yes, sir?'

'Mrs G will come and speak to you in a second.'

He began to walk out with his pipe in his mouth, so I gathered up my courage and said, 'Sir?'

He looked back at me as he took a large puff on his pipe. 'Yes, Abby?'

'Sir,' I said, 'am I in some sort of trouble?'

He walked back towards me, still puffing away. His clunky shoes echoed in the empty room. I looked up at him as he began to speak. 'Not at all, Abby. You're certainly not in trouble, don't fret; you're just fine. Mrs G will be through in a minute.'

With that he walked out at a brisker pace than usual. I sat down and waited in the empty room for close to five minutes, pulling up my socks and making sure that I looked as smart as I possibly could. Finally I heard Mrs G's squeaky shoes approaching.

I stood up as she entered and she immediately gestured for me to sit down.

'Abbas, you have a visitor coming to see you. Mehdi is coming.'

'Mehdi? To see me?' I inquired.

She nodded.

'Am I in trouble?' I asked. 'I'm not leaving school, am I?'

'Oh no, nothing like that. Don't worry about anything of that nature. I won't let it happen.'

'Then why is he coming to see me? He never comes to visit.'

There was a slight pause, and she shrugged. It seemed to make no more sense to her than it did to me.

'He should be here soon. In fact, according to what he said when he rang, he is meant to be here already. Just sit here and wait for him. Feel free to go outside when you hear his car.'

'Thank you, madam.'

'You're quite welcome,' Mrs G said as she left the room.

I sat there wondering what was going on. Mehdi did not want to visit me even when I had to leave the school. It was most unusual for him to come in the middle of the school term. I was terrified that he would pull me out of Aymestrey.

I waited and waited, and eventually the bell went for the end of siesta. I could hear everyone darting out to get changed for cricket. I walked over to Mrs G's office and knocked on the door. Mrs G came to the door and looked at me in a slightly strange manner.

'Madam, no one has come. I'm not sure whether to go to cricket or keep waiting.'

'Are you serious?'

'Yes, madam.'

'Just wait here,' she said in a very frustrated voice. 'The bloody man deserves to be shot,' she muttered under her breath.

I heard Mrs G pick up her old-fashioned rotary telephone and start dialling. After a few seconds she spoke in a low voice.

'Mr Bradford, Brian, is that you? Yes, it's Mrs Gill Griffiths from Aymestrey. I'm awfully sorry to bother you again today, and may I begin by saying that any hint of annoyance that you may hear is not aimed at you, but this poor child has been waiting for over an hour and I'm really not quite sure what I'm meant to tell him. Now is Mehdi going to show up, or is he going to pull his usual stunt? Under these circumstances his behaviour is frankly nothing short of outrageous. I understand that he is the boy's alleged guardian, but I have duties to this boy as his teacher and his headmistress. If he does not show in the next thirty minutes, I'm going to have to ignore Mehdi's wishes and take matters into my own hands. I'm sure he has other things to do, but common sense tells me that there is a more urgent matter awaiting him here ... Thank you. Good day, sir.'

I could not believe what I was hearing. What was so urgent? Why had Mrs G spoken to Brian once today already, and why was she so mad at Mehdi?

Mrs G appeared at the door looking a lot calmer than she should have looked.

'He should be here in the next fifteen minutes, so don't go to cricket yet.'

'Yes, madam.'

I walked to the exit hall and kept waiting. I looked out of the window and watched all my friends run to the cricket field. I could see them begin to play under Draggo's supervision. Another twenty minutes crawled by as I watched the game, wishing I could be with them.

Eventually I saw Mehdi's car coming up the drive. Immediately I went out to greet him. He pulled up next to me, lowered his window and looked straight at me, his face impassive.

'Your mother's dead.'

Those were his only words. He rolled up his window and drove away. I watched him as I replayed those words over and over in my head.

Your mother's dead – your mother's dead – your mother's dead – your mother's dead.

What had he just told me? I fell to my knees on the gravel and buried my head in my hands and wept as if my life had just ended. I felt as if someone had punched me really hard in my stomach – I was so winded it was hard to breathe. Tears rolled down my cheeks, and I stayed there on my knees and cried until I felt Mrs G kneel beside me on the gravel.

'I'm so sorry, my dear boy. I'm so sorry.'

I kept crying, wondering why this was happening to me. Was it some cruel joke Mehdi was playing on me? Everything had slowed right down, and I continued to cry until I felt emptied out. Eventually I had enough breath to speak.

'Madam, how did it happen? How did my mother die?'

'He didn't tell you?'

'He just told me my mother's dead. Nothing more and nothing less.'

I could see the shock on Mrs G's face. She stood me up and started to brush the dirt off me.

'I was told she died from a heart attack. That's what Mr Bradford said – Brian. That is as much as I know. I was hoping Mehdi could fill in some gaps for us, but apparently that didn't happen.'

I stood there, holding my face in my hands. I could not stop crying. I didn't care about being embarrassed, or about crying in front of Mrs G. I didn't care about anything. The only thing I had looked forward to, the only thing that had kept me going thus far, was the thought of being reunited with my mother and building a life with her in England. What had Istanbul been for? What had enduring all of Mehdi's abuse been for? What had my broken ribs been for? Why was I trying so hard at school?

'Come on, Abbas. There's only one way to deal with situations like this.'

I tried to stop crying and listen as Mrs G held my shoulders tightly and looked me in the eyes.

'You have to keep your chin up, young man. You have to keep that chin up and continue to live your life the way you have been. It's times like these that we really find out a lot about ourselves. I know you have it in you, Abbas. Few do, but I see it in you. Mr G sees it in you. Now, you go down to the cellars and put on your whites and go and hit some runs.'

'Yes, madam.'

In my teary reverie I walked away from Mrs G and went to the cellars to get changed. I slowly took off my clothes, the tears rolling down my cheeks all the while. I felt as if I were being punished. I felt as if I had made a huge mistake. I did not know how I was going to get through cricket. Slowly I walked to the fields. It was a bright, sunny day, and I looked up at the sky, as if I could see my mother there if only I stared hard enough.

As I approached the field Draggo shouted, 'Abbas, go to square leg and remember to walk in.'

Draggo was pretending it was business as usual, but I could see all the boys staring at me. I could see that they all knew. It seemed I was the last person to find out. They all waved at me, and I could see the pity in their eyes, a pity that didn't make me feel any better or help me in any way. Throughout the match I did not speak to anyone, nor did anyone try to say anything to me.

After the showers the others changed hurriedly as usual, but I sat on a bench, my clothes in my towel, not having the energy to do anything. Draggo did not say a word; he just let me be. Eventually Murphy came up to me and put his hand on my shoulder.

'Abbas. I'm so sorry, mate. I really am. If you need anything, let me know.'

As much as I appreciated what he'd said, it made my mother's death a reality. I immediately began to sob into my hands. I couldn't help it. I felt nauseous, and could almost taste the sick in my mouth as I wept. After Murphy, every other boy in the school came up to me in turn and offered me their condolences. It meant a lot that each member of the school cared enough to come and see me personally.

Eventually, after everyone had left, I slowly got up and began to get dressed. I leant my forehead against the wall. My ears were full of tears as I thought about how empty my life was. I had nothing to live for. Everything I had achieved since leaving Iran I had done in the hope of seeing my mother again.

I remembered that last conversation with her, when she had begged me to be strong. I was almost sure she had heard me afterwards, discussing working in Mehdi's kitchen with my father – and if she had known that I was suffering, she would have been devastated. She had probably blamed herself, and perhaps the guilt had got to her. I knew that she could not have lived with the knowledge that I was alone and being mistreated.

I was almost sure that I had been the cause of her death; I could only blame myself. I felt so guilty and so responsible for her. She was only thirty-seven years old. All I had ever wanted to do was look after her and make her proud. Instead, I felt as if I had killed her. As these thoughts were going through my head I began to slap the wall with both hands, crying and groaning.

Draggo walked up to me as I began to calm down. He had been in the cellars all that time.

'It's okay, Abbas. Take your time. I know you're hurting

right now, and I don't blame you. I just wanted to share something with you.'

He handed me a piece of paper, then walked out. I unfolded the paper to see a photocopy of a poem.

If I Should Die

If I should die and leave you
Be not like the others, quick undone
Who keep long vigils by the silent
dust and weep.

For my sake turn to life and smile
Nerving thy heart and trembling
hand to comfort weaker souls than thee.
Complete these unfinished tasks of mine
And I perchance may therein comfort thee.

THOMAS GRAY (1716–1771)

As I read it, even if it was in a different tongue to my mother's, I could just imagine her saying these words to me.

I had a pounding headache and I did not want to be near anyone, but there was really nowhere I could go, so I rejoined the school for the rest of that long, silent day.

That night I could not sleep. I kept reliving the scene with Mehdi from that afternoon. How could he be so cruel to me? I knew that he did not like me, but what had I done to deserve to be treated that way? I had so many questions, but I had no one to ask.

I wondered how my father was coping. At Aymestrey the general rule was that students were not allowed to receive or make calls, but I thought they would probably make an exception and allow me to call my father under these circumstances. Then again, he had given no indication that he wanted to talk to me. Why hadn't he called me? I was sure Mrs Griffiths would have told me if he had, even if she'd not allowed me to actually take the call. Why hadn't he wanted to?

Eventually I walked downstairs and sat in the bathroom looking out of the window. I was alone and the view was peaceful. I had tears in my eyes; I thought of my poor mother in her last days without me being there for her.

I felt a hand on my shoulder. It was Mrs G.

'Hello, young man.'

'Sorry, madam.'

'You're all right, Abbas. You can stay here for a little bit,' she said sympathetically. 'I would be the same if I were in your shoes.'

I kept looking out of the window while she spoke.

'You know, this is a very, very important time in your life. It's an event like this early in your life that shapes you into the person you will become. I know what you went through to get here, and that also shaped you, but Abbas, this is life-changing.'

Mrs G paused to see if I was listening. I looked at her and nodded for her to carry on.

'You see, Abbas, there are only really two paths that one can take in life – the right one and the wrong one. There are sometimes more options, but when you really dissect it, the road is either the right one or the wrong one. You follow me so far?'

'Yes, madam,' I said.

'Up till now you have stayed on the right path and done everything in a way that made your mother proud, correct?'

'Well, I'm not really sure, madam, but I hope so.'

'She was proud of you, trust me. Now, I know what you're thinking. Why did you bother trying so hard and working so hard, just for your mother to be taken away? Correct?'

I gave her a little nod.

'And you feel cheated,' she continued, 'and as if you have nothing to be good for anymore, because your mother will not be coming to England now, right?'

Tears were flowing down my cheeks again. Mrs G had managed to get right inside my head once more.

'Right, madam,' I said in a whisper.

'Well, you cannot … you cannot stop doing the right thing, because your mother made sacrifices for you, sacrifices that caused her pain, and caused her heartache. Now, turn to me and look at me. Look at me, Abbas.'

Mrs G twisted me around and looked very seriously into my face.

'You tell me, Abbas,' she said in a gentle voice, 'do you want all that sacrifice to have been for nothing?'

'No, madam,' I responded immediately. I was shocked that she could even ask me that.

'Well, it will be for nothing if you give up on yourself – your talents, your potential – and start making poor decisions in your life. Now from this day forward, every single day, with every decision that you face, before you make that decision, just ask yourself one question: *Would my mother approve of this decision? Would my mother be proud of me? Would my mother agree with my action or inaction?* You now have a huge responsibility, greater than anything you have had before – you have a responsibility to your mother to do the right thing. You have to make her life mean something. You have to memorialise her sacrifices and her death with your achievements and dedicate them to her. If you don't do that, she will have wasted her life, and her memory will fade. And I know you better than that, Abbas. I know you won't do that. I know how much integrity you have and what potential you have. Now go to bed and think about everything I have said, and start your new life with your new responsibilities tomorrow. Okay?'

'Yes, madam.'

I went back to bed and lay there thinking about everything that Mrs G had said. It all made sense. There was no way that I would let my mother's memory die. I knew I had to succeed. Failure was not an option for me, because that night I promised myself that I would make the sacrifices of Marzieh Kazerooni worth something.

EIGHT

For the next four weeks I did not really speak very much. Those around me allowed me to keep to myself. School was all I had to cling to, and schoolwork kept me busy, even though I was continuously thinking about my mother. My unanswered questions and the manner in which the news had been broken to me were also constant preoccupations. Mrs G told me that with time the hurt would ease. She had never lied to me – she had more than earned my trust – and so I decided I had to take her word for it. I tried really hard to do as she advised, but at times I would find myself crying. I just couldn't help it.

For a while Draggo treated me gently, and on a few occasions when we went running, he would drop his pace and run along beside me. He would talk about a range of subjects, continually trying to stimulate my brain. Despite his rugged, grumpy exterior, he was clearly a good and caring man.

There were now only a few weeks until the end of term. I was sitting in my usual place in Draggo's English class one day listening to him explain the genius of John Donne and Andrew Marvell. There was a knock at the door, and before Draggo could answer, Mrs G entered the classroom. We all stood up in unison to show our respect. In one movement, Mrs G waved us down and began to speak.

'Thank you. Please sit,' she said. 'Mr Driver, could I borrow Abbas from the class, please?'

Everyone looked at me with great curiosity; this was an extremely unusual event. I dreaded what might be coming at me. In the past when Mrs G had come to get me for something, the results had been catastrophic.

'By all means,' Draggo replied, looking over at me with some concern. I was not sure if he already knew why Mrs G wanted me, or if his concern was just him looking out for me.

When we were both standing on the newly polished floorboards next to the grand piano in the main school hall, Mrs G said to me, 'I need you to get your blazer, go to the assembly room and wait for Mr and Mrs Bradford.'

'What's happened, madam?' I asked, my voice trembling with anxiety and my heart racing. I could not take another blow. My mind was working overtime trying to figure out what had happened. Mrs G could tell how stressed I was and that I could not hold back my tears much longer, because my eyes had welled up and I was beginning to shake. If I had spoken another word, I would have broken down. Even though it might not be bad news, my emotions were too fragile to cope with the suspense.

'It's okay, Abbas, really,' she reassured me. 'Mrs Bradford called me and told me that it is Mehdi and Kate's wedding tonight.'

I was shocked. This was the first I had heard about a wedding. Why was I being pulled out of class for it?

'I didn't know, madam.'

'I know. Mrs Bradford told me she had assumed you knew all about it and that when she found out that was not the case, she insisted she would not go unless you went, too. She also didn't know that they had not visited you since … well, you know.'

'Oh,' I responded, slightly shocked. 'I see. So am I leaving school?'

'Yes. It's Saturday anyway, and there's only one class that you'll miss. They said they would bring you back either late tonight or tomorrow morning.'

'Madam,' I said, slightly taken aback, 'I am not even officially invited and I have nothing to wear. I have outgrown most of my casual clothes, especially my trousers and button-up shirts.'

Mrs G smiled at me.

'Well, first, my dear boy, Mr and Mrs Bradford invited you. Traditionally the parents of the bride send the invitations, and if they say you're invited, then you're invited. As for the clothing, you have your blue school shirts. I will ask Mrs Barnett to find you a clean pressed one. Wear that with a pair of your Sunday trousers, and I'll lend you one of Mr G's ties. You should be set then.'

'Thank you, madam,' I said, feeling a little embarrassed about the clothing, 'but do you think I should go?'

'Why shouldn't you go, Abbas?'

'I'm not sure, madam. I just don't really feel like it, and I would not want Mehdi and Kate's day to be spoiled if they did not want me there.'

'Now you listen to me,' Mrs G said sternly, kneeling down so she was at my level, 'you absolutely should go. Mr and Mrs Bradford want you there so badly they will not go to their own daughter's wedding if you don't. So look at it this way: you would actually be helping Kate, because without you, her parents would be missing and that *would* ruin her wedding.'

'Yes, madam.'

'Now off with you, and make sure you have fun.'

'Thank you, madam.'

I gathered my few things and went to the exit hall. Within minutes, Nancy and Brian pulled up. Nancy flew out of the car and ran towards me, hugging me so hard she almost squeezed the life out of me. As she held me, she whispered in my ear, 'Abbas, I had no idea, I'm so sorry.' Her voice shook.

'It's okay, it's only a wedding.'

'No, not just that. I only found out a few days ago that Mehdi and Kate have not been to see you since you heard about your mother. I had no idea. That's just unforgiveable. I'm so, so, so sorry.'

I was still in her embrace, but I could tell from her voice that she was crying now.

'It's okay. Thank you, Nancy. I'm okay.'

Despite what I'd said, Nancy's hug, and her sorrow, had stirred up my emotions and my eyes welled up again. I tried desperately not to cry. Nancy was clearly distraught about the situation, and I did not want to make her feel any worse.

'It's not okay, it's just not okay. You deserve better than that.'

'Come on, guys,' Brian said in a cheery tone. 'We have a wedding to get to.'

Nancy reluctantly let go of me and led me to the car. Brian approached and shook my hand.

'Hello, fella. It's just too bad, old chap. It's a terrible thing.'

'Thanks, Brian.'

We got into the car. Nancy was still upset and kept looking at me to see if I was okay, while Brian was obviously trying to think of something jolly to talk about. I was happy to see Nancy and Brian, but I really did not want to go to the wedding.

'Abbas,' Nancy said, 'we are so sorry that you did not get an invitation earlier. We really did think that Mehdi and Kate had told you.'

'Oh, it's no bother. I'm sure they have been very busy.'

'Oh, sure,' Brian chuckled. 'So busy I'm unsure whose wedding it is, mate, ours or theirs, because we seem to be doing everything.'

'Knock it off, Bri,' Nancy said, giving him a playful slap on the shoulder. 'He's exaggerating, Abbas.' After a pause she went on: 'I want you to know that the wedding just wouldn't be the same without you, and we wouldn't have it any other way.'

'Thank you.'

'How is the trusty 405?' Brian asked, trying to change the subject.

'It's amazing,' I said with a little smile. 'I made the team like I told you in my letter. I knocked a fifty with it against Saint Richards last week.'

'No – you didn't!' Brian exclaimed. He was so excited.

'Well done you, Abbas,' Nancy joined in.

'Thank you,' I said shyly. 'But I got caught on sixty-two. Mr G said it was a good knock but I need to keep my bat straighter.'

'I think he's being harsh. Sixty-two is a bloody good knock, old boy.'

'It really is, Abbas. Good for you.'

'I told you he's a natural.' Brian turned to Nancy. 'This boy's going far, you watch.'

'He most certainly is.'

I was unsure if this was a show they were putting on for me or whether they really were excited for me. I knew they cared, though, and that was all that mattered.

It felt good to be someone's pride and joy. I knew Draggo had made me his pet project, but I was never sure if it was because I worshipped him or because he saw something in me. Either way, Draggo rarely let me see he was proud of me or showed any emotion other than frustration and anger. By contrast, Brian and Nancy put me on a pedestal and followed what I did as if I were their own son.

Fifteen minutes after leaving Aymestrey we arrived at their house, which was a complete mess: people were staying from out of town, there were boxes all around the house, and everyone was running about like headless chickens. I went to the bathroom and changed, then walked into the back garden and sat in a garden chair and waited. I knew I would be in the way inside, and I was in no mood to socialise with complete strangers. I sat there for an hour or so before Brian came out to see me.

'You okay, Abbas?'

'Yes, thank you.'

'You ready?'

'Yes.'

'You go along to the church with Nancy; I have to go in the car with Kate. Mehdi should already be at the church.'

'Sure.'

Nancy and I drove to the church, which was almost full with their family and friends. Mehdi was at the front talking to the vicar. Nancy took my hand and we went to the first row. She pointed to the opposite row, on Mehdi's side.

'Traditionally this side is the bride's side, so I have to sit here. You have to sit over there.'

'No problem.'

I walked over, but there was really no room in the front row. I began walking to the back where there was more room, then I heard my name echo through the church. Nancy had made a couple move from the front row and sent them to the back.

'You're immediate family, so you sit in the front.'

'It's okay, really.'

'I won't have it any other way, Abbas.'

She smiled as she watched me sit in the front row. Mehdi had still not made eye contact with me. I watched him look at Nancy, who rolled her eyes with contempt and was probably wondering how she was going to cope officially being part of Mehdi's family. Nancy's feelings about Mehdi had become more and more obvious as time had passed. Evidently, Kate was marrying him despite strenuous opposition from her mother.

The ceremony went without a hitch and we were taken to the hall where the reception was going to be held. I did not really know anyone. There were chairs around the walls of the hall, so I went and sat down and waited for further instructions. A man came by and offered me some lemonade, which I gladly accepted. The hall was at capacity and the DJ was already mixing his cheesy hits.

I felt a sudden tap on my shoulder, from a tall dark man who had a beautiful English lady standing next to him. Beside them was a boy who must have been five or six years younger than me. He had a mischievous look on his face. The lady held his hand as the man leant down to speak to me.

'Hi, are you Abbas?'

'Yes, sir,' I replied. How did he know my name?

'I'm Fereydoun, your cousin from Iran. You don't know me, but we are first cousins.'

'Oh wow, really? One of Aunty Beebozorg's sons?'

'Yes.' He smiled. 'I'm the youngest. I have heard so much about you from my mother, and I knew you'd be here tonight. Between you and me, that's why we came.' He paused, then turned to his wife and boy and added, 'By the way, this is Nadine, my wife, and this is Firooz, my son.'

'Hi,' Firooz said with a naughty little smile. 'Can we go and play now?'

'Hold your horses, Fiz,' his mum said, then turned her attention to me. 'Hello, darling. How are you?' She had a lovely smile. 'We are so excited to meet you after all this time.'

'Hello,' I said, standing to greet her. I put out my hand to shake Fiz's hand, too, but he hid behind his mum.

'You'll have to forgive him – he can be a little shy about some things, but once he knows you, God help you!'

We all laughed at Fiz, who looked like he was getting annoyed.

'So, how have you been doing, Abbas?' Nadine asked.

'Very well, thank you. I just came from school today.'

'Oh wow, you were at school on a Saturday?'

'Yes, I go to boarding school, madam.'

'Ha, you can call me Nadine. None of that madam stuff needed here,' she insisted. She glanced at Fiz. 'See, Fiz, if you don't behave you're off to boarding school with Abbas!'

'Muuum,' Fiz protested.

'How are you finding the school?' Fereydoun asked.

'I love it, actually. It's amazing. So different to Iran.'

'It's probably different to what most children experience in England, to be honest,' Nadine commented.

'I'm sure,' I responded with a smile.

'Well, it's great to meet you,' she said. 'I hope we get to see a lot more of you. Make sure we speak again tonight.'

'Absolutely.'

Fiz took this as his cue to drag me away to play with him – he was tired of adult company. We wandered around for a little while, and he told me about all his Transformers and his friends at school. Then we played some board games until he fell fast asleep, stretched across three chairs.

I sat next to Fiz, minding my own business, wanting the night to finish. I watched Mehdi work the crowd with his pretentious affable persona, which most people seemed to buy. I knew Mehdi loved the idea that he was well liked and highly regarded. Nancy and Brian watched from the sidelines, too. Poor Kate seemed happy enough, but I believed that in her heart she must have known this man was not the right person for her. At one stage she looked at me from afar with a wry little smile. It felt as though the only person in the room who really understood was me, and she knew it. I felt bad for her.

People were very drunk and the party was in full swing. Fereydoun and Nadine came and sat on either side of me, and Fereydoun put his arm around me and leant in a little so that we could talk.

'Abbas, I wanted to let you know that I … that we, Nadine and I, know … well …' He paused and looked at Nadine and then tried again. 'How can I put this? Mehdi … We know that he is not the—'

'We know that he can be a real shit,' Nadine interrupted. 'Tell it for what it is. Abbas, I know you don't know us, but if you ever want somewhere else to stay for a little while – for the holidays, or for a weekend – you can always stay with us. We would really like that … and Fiz loves you already.'

'Here.' Fereydoun gave me a card. 'This is my business card, and I've written my mobile number on the back of it. If you ever need anything – I mean anything – you call us.'

'Fereydoun, why don't you take Fiz to the car and I'll be right behind you?' Nadine said.

'Sure,' Fereydoun said as he patted me on the back. 'Bye, Abbas.'

'Bye.'

Nadine and I watched Fereydoun pick up Fiz and head for the exit.

'I can tell you're not happy, Abbas,' Nadine said, 'and I don't want you to feel pressured about anything. Just know that if you want to come and spend a few weeks with us, you don't even need to ask – you already have an invitation.'

'Thank you.'

'And of course this little conversation is strictly between us.'

'Thank you,' I said with a sigh of relief.

'You're welcome.' Nadine smiled. 'Now look into dates for your holidays and let us know, okay?'

'I will. Thank you so much.'

With that, Nadine said her goodbyes to me and left quietly. It had been a strange encounter, but I'd really liked Nadine, Fereydoun and Firooz. They were kind-hearted people, and for some reason they really did care about my welfare.

I sat on the chair at the edge of the hall and watched the older aunts and uncles break out their funky moves, to the amusement of the twenty-somethings. Nancy came up to me, sweating, with a huge smile on her face.

'I'm drenched. I've been dancing with Aunty Maureen. She's a hoot.'

I gave a little laugh. It was good to see Nancy so happy.

'Now, are you going to let me stand around without a dance partner?'

'Oh … well … Nancy … you know …'

'Don't be silly, Abbas. I'm sure Mrs G will not take too kindly to you leaving a lady unattended!'

'Okay,' I said with a reluctant smile.

We began to dance, and before we knew it Brian and a few of Kate's cousins had joined us. I was starting to enjoy myself, laughing and chatting with Kate's extended family. They were all so lovely and so attentive to me. I was not sure if they knew about my mother's recent passing or whether they were always this nice. Either way, I decided to take Mrs G's advice and have some fun.

Eventually Kate made her way over to us and we all danced with her. She looked beautiful in her wedding dress and deserved to be the centre of attention. She even danced with me for a little, then hugged me and kissed my cheek. Everyone circled around us, watching and whistling. As Kate drifted on to dance with the next person, I felt a firm grip on my shoulder. Mehdi's alcohol-tainted breath was hot against my face as he hissed in my ear, 'Stop making a show of yourself and go and sit down – you're embarrassing me.'

'Sorry,' I said, without even looking at him. I knew there was no point in trying to reason with him and explain that it had been Nancy's idea that I dance in the first place. He sounded furious, and not at all like a man should on his wedding night.

I walked over to the edge of the hall and sat down again, trying to blend in. A few seconds later Brian came and sat next to me.

'How are you, Abbas?'

'Well, thank you, Brian. Congratulations. The wedding has been amazing.'

'Thank you,' he said in a slightly deflated voice. 'It was all right ... It was all right.'

I wasn't sure whether I should ask if he was okay or not, but I decided against it. 'So what happens now? Do people dance till it ends?' I asked instead.

'I guess. We have to see off the couple, and then we dance a little more and go home.'

'Where are they going?'

'On their honeymoon. It's a tradition that the newlyweds go on their honeymoon the same night.'

'Oh, okay. Where are they off to?'

'Greece.'

'Very nice.'

There was a slight pause before Brian asked, 'Abbas, how are you and Mehdi related again?'

'Cousins. We're cousins.'

'I have no idea how you two could even be remotely related.'

'Why?'

'Oh, it's nothing. Just don't stop being you. And do as they teach you at school, not as us adults behave.'

'Okay, Brian.'

'I'm sorry. I think I'm a little drunk, but I hope you understand what I'm saying.'

'I do.'

He was clearly expressing his disapproval of Mehdi. I

took it as a compliment. But at the same time, it scared me that everyone was expressing their preference for me so openly. If Mehdi found out, I would bear the brunt of his anger, and possibly Kate might, too.

Soon Kate and Mehdi were gone. I immediately felt more relaxed and tried to have a bit of fun. But I purposely stayed out of as many photos as I could so that Mehdi would not see me dancing or enjoying myself.

At around one a.m., I helped Nancy and Brian clear up and we drove back to their house. Since they had guests, I slept on the floor on a blow-up mattress.

The next day Brian took me back to school. All the boys had wondered why I had been dragged out of class, and all of them were jealous that I had been allowed to leave school on a weekend that was not an exeat.

The last couple of weeks of term passed swiftly. When school ended, once again I was the last person left at school. I was not sure whether Mehdi and Kate were back from Greece. Mrs G had tried calling Brian and Nancy, but they were out. I ended up having to stay an extra night, to the agitation of Mrs G, but bored as I was, an extra night at school was one more night away from Mehdi.

At lunchtime the next day Mehdi showed up with Kate. Both of them were tanned. Kate was in a merry mood, having just come back from her honeymoon. Unsurprisingly, Mehdi was his usual sullen self. I was happy that Kate was in the car, but that left the question: where were they taking me?

'How was your holiday, Kate?'

'Amazing. It was wonderful. Didn't want to come back.'

'Wow. I'm happy you had fun.'

'So how are you?' Kate asked. 'How is school?'

'Great, thank you. I've made it to the top of my class. It's the first time I have managed it.'

'Well done, Abbas! Now that your English is so much better, I'm not surprised. Not a dummy, this one.' She tapped Mehdi, asking him to acknowledge me.

'Yeah,' Mehdi grunted. 'He's certainly no dummy.'

'Your English is fluent now. So why do you want to go and learn English in your holidays again?' Kate asked, looking at me and then Mehdi.

'Erm …' I was stuck. I glanced at Mehdi, who was giving me a death-stare in his rear-view mirror.

'It's not so much the English now. He just likes the after-school activities. Keeps him busy,' Mehdi interrupted.

'Oh, yeah. I get to go and see lots of things and have fun with the other kids.'

'See, I told you,' Mehdi said to Kate.

'I guess,' Kate said, still confused, 'but won't you just go to the same places as last time?'

'Erm … yeah, kind of … but there are so many, and we don't always go to the same places each time. Like in London we might go to the Tower of London, do the river trip or go to the Natural History Museum. There's loads to do, and I get to tag along.'

'Good for you, Abbas,' Kate said proudly. 'No wonder you're so smart. Colin and I would never had done any of that at your age.'

'Maybe he should slow down or his head will explode,' Mehdi joked. Kate laughed, but I could sense the resentment in his comment.

Soon we were back at Abbey International.

'Okay, evening activities will start at seven p.m. in the usual place. There'll be a note up with directions as usual.'

'Oh, nice. Cheers.'

I knew that this was code for me having to go to the kitchen, but I did not have the back-door key.

'Will I find my student access key in the dorms?'

'Yes, in the top drawer of your side cabinet. I asked the night matron to put it there for you.'

He had clearly thought this through, anticipating that Kate would want to come with him to collect me and planning things so he didn't have to give me the key in front of her.

'Great, thank you,' I said.

When we arrived, Mehdi and Kate sat in the car as I dragged my trunk out of the boot. I started to haul it down the pathway as usual. Before I knew it Mehdi was out of the car shouting, 'No, you always do this. He can do it. He does it every time.'

'Well, maybe if you acted like a human being he would never have to do it by himself,' Kate shouted back from within the car.

Mehdi slammed his car door shut and started walking furiously towards me. I stopped with fright and just waited to see what would happen. He lifted the other end of the trunk and I immediately lifted my end up. I was at the front and he was pushing me forward, hard and fast. I was struggling to lift my end and keep pace, but I managed to hang on. I was too scared to let go. Mehdi was furious.

As soon as we were out of sight of Kate, Mehdi dropped his end and stalked off. I was relieved that he was gone. I continued to drag the trunk towards my damp little room, but I had only gone a few yards when I heard Kate's voice.

'Abbas?'

I dropped the trunk and started to run back towards the car. I didn't want her to see that Mehdi had dropped the trunk short of the room; nor did I want her to see my accommodation for the holidays.

She smiled at me as I approached her. In the distance I could see Mehdi sulking in the driver's seat of the car.

'I almost forgot,' Kate said. 'Mum and Dad gave me this envelope to give to you.'

'Thank you,' I said, looking at it. 'Thanks so much.'

'Don't mention it. I wish my parents liked me the way they like you,' she joked.

I chuckled and watched her return to the car.

I went to my trunk and eventually reached my room. To my surprise, the room had been decorated, and it was a lot nicer. There was new paint, a new sink and an actual bed there now. I looked inside the bedside drawer and, as Mehdi had said, there was the key.

I sat down and looked at the envelope again, on which Nancy's handwriting said, *To the New Class Number One – Abbas*. It made me smile. I opened it to find a card with a picture of a bear inside, with *Congratulations* written above his head.

Dearest Abbas,
Brian and I called Mrs G to ask how you were
doing. We were delighted to hear that you aced
the exams this term. You are such a star. We are so
proud of you. Brian and I wanted to pick you up at
the end of term but we had a trip planned. So we
are giving this to Kate to give to you. We will take
you for a celebration meal when we get back. You

*really have achieved so much in so little time. We
hope you know that.*

   Lots of love,
   Brian and Nancy xoxoxox
   P.S. Our little secret!

Inside the card was forty pounds. I could not believe my
eyes. They were so kind to me and cared for me as if I were
their own child.

Before work started I knew exactly where to go: to see
Chris at the tuckshop. He was his usual cheery self and was
happy to see me. I bought a Mars Bar and got some change.
I had not talked to my father since receiving the news of
my mother's passing.

With trepidation I walked over to the phone box and put
some change into the telephone. My heart started racing
and I had tears in my eyes already as I listened to the phone
ringing. I wanted to know what had happened, but at the
same time I did not want to talk to my father. I was sad
and somewhat angry with him. Why had he not called me?

The telephone kept ringing and ringing until it just went
dead. I tried calling another two or three times with the
same result. He was not home.

I headed back to my room, trying to take my mind off my
father by opening my Mars Bar, but I had not taken a single
bite before tears started rolling down my cheeks. I tried to
pull myself together, but my emotions overwhelmed me. I
did not know why I was crying: because I missed Maman,
because I felt alone, or because my father had deserted me.
Perhaps it was a bit of everything.

I arrived in the kitchen at seven p.m. sharp to find the
usual note from Mehdi. It was summer, and I had over six

hundred packed lunches to make. I immediately set to work and tried to focus on finishing on time.

That summer was really hot, and I remember sweating that first night. I would splash my face with water every hour or so to try to keep cool and then get back to my counters lined with bread.

My system always came back to me quickly. Every strange noise would put me on guard, though; the memory of Mehdi's visit some seven or eight months before was still vivid in my mind.

I almost didn't make it, but managed in the end to pack the last box by about 4.15 a.m., then I walked down to the pool to take my daily shower and noticed the sun was coming up. I stood in the shower looking at the orange sky, wondering if Maman was looking at me. It still hurt so much.

NINE

Two weeks went by without incident, but every night I struggled to finish my work. The number of sandwiches required remained high and the weather remained hot.

One Tuesday I was finally sinking into a deep sleep after tossing and turning uncomfortably in bed due to the heat for perhaps four hours when there was a loud knock on the door. I leapt up and looked through my small window. It was Mehdi.

'Get your stuff ready,' he said when I opened the door.

'It's not time to go back to school yet.'

'Yeah? No kidding. You never cease to surprise me with your ability to make new friends.'

'Sorry?' I had no idea what he was talking about.

'Apparently Nadine has taken to you and wants you to have a holiday with them. Fereydoun is coming to pick you up in an hour.'

'Oh, sorry. I had no idea—'

'What the hell am I meant to do now?' he interrupted.

'I don't have to go. Say we have plans.'

'Sure … *Nadine, sorry, Abbas can't come, he's working in my kitchen*,' he said sarcastically. 'I'm sure that would go down well. You'd love that, wouldn't you?'

'But school is free now. So that does save you something.'

His glare meant that I should shut my mouth. I didn't say another word. 'Just for once, for once, can you not have a smart-arse response for me?'

I packed my trunk and dragged it to the top of the hill to wait for Fereydoun with Mehdi. Right on time, Fereydoun pulled up in his car. Mehdi went and spoke to him first and then came back to see me.

'Okay, have fun,' he said sarcastically. 'They'll take you back to school directly afterwards.'

'Thanks.'

I walked over to Fereydoun, who picked up my trunk with one hand and put it into the boot of his car.

'How are you, mate?' he asked.

'Well, thanks. You?'

'Great. Fiz is so excited that you're coming, asking about you every day. He'll probably wet himself when you arrive.'

We both laughed as he drove onto the motorway. Fereydoun, I discovered, loved to speed. He had a roll of mints in the front, and every fifteen minutes he would order me to have one and to give him one.

'So this should be fun,' he said. 'It will be a good holiday for you.'

'Thank you.'

After about two hours we got to Aylesbury in Buckinghamshire where Fereydoun and Nadine lived. As soon as we pulled up Fiz dashed outside and jumped on me like a monkey.

'Abbas! I thought you'd never come. We have so much to do,' he shouted.

Fereydoun carried my trunk in and Nadine came out to greet me with a big hug. 'How are you, sweetheart?'

'Well, thank you,' I responded. 'How are you?'

'Great. We're so excited to have you. Are you excited about the trip?'

'Trip?' I asked. 'What trip?'

'You didn't tell him?' Nadine asked Fereydoun.

'Well, I told him he was going on holiday.'

'Oh, you mean we're actually going somewhere else?' I said with a huge smile. I couldn't believe that they were actually going to take me with them on their family holiday.

'Not Dad – he's working – but you, Mum and me. We're going to Turkey,' Fiz said.

My face dropped. I hadn't thought very much about Istanbul since I'd arrived in England – I'd tried to put it all behind me. I didn't know how I felt about returning to Turkey.

'It's okay, love,' Nadine cut in, clearly noticing my reaction. 'We're only flying into Istanbul. From there, we're going straight to a resort at Bodrum. It will be wonderful. You'll see. We will only be at the airport in Istanbul. Is that okay?'

'Of course,' I said politely. 'Thank you very much.'

We spent the rest of the day talking about the trip. To my great surprise we were leaving the very next morning. Mehdi had already given my passport to Fereydoun and we were all set. Nadine asked if she could help me pack. With huge embarrassment I opened up my trunk and showed her that I had no suitable clothes.

'Come on, love,' she said without hesitation, 'let's go grab you a few things.'

I felt humiliated that I had nothing to my name, not even decent casual clothes. Nadine took me to the shops to buy me new trainers, jeans, shorts, T-shirts, swimming shorts, casual shoes and underwear. All I could keep saying was 'thank you'.

Eventually Nadine cut me short. 'Abbas, sweetheart, really, it is our pleasure. Stop thanking us.'

I just nodded and sat quietly after that.

Nadine and Fereydoun did everything they could to make me feel welcome and a part of their family, but I was still not fully at ease in their home. Even so, it was good to be in a comfortable house with no work to do.

That night there was a telephone call. Fiz ran to answer it. 'Hello?'

'Who is it, Fiz?' Nadine asked.

'Mehdi.'

'Hand it over,' Nadine said.

'Hold on, Mum,' Fiz said. It seemed he loved being on the phone. He started to laugh at whatever Mehdi was saying. 'No way, really?'

'What is it?' Nadine asked.

'Mum, Mum, Mehdi promised me that he'll take me and Abbas camping next weekend when we get back from Turkey.'

The excitement on Fiz's face was priceless, but I felt sad for him because I knew already that Mehdi would let him down.

'I'm sure,' Nadine said suspiciously. She took the phone from Fiz and walked out of the room, coming back a few minutes later and winking at me.

'Everything okay?' I asked.

'Yup,' she said confidently. 'He was just checking when we're going.'

She went into the kitchen to talk to Fereydoun, and I overheard her explaining that Mehdi had wanted me to return but that she'd told him it wasn't right to disappoint a child like that. I guessed he hadn't been able to find a replacement for me to make the packed lunches, which meant that he would have to make them himself.

The next day I got on a plane with Nadine and Fiz and flew back to Turkey. I felt nervous when we arrived at Istanbul, but as Nadine had promised, a small minibus took us from the airport to Bodrum, a seemingly endless journey.

Bodrum, I discovered when we arrived, was full of British and German tourists, and nothing like Istanbul. I spent the week getting to know Nadine and Fiz and lying by the pool, happy to be out of the kitchen and well fed for a change.

I was glad I'd met these generous people, even though I had no idea what this new relationship might mean. Perhaps there would be future opportunities to spend more time with them rather than with Mehdi. I felt worried I might spoil my chances of this happening by behaving in a way that Nadine or Fiz didn't like, though, and as a result, I could not really be myself. Nadine tried hard to break me out of my shell, but I could not allow myself to cross the barrier that I had created for myself. I just wanted Nadine to be happy with me, because I cherished this holiday she and Fereydoun had offered me.

When we returned to England after a week in the sun, I didn't know whether I would get to spend the rest of the holidays with them in Aylesbury or would have to return to Mehdi as he had requested when he'd called before we'd left. I expected the worst, but hoped for the best.

As it turned out, the only time we spoke about Mehdi was that Sunday. I saw Fiz dragging a packed bag down the stairs like an excited puppy.

'What are you doing, Fiz?' Nadine asked him.

'I'm ready,' he said with a huge smile on his face. 'Mehdi said he'll take us camping today, remember?'

I looked up at Nadine, wondering what she would make of the whole situation. Nadine's face dropped; clearly she knew as well as I that there would be no camping.

'Sweetheart, I'm not sure if Mehdi's coming.'

'But he said he would,' Fiz cried, taken aback. 'He's coming, right, Abbas?'

'I hope so, mate,' I said, trying to let him down gently, 'but I don't think so, to be honest.'

'Why?' Fiz demanded. 'He promised.'

'Yes, I know, honey,' Nadine said, holding him, 'but it's not always that simple.'

'But if Dad promises...' His voice trailed off and he allowed his mother to comfort him.

'Come on, Fiz,' I said. 'We can go and have a kick-about, if you'd like?'

'No, thanks.'

Fiz walked upstairs, dragging his bag behind him. I felt sorry for him – he had really wanted to go camping – but he did not know what he'd been wishing for!

———

I stayed with Fereydoun and Nadine for another three weeks. One Sunday night we were all watching television when the phone rang. Fiz ran to pick it up.

'Hello? Yes. Yes. Who is calling, please? Abbas,' he said, 'it's for you.'

'What? Me?' I asked in shock.

'Yeah, it's Brian Bradford. For you.'

'Oh,' I replied. I hadn't realised Brian even knew where I was. I was happy to speak with him, though. I took the telephone from Fiz and said, 'Hello?'

'Hi, Abbas. How are you?'

'Really well, thanks. You?'

'Oh, not so bad,' Brian said. He sounded a little deflated.

'How is Nancy?' There was a slight pause. I waited for a response and then said, 'Brian?'

'Oh, sorry,' he said as he snapped out of his reverie. 'Yes, she's okay. She says hi.'

Something was not right, but I was not sure whether I should push the subject or not.

'Oh, good. I got to go on holiday to Turkey! Do you remember Fereydoun and Nadine from the wedding?'

'Of course. Yes. That's great. I'm glad you're having fun.'

'Thanks.'

'Listen, Abbas, your father called here today, and from what I could understand he said he will ring again the day after tomorrow. I tried afterwards to have Mehdi contact him and have him call you there in Aylesbury tomorrow instead, but Mehdi said you should come back to Malvern anyway. I'm sure one of us can then take you back to school when it starts in a week?'

'Oh,' I said, 'sure, I guess. Can you hold on a second?'

'Sure. Take your time.'

I turned to Fereydoun and Nadine. 'Brian says my dad's going to ring me the day after tomorrow and Mehdi won't tell him to call here, so I need to get back to Brian's place in Malvern. I haven't spoken to my dad in...'

'Of course, sweetheart, but do you want to go back?' Nadine asked.

'Yes ... please,' I said hesitantly. I did not want to upset Nadine, but I did want to speak to my father. 'Maybe I can get a train tomorrow?'

'Don't be silly,' Fereydoun said. 'I'll take you myself.'

'Thank you.' I turned my attention to Brian again. 'I can get a lift with Fereydoun tomorrow. I'll be there.'

'Okay, great, Abbas. If no one is in, I will leave a key under the doormat for you. Just let yourself in.'

It was a really strange conversation. Brian just wasn't himself. I went upstairs and packed my trunk and got myself ready for the next day.

As promised, the next morning Fereydoun helped with my things and put my trunk in the boot of his car. Fiz and Nadine stood at the door waiting to say goodbye to me, and I could see tears in Fiz's eyes. I was going to miss the little rascal, and apparently he was going to miss me.

I gave him a hug. 'See you soon, mate. Look after yourself.'

'Bye.'

His mouth was turning down into a pout. Rather than cry in front of me, he hurried back inside.

'Bye, sweetheart,' Nadine said to me. 'You can see how much we all love you, especially Fiz. Please come again soon.'

'Thank you so much for everything – for having me, for the holiday, for my clothes, for everything. I really appreciate it.'

'You are so welcome, my dear. You be good and take care of yourself, okay?'

'Okay.'

The journey back was mostly silent. I could see that Fereydoun wanted to say something but was thinking about how he could phrase it correctly.

'You know you can stay with us anytime you like, Abbas,' he said eventually.

'Thank you. It means a lot.'

'Fiz has really taken to you,' he said, glancing at me. 'It makes him happy when you are there.'

'I love hanging around with him, too. He's very good to me.'

When we drove into Brian's driveway, before we got out of the car, Fereydoun reached into his pocket and handed me fifty pounds.

'In case you need anything,' he said. 'You never know.'

'Thank you so much,' I gasped. 'You really don't have to—'

'Don't be silly,' he insisted. 'It's my pleasure. Let's keep this between you and me.'

'Fereydoun, thank you, really,' I said, shocked at his generosity. 'Thank you so much.'

We got out of the car, and soon enough Brian and Nancy were standing in the doorway welcoming us. I could not believe what a good holiday I had had and how generous Fereydoun and Nadine had been. They really cared for me and had been so good to me, and they expected nothing in return. It had been a while since I had experienced such unconditional affection from a family member.

'My dear boy,' Nancy said with her glowing smile and open arms, 'it's good to see you.'

I ran up to Nancy and gave her a warm hug. I had really missed her. The feeling I always had when she held me in that motherly way was very special.

Fereydoun headed home immediately after saying his goodbyes. He was not a terribly emotional man – he merely shook my hand and left – but he was always kind and caring.

That evening, Nancy, Brian and I sat around the television eating sandwiches until Nancy broke the silence.

'Well, I told Mehdi you are staying with us this week and we will take you back to school afterwards.'

'Oh, great,' I said excitedly, 'thank you! I hope that's no trouble.'

'Really, Abbas?' Nancy asked, rolling her eyes at me.

I smiled as Brian winked at me.

———

I woke up the next day to the sound of Nancy's knock at the door.

'Abbas, dear, you have a call. I think it's your dad,' she said. 'Hurry up.'

I leapt out of bed, ran downstairs and picked up the receiver. 'Hello?'

'Abbas?'

'Hi, Baba.'

'Hi,' he said. Then, after a long pause, 'So how are you?' It was obvious that he was lost for words.

'Okay.'

'What are you up to?'

'I just woke up.'

The conversation was slow and painful. I had tears in my eyes and wondered why it had taken him so long to call me, and why now, when he finally did, he still did not talk about Maman. She was all I thought about every day and he did not seem to care.

'Everyone here says hi to you,' he said. 'I hadn't realised how popular you are!' This was Baba's attempt at humour.

'Say hi.'

'So when are you going back to school?'

'Next week.'

'So...'

'So,' I parroted. My sadness was edging towards anger.

'I just wanted to say...'

'Yes?'

'I'm so sorry for not...' He could not carry on.

'It's okay.'

I gave him the easy way out. Tears rolled down my cheeks. I forgave him out of sadness, even though he still had not asked how I really was.

My heart broke, because I felt so alone. Baba was not being the father I needed him to be. He seemed to need me to be this *man* that I clearly was not.

I cannot remember the rest of the conversation. I controlled my voice so he could not tell I was crying, and he spoke to me about meaningless events. I missed Maman; only she could make me feel better, and she was not there anymore.

TEN

Before I knew it I was back at Aymestrey with my friends, and had slipped back into the routine of school.

I was still not myself, though. Since my mother's death I had become more inhibited and an air of sadness surrounded me. Although a little time had passed, it was not getting easier to accept my loss. I would find myself unable to sleep at night, and tears would sometimes roll down my cheeks for no clear reason. Life just didn't seem fair; nor did I feel I had a purpose anymore. I would watch my friends asleep in the dormitory without a care in the world and wonder why I was being punished. This was a thought that recurred over and over again. I tried not to feel down, but it was hard.

A deep sense of loneliness had hit me, too. In Istanbul I had been alone, and far more vulnerable, but there had always seemed to be a way out – my mother was always going to be there at the end. Now she wasn't, and my father's behaviour only exacerbated that sense of loss. The idea that I was alone at the age of just eleven was hard to accept.

One day, I had been thinking about Maman throughout an entire algebra class. The class passed me by, and when the bell rang the other boys ran to the next class as usual. I was trailing behind when my books fell out of my hands. As I bent over to pick them up, I began to cry for no real reason, tears flooding onto the floor beneath me despite my efforts to control myself. As I was about to get up, Mrs Griffiths knelt next to me and put her arm around me.

'My dear Abbas,' she said softly, 'what is the trouble?'

I shook my head apologetically, trying to indicate that I was pulling myself together. Mrs Griffiths helped me up, took me by the arm and walked me into an empty classroom.

'Your mother?'

'Yes, madam.'

'I have seen a change in you, Abbas.' She shook her head sadly. 'It is only to be expected. You had been through a lot already, and you didn't deserve this.'

I stood still and listened.

'But as we have discussed previously,' she continued in a firmer, more rallying tone of voice, 'your mother sacrificed much so that you could be here, wanted so much for you, and I think you are beginning to give up. This won't do, young man. You cannot just feel sorry for yourself and walk around like the world owes you something. You need to hold your head high and be even more courageous than before … to work hard, and do your best for your mother. You owe her that.'

'Yes, madam,' I said, listening intently.

'Let me tell you, young man, the right path is almost always the hardest path. I know it hurts, but you can work through this. Do you understand what I'm telling you, Abbas?'

'Yes, madam,' I said pensively. 'Thank you, madam.'

That night, I stayed awake thinking about the conversation. Mrs Griffiths was right. To this day, I believe that the advice she gave me, then and in our previous conversation about my mother, was the best advice I have ever received. It changed my life.

I once again decided that I would make the most of myself, and that I would do everything for my mother.

As the term progressed, although I was still grieving, I began to cheer up. School was going splendidly and I was excelling both academically and in my extracurricular activities. I went to friends' houses for the exeat weekends, and had not seen Mehdi all term.

I had written a few letters to Nancy and Brian but, uncharacteristically, Nancy had not responded. I eventually received a letter from Brian saying that he would probably come and get me for the next exeat weekend. The uncertainty of his offer was unusual, but I replied saying I would not make any other plans, because I wanted to see both Nancy and Brian.

At the next exeat all the other boys left and I began to think Brian must have forgotten about me. Usually I would be one of the first to be picked up if he or Nancy were collecting me. Mr Griffiths checked on me and, as usual, he felt sorry for me and gave me a pack of Cherry Drops to keep my morale up. I was not upset, though; I just knew something was wrong, because Brian and Nancy never behaved like this.

Time passed, and I eventually gave up on the weekend and began to play snooker. To my surprise, though, soon after that Mr Griffiths came up to see me with a smile, followed by Brian.

I was shocked by Brian's appearance. He looked as if he hadn't showered for a week, he was unshaven and his hair was messy.

'Hi, Abbas,' he said in a broken voice.

'Brian, what's wrong?'

There was a silence as both men towered over me, neither knowing what to say.

'Abbas,' Brian said softly in the end, 'why don't we get out of here and let Mr and Mrs Griffiths enjoy their break?'

'Sure.'

I followed Brian out to his car in silence. He seemed awkward, and we got in the car and buckled our belts without a word.

Brian began to drive.

'Where's Nancy?' I asked, to break the silence.

'We…we…we'll see her in a bit,' Brian said softly, blinking hard.

'Oh, okay.'

'And, actually, she's not at home.' He was really trying to control himself now. 'We are meeting her…out.'

I felt sick inside. Was it Mehdi? What if Nancy was with Kate because he'd done something to her? Would it mean I could not see Brian and Nancy anymore?

'Sorry to ask, Brian, but…has Mehdi done something bad?'

'Probably,' Brian said with a wry grin, 'but nothing recently that I'm aware of.'

'Oh, okay then,' I said with relief.

A little while later Brian stopped at a teashop. We went inside and Brian ordered a pot of tea and some scones.

'I know you're always hungry when you leave school.'

'Thanks. You're not wrong!'

The tea arrived and Brian poured us a cup each. I started to munch on the scones and sip at the tea when I realised Brian was crying over his cup.

'Brian, what's wrong?'

'Abbas.' He looked up at me. 'I have some really terrible news.'

'What's happened, Brian?' I put down my scone. My stomach was churning and I suddenly felt nauseous.

'Nancy is very ill.'

'How ill?'

'Really, really ill. She has cancer.'

Brian broke down, burying his head in his arms on the tabletop.

'When did this happen, Brian?' I asked. 'When I saw her at the wedding she was fine.'

'I know.' He shrugged. 'She was having stomach pains, and they sent her for tests. Apparently she has had cancer for a long time and no one picked up on it.'

'How can this happen? She's so healthy – she plays tennis and walks the dog…' I couldn't get my mind around it.

'Abbas, she wants to see you, but she is not in a good way.'

'I want to see her, too,' I said immediately. 'Where is she?'

'At the hospital.'

'Why didn't anyone tell me, Brian? I love Nancy.'

'I know, and she loves you, too. But that's why we thought it best we wait. We wanted to see how bad it was and … with you recently having lost your mum … it is a tough thing to deal with.'

'She can fight this, right?'

'It is really late-stage cancer, Abbas. You'll see when we get to the hospital.'

I could not stay in the teashop any longer. 'Excuse me, please, Brian.'

I went outside and sat on the kerb. I was breathing heavily and trying not to cry. I had to be strong for Brian, but I was so worried about Nancy. I just wanted to see her.

Brian came out and we drove to the hospital in silence. I followed him inside, scared, almost not wanting our walk to Nancy's ward to end. When we arrived Kate was there, pacing back and forth outside the room. Her eyes were red. She gave me a big hug.

'You okay, Abbas?'

'Yes, thank you, Kate. You?'

'I've been better,' she said. 'But you must know how this feels.'

'Yeah.'

'I'm going to get a drink. I'll be back.'

'Okay.'

Brian led me into the darkish room and I saw Nancy lying on an elevated bed. Her stomach had grown so much that she looked pregnant, but the rest of her body, including her face, looked malnourished. Only a few patches of her hair remained. As soon as she saw me she smiled, but I could see that even smiling was painful for her. She waved me over to her weakly. I approached slowly and she put out her hand for me to hold. As soon as I touched her I began to cry; I couldn't help it.

'Shhh … it's okay,' she whispered. 'I'm okay … I'm okay.'

'I'm so sorry, Nancy.'

'Don't be.' She gestured for me to come closer for a hug. It broke my heart seeing her so ill. As she held me, she whispered in my ear, 'I had to see you. Meeting you has had such a huge impact on my life, in such a short time.'

'Thank you … and you on mine,' I whispered, struggling to control my tears.

'You are a good boy, Abbas. I know Mehdi bullies you, but you are a good, good boy. Just keep on the way you are going, and you will do great things.'

'Thank you, Nancy. You have helped me so much since I've been here.'

'You help yourself and be good and people will always want to help you. Just know that I'm so proud of you. I have grown to really love you.'

'I love you, too.' I began to sob openly as she held me. I felt Brian's hand gently touch my shoulder, and as I lifted my head he gestured that we should leave.

'Hey,' Nancy whimpered, pointing to her cheek. I leant over and kissed her, and she held my hand one more time. I gave her one last loving look and left the hospital room with Brian.

Outside I sat on the bench in the corridor beside Kate and we both cried for a long time in silence. Brian had gone back in to Nancy. Eventually I sniffed and said, 'Kate, where is Mehdi?'

'I don't know,' she said. 'He's only been here once, to drop me off.'

'Can I stay here with you, please?'

'No,' she said softly, 'you have to go back to school. Dad and I will stay.'

'But it's exeat.'

'Mrs Griffiths said you can go back.'

Brian soon came out of the room and took me back to school. I had started that day thinking I would be in Malvern with Brian and Nancy having a nice dinner, but within a few hours I was being driven back to school with the worst possible news. Mr Griffiths met me at the large oak doors.

'How are you holding up, old chap?'

'Well, sir, thank you.'

'Good, good. Let's get in a game of snooker before dinner, shall we? What do you say?'

'I'd like that, sir. Thank you.'

The rest of the day dragged, because I was alone at school with very little to do, when all I wanted was to be with Nancy.

On Sunday I woke up thinking that at least my friends would be back later in the day. As I sat down to breakfast with Mr and Mrs Griffiths, we heard a car pull up on the driveway outside. Mr Griffiths went to investigate.

'Abbas, were you expecting a visit today?' he asked when he came back.

'No, sir.'

'Well, it seems Mr Bradford is back again. Go on and see what this is about,' he instructed.

'Yes, sir.'

I met Brian outside. He looked dishevelled and tired.

'Hi, Brian.'

'Hi, Abbas.'

'How is Nancy?'

The question stopped him in his tracks. He looked at me and tears started to roll down his face. I knew what was coming.

'Abbas ... I'm so sorry.' He was finding it hard to speak. 'Unfortunately we lost her late last night.'

'I am so sorry, Brian,' I said, starting to cry, too. We stood side by side in the open air, looking out over the Worcestershire countryside, and wept for Nancy.

Finally we pulled ourselves together and he looked at me. 'I wanted to tell you myself. Nancy wanted it that way.'

'Thank you.'

'I'm sorry I can't stay,' he said. 'I have to go home and change and start funeral arrangements.'

'Of course.'

'Oh, and one more thing.'

'Yes?'

'She wanted me to tell you that she really loved you.'

'Thank you.'

I held myself together until Brian's car disappeared. I thought about seeing Nancy at the hospital. She'd known that she was dying and she'd taken the time to say goodbye to me.

I knew that I would really miss her.

Mr Griffiths came outside to see if I was all right.

'You know what they say, Abbas.'

'No, sir.'

'When it rains, it pours.'

'It does, sir.'

ELEVEN

The next year was hard. Recovering from my mother's and Nancy's deaths was slow and painful. I did not see Brian as much, and so my life was split strictly between school during term time and the kitchen at Abbey International College during holidays. Conversations with my father had become even less frequent, and I was lonely. I would find myself sitting on my bed at Abbey International waiting to go to work, wondering where I fitted in the world.

My only solace was school, where I fitted in and appeared normal. My friends always had better things than I did – better trainers, better football boots – but none of that mattered. I just liked their company. The fact that I was held to standards consistent with others of my age helped me feel secure, and I was able to excel.

In my following, final year at Aymestrey I was elevated to Head Boy. This meant a lot to me; it was the most prestigious position a student could hold at a boarding school, and I loved that I had been given the opportunity to earn it in my parallel happy world.

Towards the end of fifth form, I took the entrance exams for some of the high schools near Aymestrey and was accepted for an assisted place at the King's School in Worcester. My last day of school at Aymestrey was very emotional and very sad for me. Mr and Mrs Griffiths and all the teachers, including Draggo and Mr Goodyear, had taken a special interest in me. I felt as if I was leaving home once more, this time at the age of thirteen. I knew that I would never forget my time there.

The issue with King's was that I had only been accepted as a day boy. I could not be a boarder because, while my schooling was once again free, boarding fees were extra, and expensive. Mehdi and Kate lived an easily commutable distance away, just half a mile from the school, though in a very rough area of Worcester. My main concern was not the threat outside their front door, however, but behind it; I did not want to live with Mehdi full-time.

The summer before I began at King's I was back in the kitchen at Abbey International College. The mundane repetition of life there had got easier to endure; I was accustomed to the routine, and the days merged into each other.

One afternoon, just two days before the new school term was due to begin, I was sleeping in my room, waiting for night-time, when my door burst open.

'Get up,' Mehdi ordered.

'Okay.'

'I've quit. I have a new job. I'm opening a bar in Cheltenham,' he said, clearly happy with himself.

'When?'

'Next week.'

'So … am I moving to Cheltenham?' I asked.

'No.' He spoke as if the mere idea were ludicrous. 'You will stay in Worcester, at the house.'

'With Kate?'

'No.'

'Kate's going with you, then?'

'No, we're getting divorced,' he snapped. 'Stop asking about things that have nothing to do with you.'

'So I'll be alone?'

'What, a whole house to yourself is not enough for you? Do you want me to get you a butler, too?' he barked.

'Sorry,' I said. 'I just wanted to know.'

Secretly I was delighted. Even though I was only just thirteen years old, I was more than capable of taking care of myself. The fact that I did not have to live with Mehdi made me so happy.

Mehdi drove me to the house with all my things that very hour. We did not speak to each other at all until we arrived.

'Here's the key to the house,' he said. 'I'm not coming in. Kate is not leaving until tomorrow.'

'Okay.'

I got out of the car and dragged my trunk up the stairs to the door. My new address was 80 Wyld's Lane, Worcester. Across the street was a newsagency, and further down the road on the same side as the house were two rough pubs. I watched various unsavoury characters walk by, each one giving me a knowing look. It was almost as if they knew that I was new to the neighbourhood. I was a teenager now, and losing my childhood charm; I knew I could no longer rely on receiving the same consideration I had been shown previously in difficult situations because of my age.

Inside, the entire house was empty; Kate had already left. There was no furniture, including no beds in the bedrooms.

In the kitchen Kate had left behind two plates and a glass, a few pots and pans and a few pieces of cutlery. There was no washing machine.

I walked into the bathroom and stared at myself in the mirror, wondering whether this was better or worse than my accommodation at Abbey International. I looked down and turned on the tap. The sight of running water was a relief.

Since there were no cupboards or drawers in which to store anything, I just put my trunk against the wall in one of the bedrooms and used it instead. I did not know what I was going to sleep on at night: I had no blankets and no pillows. The floors of the house were concrete, covered by very thin carpet, and the house was slightly damp and cold. It was quite dark even in the daytime as most of the light bulbs had blown.

I returned to the kitchen. As I sat there, the door opened. It was Mehdi, with a bag in his hands.

'Kate called and told me she's already left. I don't have to be in Cheltenham until later.'

He had a smile on his face. I did not trust it. Mehdi being nice set off alarm bells.

'You hungry?' he asked.

'Yes.'

'Go unpack your clothes and I'll cook you something to eat before I leave.' He smiled. 'I bought some groceries.'

'Thank you, but there is nowhere to put the clothes.'

'Well, go into the next room and read a book or something.'

'Okay.'

I went to the living room as he'd suggested, relieved there would be a meal that night but still feeling more scared than happy. I imagined there was something ominous in the air, but I could do nothing except sit and wait.

Eventually Mehdi came out with a plate and gave it to me. The dish consisted of meat and vegetables covered with a heavy spiced gravy. He stood over me and smiled.

'Are you not eating?' I asked him.

'No, I'll eat later in Cheltenham.'

I nervously took a bite, and he watched me eat. The food tasted okay, but the texture was jellylike. I ate it all because I was so hungry, and the entire time Mehdi stood over me, watching me like an excited child. At last I got to my feet to take my plate to the kitchen.

'Thank you for the meal; it was very nice of you,' I said.

'Oh, you are most welcome,' he responded sarcastically.

In the kitchen I started to wash my plate. Mehdi followed me and leant in the doorway, watching me with a knowing smile.

'Look in the rubbish,' he said.

'What?' I asked.

'Just look in the rubbish,' Mehdi snapped.

The brown paper bag he had used to bring the groceries in was now the rubbish bag. I bent over and looked inside. There were some vegetable peelings and a tin. I reached down and turned the tin around so that I could see the label. In bold letters I saw PEDIGREE CHUM, with a picture of a dog underneath. I looked up at Mehdi, still holding the tin. He was holding a camera. The flash went off and he roared with laughter. I could see the hatred in his eyes.

I just stood there, wondering what he must have been thinking and feeling to make him do such a thing to me. He had gone to considerable trouble to humiliate me. I felt my eyes prickle with tears but would not give him the satisfaction of seeing that he was getting to me. My stomach contracted and I ran for the toilet. I could hear his bellow of laughter and his shout, 'That would be the special ingredient I added.'

I knelt over the toilet and vomited violently. I could not stop. Tears were rolling down my face. I had no idea why Mehdi hated me so much. I had always done what he asked, and stayed out of his way.

'Oh, hold on, maybe it's because the dog food was two years out of date,' I heard him cry.

And then there was silence. I continued to retch until there was nothing left to come up but bile. I washed my face and returned slowly to the kitchen. Mehdi was gone. The bag of rubbish was still there, as a reminder of what had just transpired.

I decided to take out the rubbish immediately, but when I leant down to pick up the paper bag I was overcome with extreme emotion. I tried to hold myself together, but I could not do it. I fell to the ground and cried. It was not the eating of the dog food that had upset me so much as the fact that Mehdi hated me as much as he did, combined with the long periods of solitude and loneliness I'd been through. I had not heard from my father for weeks, and the solace of Aymestrey was gone. I was alone.

———

I sat in the kitchen for hours. Darkness fell, but I hardly noticed. At last I heard the door open. Fearing it was Mehdi again, I thought about hiding but couldn't be bothered. I just sat there and waited to see what he would do.

A light went on in the corridor.

'Abbas?'

It was Kate.

'Hi,' I called softly.

'Hello?' she said, looking for me. 'Where are you, sweetie?' Kate walked into the kitchen and turned the light on. 'What are you doing in the dark?' she asked, concerned.

'Oh, nothing. Fell asleep.'

'With the rubbish in your hands?'

'Yes, sorry.'

'Don't be sorry,' she said. 'I knew you were here and I wanted to bring you a few things.'

'Oh, thank you. You didn't have to.'

'I brought you a few blankets,' she said, then paused, looking like she was struggling to maintain her self-control. 'I cannot believe you are here by yourself.'

'I'm fine, really.'

'This isn't right, Abbas,' Kate said harshly. 'You shouldn't be alone.'

I didn't know what to say. 'I am so sorry about you and Mehdi splitting up, Kate.'

'Don't be. I'm happy it's over.'

I wished I could just leave the way she had.

'I know you have to buy a uniform and I know Mehdi won't give you any money,' she said, reaching into her pocket. 'I don't have much right now, but here is five hundred pounds.'

'Kate,' I said, shocked by the amount, 'you really don't have to—'

'Just take it,' she ordered. 'You have worked so hard, and God knows what Mehdi has been putting you through in the holidays all these years. You deserve much better.'

'Thank you,' I said, 'it means a lot.'

Kate leant over and kissed me on the head.

'I'm not sure how much I will get to see you from now on,' she said. 'You're the only thing I will miss from this part of my life.'

She held me close, and I could feel her tears wetting my hair. This really was the end of a chapter in her life. I was going to miss Kate. I had forgotten about the new uniform, and the fact that she even thought of it really touched me. I had no idea where I could have got the money otherwise. Kate gave me one last kiss and left the house in tears.

I took the blankets upstairs into the room with my case and laid them on the ground. I lay on one and spread the other over myself, thinking about how I would make this situation work. I needed a job. I didn't have work papers, due to my immigration status, and even if I had, I was only thirteen years old. I knew there had to be a way to make money, but I couldn't imagine how. I lay there thinking that my father would be able to solve the problem if he were me and so should I. It was cold. The house was dark and felt ominous. Time was passing so slowly and I could not sleep.

As my eyes became accustomed to the darkness I began to imagine I could see faint shapes. There was a smell of must and mould in the house, and I was very cold. The floor was hard and I kept rolling from one side to the other to try to get more comfortable. Eventually I drifted off to sleep to the noises and shouts coming from the pubs a few doors away.

The next morning I woke up feeling extremely stiff. It was my last day of summer holidays, so I knew that I had to go to King's to buy my uniform.

I went to the shower and waited for the water to warm up. After a few minutes it became apparent that there was no hot water – the boiler must be on the blink. I darted under the shower and hopped about washing myself as quickly as possible. I brushed my teeth and went to look inside my trunk. I really did not have much to wear – very few of the casual clothes Nadine had bought me still fitted. I wanted to make a good impression at King's, though. In the end I put on my Aymestrey uniform trousers and shirt without a tie and blazer; it was the best I could do.

King's was about a ten-minute walk from the house. I made sure the front door was locked behind me and then turned left down Wyld's Lane, which was a narrow, dirty street with broken glass and puddles of vomit on the footpath outside the pubs. I saw an Indian man in the doorway of the newsagency, and as I walked by he looked at me. I smiled and waved at him and he waved back as I continued down the street.

There was a grim-looking park to the left, and a group of older boys had congregated around its gate. They fell silent as I passed on the opposite side of the road, staring at me menacingly. One of them stepped forward and started to shout. 'Hey, Paki. Where the hell do you think you're going?'

I kept my head down and continued to walk. They were all white and probably three or four years older than me.

'Paki. I'm talking to you.'

I looked back at him and said in my perfect English accent, 'I'm sorry, I'm just minding my own business.'

'No, you ain't – not when you're on our turf,' one of the other kids shouted.

I kept walking, looking down at the filthy cobbles and hoping that the boys would leave me alone. But I heard the brushing sound of parachute pants behind me, coming closer and closer. I turned around to see the white boy who had just shouted at me and felt the force of his fist to the side of my face. I had not been expecting the attack and the punch knocked me against the wall.

I did not want to do anything to antagonise him; he had several of his friends behind him. I kept my head low and tried to keep walking.

'That's right, Paki, you keep f—in' walking.'

Suddenly I remembered that I was carrying five hundred pounds in my pocket. I could not afford to lose that.

I walked a little faster, but just as I thought I was getting away I felt a hand on my shoulder. It spun me around and I was immediately slapped in the face. Then they were all on top of me, pushing me to the pavement. I curled into a foetal position and covered my head with my arms, while each of the boys tried to land a punch or a kick on me before they all ran away.

I looked up warily to see if they were still lurking nearby, surprised that it had not hurt as much as I had anticipated. My head throbbed a little and I felt slightly sick, but I only had a graze I could feel above my left eye. I was hoping it would not bruise before I arrived at the school.

I had felt much harder blows before, but I was shocked by such unprovoked animosity and hate. My body was shaking and I was on full alert.

I had never been attacked before because of the colour of my skin, and I was not even Pakistani. I realised I was now living in a part of the city that was culturally very different from Aymestrey, where all my best friends had been white but they had all treated me as if I was one of them. I hoped that King's would be the same.

I made my way to the school and started looking out for any signs indicating the way to the school uniform shop. Lots of other children were arriving with their parents for the same purpose, in their fancy cars. There were both boys and girls: King's, once just for boys, had been accepting girls into only its top two year levels since the seventies, and this year was taking girls into its junior and middle schools for the first time. My year, though, was to be the last one ever to comprise only boys until we reached the top two levels when girls were introduced.

The children were all dressed in expensive designer clothes, looking very preppy. I noticed the looks I was getting, in my shabby old school pants and shirt, but I kept my head down and followed the crowd to the school shop.

Four families were ahead of me in the queue. A boy my age with long blond locks, dressed in corduroy trousers and a designer shirt, was staring at me. He smiled at me patronisingly and turned to say, 'Mum, I thought you said this was a good school. Look at that boy. He's dressed like a peasant.'

He chuckled, obviously thinking he was hilarious. His mother smiled and blushed, then hissed, 'Dom, shhh. You can't say that.'

I was the centre of attention, everyone either staring at me or avoiding staring at me. I felt intensely humiliated – small and insignificant, but not small enough to disappear, as I wished I might.

I was alone in a world I did not know. These people were really rich. As each family reached the front of the line, I could hear the mothers' murmured requests – 'The scarf please', 'The extra blazer' – and the sums they were being charged. I did not witness a transaction that was under fifteen hundred pounds. What could I do? I had only one-third of that amount.

By the time I reached the front of the queue, there

were five or six families behind me and I was almost too embarrassed to speak.

The lady at the counter greeted me with a welcoming smile. 'Hello, young man. My name is Mrs McDonald. Are you here to buy your uniform?'

'Hello, madam. My name is Abbas, and yes, I am. I am here to buy a uniform,' I whispered.

'You are going to have to speak a little louder, my dear. It's quite noisy in here.'

'Sorry,' I said a little louder but still in a whisper. 'I was wondering if you sell any second-hand clothes?'

I felt as if everyone in the shop had fallen silent just in time to hear what I had said.

'Not usually,' Mrs McDonald responded with a quizzical look. 'Why would you want second-hand clothes, my dear?'

I glanced over my shoulder to see if anyone was listening. Everyone was staring at me, and I felt very uncomfortable.

'Would you like to come to the back room, dear?' Mrs McDonald said kindly. 'You can see our full selection there.'

I knew that she felt my discomfort and was trying to help me. 'Thank you very much,' I said as I followed her back. 'I am sorry you had to do that.'

'Don't be silly. Are you all right?'

'Yes, thank you.'

'So, where are your parents?'

'Well, actually, madam…' I said hesitantly. 'I have a guardian…and…well—'

'You don't live with your parents?' she interrupted.

'No, madam,' I said, 'and so…'

'It's all right, my dear. You can tell me,' she said sympathetically.

'Sorry. I am in a very difficult spot. I don't have very much money, and I know how much your clothes are … and …'

'Shhh. It's all right. Abbas, is it?'

'Yes, madam.'

'Well, Abbas, let me look you up.'

Mrs McDonald looked to be in her fifties. She was pale, with long auburn hair that had most likely been dyed, and she wore a long tweed skirt with a button-up blouse tucked into it. She was very proper and spoke with a perfect English accent. She walked over to a computer in the corner of the back room, put on a pair of spectacles and tapped my name into the keyboard. After a few minutes she returned to me with her friendly smile.

'I see you are on an assisted place.'

'Yes, madam.'

'Well, may I ask how much money you do have?' she asked politely.

I pulled out the money I had in my pocket and put it on the counter.

'Five hundred pounds, madam,' I said quietly.

Mrs McDonald tried hard not to react, but I could see on her face that this was not very much money.

'Well, let's see whether we can work with that, my dear,' she said, clearly trying to make me feel better.

'Thank you. What do I need?'

'Well, you are joining us at the high-school level,' she said as she walked about the shelves picking out clothes. 'I think we may be able to squeeze what you need into your budget if we find some second-hand garments, but you mustn't tell anyone, because it is against the rules.'

'I really appreciate it,' I said with a smile. I just hoped she could actually make it happen.

I watched her come and go as the pile of clothes in front of me grew. She then started to ring up the clothes on a cash register, checked the total and took some of them away again. As she did all of this, she began to look more and more anxious, probably because the queue of impatient families outside must have been growing.

She looked up at me, her face sombre. 'I took away a second pairs of shorts, and I gave you a second-hand blazer, second-hand trousers, but it still comes to six hundred and seventy-five pounds.'

'Oh,' I said in shock. 'Is there any way I can take it on credit and pay by the end of the term?'

'Pfff. I wish you could, my dear, but that is not allowed.'

'Okay,' I said, 'then what can I do?'

I must have sounded disheartened. 'Ah!' she said suddenly. I watched her tap some more figures into the register and then smile. She put my money into the till, took out a twenty-pound note and some change and handed it to me. Then she put all the clothes in a bag.

'Here you are, my dear.'

'How did that just happen?' I asked.

'It's all fine. I have a friends-and-family discount. We know each other now, right?' she said with a wink.

'Yes, madam.'

'This is just between us, you understand?'

'I do. Thank you so much. That is so nice of you.'

'A pleasure, my dear. Now, you do me proud.'

'I will, madam. And thank you again.'

I took my clothes and walked past the queue of staring families with my head down. I knew I was being judged, but I was happy that my money had stretched far enough to buy the uniform I needed. I even had change to buy a few things for the house and for tea – I had been wondering what I would eat.

On the way home I went to Sainsbury's to buy food. I did not know how long this money would last me. I remembered my days in Istanbul, where I had to ration my food. I went to the bread section and bought value-brand bread, four cans of baked beans, and as a treat some value-brand orange juice.

I hung my head as I put the striped value-brand food on the counter. This supermarket was right opposite my school, so I knew that there would be parents of children from my school shopping there. I dreaded being judged by them because I was poor.

I turned for home and realised that I'd have to walk past the park again to reach the house. I set off with great trepidation, hoping that I would not run into those kids again. I was scared. I also did not want them to see the uniform I'd just bought, from my prestigious new school, because I was sure that it would create more resentment in them.

I edged my way into the mouth of the street. I could hear them in the park, shouting and guffawing. I crossed the street to the park side so that I could shelter behind the quite tall retaining wall edging it – that way, hopefully they would not see me.

I made it past the park, relieved. There was a Pakistani boy on the other side of the road, looking almost my age, and he was waving me over. I did not feel afraid of him – he was alone, and besides, he wasn't white like those other boys, he was Asian. I walked over.

'Mate, what the f— are you doin' walking past the park?' he asked in a whisper. 'They'll kick your head in if they see you.'

'They already did earlier.'

'Well, they'll do it again. They hate us.'

I didn't know what to say.

'Thanks, mate,' I said after a pause. 'They're not a good crowd. I'll just have to keep my distance, I guess.'

'Yeah, man. They're bad news.'

'Well, cheers. I'd better be going.'

'Yeah, peace. By the way, my name is Jaber.'

'Abbas.'

'You from Pakistan?'

'No. I was born in Iran.'

'Ah, I knew it was a Muslim name. Wicked, man.'

With that, Jaber left. I walked in the shadows to avoid detection, clutching my clothes and my food. I wondered why the religious origin of my name mattered to Jaber. Everything seemed to be based on race or religion here. I did not even practise a religion. I had indeed been born in a Muslim country, but my parents had not raised me religiously, nor had they ever tried to convince me of the merits of one faith over the next. I had always believed in God, but had never considered which God I had been praying to. For the first time in my life, I realised that I was a believer without a religion.

I was jolted out of my thoughts when I heard a huge crash and men shouting. A fight had broken out in the pub a mere fifty feet from my house, just as I passed. I looked through the grimy window and saw about five or six men in a violent struggle. One of them smashed a beer bottle over another's head; blood ran from his forehead, but his assailant had no mercy, continuing to punch the wounded man with his bare knuckles until he was on the floor.

'Hey, you,' I heard a man say from behind me in a heavy Indian accent. 'You!'

'Me?' I asked.

The Indian man from the newsagency waved me over. He was dark, of medium height and extremely thin, with kind eyes, and he was wearing an old jacket and grey trousers with modest brown shoes. I crossed the street towards him.

'Why you want to watch that?'

'I don't. It's horrible.'

'Good. This is no place for a boy. You should get home to your parents.'

'I don't live with them,' I said, realising as soon as the words left my mouth that I should not have told him that.

'Who do you live with?'

I paused, not wanting to say more, and he could see that I was uncomfortable.

'It's okay,' he said gently. 'I apologise for asking such a personal question.'

'It's okay.'

'My name is Patel. I own this shop.'

'Abbas. Nice to meet you, Mr Patel.'

'If you need anything, come and see me, okay?'

'Thank you,' I said politely.

Mr Patel seemed nice. With his words of advice fresh in my mind, I walked briskly back to my dark, empty house. As I entered, the smell of mould met me on a cold draught, despite the relatively warm summer day outside. The broken boiler powered both the hot water and the radiators, so I knew trying to heat the place would be useless.

I was starving. I went to the kitchen to prepare a bowl of baked beans to have with the bread, but suddenly realised that I did not have a can opener. I just stood there thinking, *Why?*

Why did I have to deal with menial things that everyone else took for granted? I was feeling upset and alone when suddenly I remembered the Swiss Army knife O'Grady had given me all that time ago: one of the blades was a can opener.

I went to my trunk and pulled out the knife. With difficulty but great anticipation, I opened the can of beans little by little, then I poured my beans into my sole pan. I put it on the stove and turned the knob to light the gas. Nothing happened. I kept trying and trying. Soon I realised that the gas had been turned off. I had been really looking forward to eating the beans because I was so cold. I even craved the heat of the stove, but it was not to be.

So I sat on the cold kitchen floor and dipped the white bread into the cold beans and ate in silence. It reminded me of my last supper with Maman and my grandmother, Mamanjoon, in Tehran, when we'd had fried onions on *lavash* bread. I had thought at the time that life could not get worse, but at least I'd had Maman with me then; at least I hadn't been alone. I had come to England for a better life, but in the years I had lived there, my struggles had just become harder.

Tears rolled down my cheeks as I chewed. I wished I could be done with this way of life. Where was my father? I had long stopped expecting anything of him. I barely spoke to him, and when I did it was idle chatter with very little warmth or emotion. I just hoped that my new school would bring some relief the way that Aymestrey had.

After tea I washed my pan in the sink with cold water and left it to dry. I had some dirty clothes I needed to wash, along with my underwear and myself. I brought my laundry downstairs and threw it in the bath, then took off my clothes, added them to the bath, ran the tap and began washing my clothes by hand with soap.

As I sat naked in that bathtub washing my clothes, I knew all this had to be worth something, but that belief was wearing thin. I had always done what I was supposed to do and I was still going backwards. It just wasn't fair. I went outside and hung up my clothes on the washing line in the small backyard.

It was early, but I had nothing to do. I trudged upstairs and lay between my blankets on the hard floor, wondering how my life would turn out. I knew that in the immediate future I had to find some money, because my funds would soon run out. There were things I had to buy: deodorant, soap, haircuts, and of course more food. This was a major dilemma, and I knew I'd have to be creative to solve it, but what this creativity would entail I still did not know.

For now, I just stared at the shadows created by the moon shining through my window as the hours passed me by, wondering what the future had in store for me. It was a little chilly, but not enough to make it intolerable – just enough for me to wish that I had an extra blanket.

I would have to earn my stripes again from scratch at King's. I was back at the bottom of the hierarchy, at a much larger school than Aymestrey – King's had over a thousand students, going all the way up to eighteen-year-olds. These kids were young adults and would be much bigger than I was.

I was feeling terribly anxious about how I would fit in at King's. But there was only one way that I would find out, and that was by going to school the very next day.

TWELVE

The next morning I woke up when it was still dark and got out my new school clothes. My shirts were all wrinkled, and I wished I had an iron. I put on my second-hand uniform and looked in the mirror. My blazer was well worn and had a few small holes in it. My tie was stained and I needed a haircut. I looked very different from the way I would have liked to look on my first day of school. I didn't have a backpack or bag for my books, but for now that didn't matter, considering our books had not been given to us yet.

I locked the door behind me and headed left along Wyld's Lane towards the main road. I was wary of boys lurking out of sight, and was prepared to run, but as I would come to discover, it was far too early for them to be out of bed. I reached the main street and set off towards King's.

I arrived early and headed for Creighton House, to which I'd been designated, according to the information pack I'd received in the mail back at Aymestrey. Luckily all the houses were signposted, as the campus was large. A great cathedral towered over the magnificent school, which I knew King Henry VIII had reopened four hundred and fifty years ago.

A man was waiting at the bottom of the stairs to Creighton House. Dressed in a pair of brown trousers and a tweed jacket with elbow patches, he was of average height, with receding hair and big ears. He had an easy face to caricature, but his broad smile was very friendly.

He held out his hand. 'Abbas, I presume?'

'Yes, sir,' I said, wondering how he knew my name.

'My name is Brian Gardner,' he said with a firm hand-shake. 'I'm your housemaster at Creighton.'

'Nice to meet you, sir.'

'All the new boys are assembling at my office outside our common area.' He gestured up the stairs. 'Go and meet some of them and we will get things rolling at eight a.m.'

'Yes, sir. Thank you.'

I walked upstairs as instructed and saw about five boys outside Mr Gardner's office. All of them were dressed in brand-new uniforms. I could see they were wondering why my uniform was not new. One of the boys, slender in stature and maybe slightly taller than me, with blue eyes and blond hair, gave me a cool, assessing look.

'I'm Kevin,' he said arrogantly, 'where are you from?'

'Abbas,' I said confidently, trying to hold my own. 'I went to Aymestrey, just outside Worcester.'

'Oh, I know that school,' said one of the other boys. 'I almost went there. I'm Joe.' Joe was a heavy-set kid with mousy brown hair who was obviously trying to be friendly.

'Yeah, but that's not where you're from,' Kevin insisted. 'Where were you born?'

'Iran.'

'Aren't they the bad guys?' Kevin asked, smirking. A few of the other boys bought into it and laughed. Joe didn't laugh, and nor did a stocky, athletic kid next to him who looked familiar.

'Dan,' the stocky kid said as he offered his hand. 'I recognise you from rugby matches. I went to Hawford.'

'Oh yeah,' I said. 'I remember you.' I recalled that he was an excellent athlete, but more reserved than most. He looked like a nice kid.

'So when did you come over here?' Kevin asked.

'I dunno. Maybe three years ago?' I answered him as casually as I could.

'So you could be a spy then,' he said, with a hysterical cackle. Again the other few boys joined in the laughter.

'Sure, if that makes you happy,' I said.

'Well, you could be. You could be an Iranian terrorist,' he said, laughing even louder.

'Why is that funny?'

'It just is,' Kevin said with a smirk. 'Only terrorists dress like that.' He indicated my uniform with a sneer. 'You do know what type of school this is, don't you?'

I didn't say anything. It was obvious from the expressions on their faces that Dan and Joe felt awkward. Thankfully Mr Gardner appeared then, sparing me from any more of Kevin's stupidity.

'Right then, chaps,' Mr Gardner said with his beaming smile, 'welcome to King's and specifically to Creighton House.'

'Thank you, sir,' we all said in unison.

'Okay, anything you need, you come to me as your first point of contact.' Mr Gardner spoke in a very animated way and clearly loved his job. 'Here is a map of the school grounds, and also your schedules. Be here at eight every morning for rollcall and announcements.'

As it turned out, Kevin was going to be in all my classes. Our first two lessons were double Biology with Mrs Knott, an elderly lady who gave the impression that she had been at King's for a very long time. The classroom contained long wooden science benches, and I took my place next to a blond boy called Timmy Morris who I recognised from playing interschool competitive table tennis against each other when I was at Aymestrey.

As soon as he saw me he stood up and shook my hand. 'Timmy Morris,' he said with a cheeky smile. 'We played—'

'Yes, table tennis together,' I said, happy to see a friendly face. 'I'm Abbas.'

'I remember.'

Timmy sat opposite me, and all was going splendidly until Kevin walked in with another boy, who came up and sat next to me.

'Jamie,' Kevin exclaimed, 'we're not sitting there.' He smirked as he walked to a different bench at the other end of the classroom. 'We don't want to be victims of a terrorist explosion.'

'What are you talking about?' Jamie asked. He was a tall, thin boy with dark, chiselled features.

'You're sitting next to Abbas the Iranian terrorist.'

Jamie looked at me, bemused, but got up and left. I just kept my head down and tried not to attract any more attention.

'Don't worry about him,' Timmy said to me. 'He's an arse.'

'Clearly.'

Timmy and I soon became close friends, and at school

we were always together. He had been at King's junior school since first form and he knew everyone. He showed me around and was always there for me. I am honoured to still call him my best friend today.

The rest of the day went by without incident. After school I put the books that had been handed out in various classes throughout the day away in my locker and set off to walk home.

When I reached Wyld's Lane I was scared I would run into the hooligans from the park, so I took off my blazer and walked briskly on the opposite side of the road. Sure enough, a kid pointed me out, and I started to run as they poured out of the park and chased me.

I must have run about a hundred yards when I heard screaming coming from the opposite direction. About twelve mostly Indian or Pakistani teenagers were running towards me brandishing sticks, bats and knives. I stopped in my tracks, too stunned to move, certain that they were going to attack me, too.

Suddenly I heard: 'Abbas, get out of the way!' It was Jaber – he was a part of the group charging me. I saw him wave me out of the way. I ran forward, realising I could reach Mr Patel's shop before Jaber's group reached me. I pelted into the shop. which was empty save for Mr Patel, who was behind the counter.

'What's wrong?' he said.

'These white kids always want to beat me up,' I panted. 'They were chasing me when the Indian kids started to charge them.'

'Oh dear,' he said. 'This is so stupid. It has been going on as long as I can remember.'

'I've done nothing to them.'

'I can't justify it to you,' Mr Patel said sadly. 'It is just ignorance.'

'I can't even walk to school…'

'I'm so sorry. These kids need a good beating themselves.'

We waited for a while. Suddenly the door burst open. It was Jaber.

He shouted an obscenity out the door, then saw Mr Patel and said, 'Sorry.' Looking at me, he said, 'That was close, but we chased them off.'

'How did you know they were chasing me?' I asked.

'We didn't,' he said in a matter-of-fact voice. 'My cousin Hussein was beaten up earlier and this was revenge. You were just lucky.'

I'd had enough of this neighbourhood already and I had barely started to live here. Jaber left soon afterwards, but I was still too scared to go home. I stayed in the newsagency with Mr Patel, wandering around looking at the goods he sold. It was a small, dingy shop, but it contained almost everything you could think of, and it smelt of spices and other goodies. He sold almost every newspaper in the country.

Suddenly it dawned on me.

'Mr Patel?'

'Yes?'

'I don't suppose you have any jobs going?' I inquired.

'Not really.'

'Mr Patel…' I stopped, trying to think how I could say what I needed to say delicately. He could probably hear the desperation in my voice.

'Yes?'

'Well, I really need a job, sir.'

He just looked at me. I knew he didn't have much, but I could see he was trying to think of something.

'Are you dependable?' he asked.

'Very.'

'Okay,' he said hesitantly, but with a small smile, 'do you want to do a paper round?'

'Of course! That would be perfect.'

'I mean it when I say that if you don't show up, you lose the job. I pay fourteen pounds a week for Monday-to-Friday deliveries.'

'Hmm, fourteen pounds a week?' I asked, trying to start negotiations.

'Yes, fourteen pounds a week,' he repeated firmly, suggesting that there was no room for haggling.

'Okay, I'll take it.'

'You start tomorrow,' he said. 'Be here at four a.m. and no later. I suggest you wear something warm, young man. You will need about an hour or maybe ninety minutes to do the round.'

'Thank you, Mr Patel,' I said, relieved. 'You won't regret this.'

It was already dark outside when I left. I crossed the dirty street and saw that the pub closest to my place was already busy. When I peeked through the window on my way past, I thought I recognised a few of the same characters leaning against the bar who'd been there yesterday.

I opened my front door and flicked on the light switch. Nothing happened. I walked into the house and tried to turn on other lights, but none came on. The electricity had been turned off. I did not know whether bills had not been paid, leaving some possibility of getting the power back if I could pay the bill, or whether Mehdi had intentionally had it disconnected. The house felt a few degrees colder than the street, and the smell of mould and damp was even more apparent after having been outside in the fresh air for so long.

I checked how much money I had left: just over twenty pounds. It was enough to keep me going for a week or two if I was careful, factoring in various supplies I needed that I was yet to buy.

I walked outside again and crossed the road to Mr Patel's shop.

'I said four a.m.!' Mr Patel joked.

'I don't suppose you have candles, do you?' I asked.

'Patel has everything!' He walked over to a shelf behind the counter and pulled out a box of eight candles. 'Why do you need candles?'

'Er, well, the light bulbs aren't working. I think there was a short in the fuse box or something,' I said desperately.

Mr Patel handed me the candles but did not let go as I tried to take them.

'Are you okay, Abbas?'

'Yes, sir,' I said, trying to keep my composure. 'How much?'

'It's okay. This one is on the house.'

'No, really, I can pay.'

He waved me off with a kind, smiling gesture. I was about to walk out when I turned around, but Mr Patel had anticipated my next move. He was holding a box of matches. I smiled and took them from him.

'Thank you, really.'

'Don't mention it.' He smiled again.

I got back to the house and felt my way down the hallway to the kitchen, where I lit a candle. I dripped a few drops of wax onto the kitchen counter and stuck the bottom of the candle to it so that it stood upright. The dim light flickered as I settled myself on the floor with my cold beans and bread, struggling to open another tin with my penknife.

I sat for a moment before eating, and thought how the evening before I had had electricity. I thought about my day: how the school was so pleasant; how much I'd liked Timmy; how much I'd disliked Kevin. I knew that one blow to Kevin's face would end his taunting, but I also knew that I could not afford to fight him. I took solace in the fact that I had a job. I was not sure how far fourteen pounds a week would take me, but it was better than nothing.

After tea I took my candle and walked upstairs to my blankets. I stuck the candle to the windowsill and lay on the floor. I did not blow out the candle, as its dim light was my only comfort in the cold, dank room. I looked at the condensation on the window and watched each drop of water make its way down to the window ledge.

The monotony was getting to me. I looked at the candle, and in the depth of my loneliness I decided to give it a name. It helped me, to imagine I had someone to talk to at night – Fred, the candle. It seemed silly, but that was what I did.

After a while, I told myself to stop this pity party and concentrate on the following day. During my induction, I'd been told that the school opened at six a.m., so after my paper round I would go to school early and see whether I could take advantage of the facilities. I blew out my candle and wrapped the blanket around me like a burrito. Though it was only September, the weather was beginning to turn.

The next day I woke up at 3.30 a.m. to the ringing of my alarm clock, put on my tatty uniform and crossed the dark road to Mr Patel's. The remains of the previous night's revelry littered the pavement outside the two pubs: broken glass and vomit. Mr Patel brought out the bag of papers.

'Nice and early, Abbas,' he chirped. 'I like that.'

'I don't like being late.'

'I'm with you on that,' he said, handing me a local map with the house numbers of the people who were to receive a newspaper written at the bottom.

It was so cold. My blazer gave me some protection, but the breeze was hitting my face and chilling me to the bone. I set off up Wyld's Lane. The road was silent and dark and empty. The milkman drove past me with his rattling bottles, which gave me some comfort.

I began to deliver the papers, and the lighter my sack became, the faster I could move. I started to warm up when I could jog a little. Memories of cross-country runs in the rain and hail at Aymestrey came back to me. I was done in less than an hour, and I knew that once I had become accustomed to my route and worked out how to deliver most efficiently, I would be able to cut that time down further still.

I popped back to the house and thought about what to do. I lay on the ground in my room and ate a slice of bread, watching my alarm clock until it reached 5.30 a.m., whereupon I picked up a small towel, placed it in my newspaper sack and walked to school. It was far too early for the boneheads to be out.

I went straight to the gym, which was behind Creighton House, and to my amazement it was open. I sheepishly went inside but no one was there. The showers were upstairs in the gym hall. I poked my head into the locker room and again it was silent and empty. I took off my clothes and turned on the tap in the shower. It was so nice to feel the hot water hitting my body. There was soap there, too. I washed myself quickly so that I would not be spotted, and sat on the wooden bench to dry myself, thinking about the day ahead.

I dressed and walked over to Creighton House. It was still before six, and no one else was there. I took my books from my locker and read until other children started to arrive in dribs and drabs.

Later on, in Geography, Timmy and I were sitting together waiting for the class to begin when Kevin walked past and said, 'Can you give me the name of the second-hand shop where you buy your clothes? If I'm ever homeless it might be useful.'

Most of the people in the class laughed, apart from Timmy, who was not impressed. 'You should kick his head in,' he snapped.

I was surprised by how concerned he was about me – we had really only just met. But he was a good kid.

'Yeah, and then I'll be suspended.'

'True.'

Last up that afternoon we had rugby practice, and my stars must have been aligned because Kevin was in my group and on the opposite team. Though it was overcast, the ground was still incredibly hard after a very dry summer. I waited and picked my time carefully. Kevin was given a hospital pass, and I hit him at the same time as the ball touched his hands. I picked him up and anger coursed through me as I dumped him on his head. A ruck formed and we stood over him. I could see he wanted to cry, but he didn't let himself. His discomfort gave me a little gratification.

'Abbas, great tackle,' our coach, Mr Rudge, shouted from the sideline.

'Sir, it was off the ball,' Kevin protested sulkily.

'No, it wasn't, Kevin,' Rudge shouted back. 'Now stop being a baby and get stuck in.'

Our coach was a short, podgy man, but he was full of enthusiasm for the game.

Kevin looked at me with hate, and as he ran past he hissed, 'No f—ing gypo terrorist does that to me.'

'Apparently one just did,' I said as I smiled back at him. 'Why don't you come see me after the game and I'll lend you a fiver to go buy yourself a felafel for your dinner, Abdul.'

He had such a sharp tongue, and although he did not know me, some of his mocking words were actually very close to the truth. That was probably why they were so cutting. It was sad that most of the people around him laughed at his jokes, which were always about race or money, because their encouragement fed his disdain.

I showered again after rugby practice and headed to the school library. I had homework to do and I wanted a desk and a chair and good lighting. The library was housed in a tower – Edgar Tower – which had been built to function as the main gate back when the school had once been a castle, almost seven hundred years ago. It was a small library, but it was full of charm, character and history.

The librarian was an old lady called, ironically, Mrs King. She had worked at the school for years. She was tall and thin and very kind. At six p.m. she walked over to me and whispered, 'Dear, we are closing.'

'Oh!' I jumped up. 'I'm sorry. I'll pack up.'

'Take your time, my dear, but we close at six every day.'

I quickly collected my books and walked down the circular staircase to the ground floor. I hadn't quite finished my homework, so I headed to the public library in the town centre, which closed at ten p.m. I smiled when I arrived – here was warmth, light and a table and chair to work on. I sat there and did my homework, watching people between my bouts of concentration. I finished up after about an hour, then picked out a book and began to read it, just so I could continue to be surrounded by people and enjoy the warmth.

About nine p.m. I could no longer ignore my hunger, so I made my way back to the house, managing to avoid the local hooligans. I had a candlelit tea of cold baked beans and bread again with Fred and made my way to bed. I was tired and I had to be up early.

That night I fell asleep without too much trouble. I was settling into a routine, and the misery was becoming more bearable.

THIRTEEN

I kept up my routine for another three weeks with very little incident.

At lunchtime I sat in the dining room with Timmy, watching him eat his food.

'Why don't you buy your food at the tuckshop, Abs?' he asked one day.

'Erm, I guess I prefer packed lunches.' It was the only thing I could come up with quickly.

'But you never eat a packed lunch. In fact, I've never seen you eat.'

'I eat.'

'Sure you do,' he retorted sarcastically.

I didn't know what to say. He was right – I didn't eat at school. Instead I sat with Timmy at lunch and pretended not to be hungry while I watched him eat.

I hoped that if I just dropped the subject, he would, too. Luckily he did on this occasion.

The weather was really cold at night and my two blankets were just not warm enough. After school one day, on my way to the public library, I stopped by a charity shop and bought a blanket for two pounds fifty.

I knew by now that I had too many expenses to survive on fourteen pounds a week. Mr Gardner had told me I was looking shaggy, and the cheapest barber I could find had cost five pounds. I had started to buy things like deodorant, soap – the kinds of things I'd never used to think about. I had not heard from Mehdi in about a month and clearly could not rely on him. I needed another job.

I found myself eating with Fred every night and thinking about how to get through the next day. The uncertainty that each day brought with it was unnerving: I hated not knowing when and what I would be able to eat the next day. I hated that I could not just concentrate on school. I felt like I was carrying the weight of the world on my shoulders.

The next morning I met up with Mr Patel at four as usual, and as usual he had a chirpy smile on his face.

'Mr Patel?'

'Yeees?'

'I don't suppose you have another round you can give me, or maybe another job?'

'Mmm,' he said, thinking about it. 'I really don't, Abbas. I'm sorry. You need more money?'

'I do,' I said softly. 'I have to make more somehow. I have too many expenses.'

'Let me see,' he said, nodding his head to show me he understood my situation. 'I think my friend who owns a newsagency near Battenhall needs someone.'

'Really?'

'Yes. I'll call him today, and after school you can go and see him.'

'Okay. Thank you so much.'

'You are a good worker – you deserve it.'

'Thank you.'

After school I went straight to the other newsagency that Mr Patel had told me about. It was located in a much better area edged by countryside, and it took me about twenty minutes to walk there. A portly man in his mid-thirties, of Indian appearance, told me his name was Mr Samani.

'Hi,' I said cautiously, 'I'm Abbas.'

'Ah, yeah. Patel called me about you,' he said in a perfect English accent.

'Yes, sir.'

'Patel says you are quite the worker,' he said, smiling as he rubbed his large stomach. 'I need you to do a rather long round every morning in my area. Do you think you can do mine and Patel's every day?'

'Absolutely.'

'How are you so sure?'

'Because I finish with so much time on my hands after I do Mr Patel's round. I know I can do it, sir. Just give me a trial, and if you don't like me, let me go.'

'Well, that seems reasonable,' he said, in a slightly mocking tone.

'Thank you very much, Mr Samani.'

'Sure, kid. I'll see you nice and early – 3.30 tomorrow. Patel has said he's okay with you doing my round first, then starting his round a little later. And by the way, the pay is the same as what Patel is giving you.'

'Thank you, sir.'

I headed back to town to do my homework at the public library, stopping at Sainsbury's on the way to buy my usual mix of cheap foods. I couldn't stop smiling, because I was going to double my income. I hadn't really smiled in a while – it was good to feel a little happiness.

Carol, the librarian, had me down as a regular. I suspected I was one of her favourites, because she always talked to me and asked me how I was doing. She must have found my presence in the library every night strange, but she did not ask questions. She was in her forties, with greying hair, and she always wore very long skirts and cardigans. She may not have cared much about her appearance, but she did care about her cats, which she told me about constantly.

That night, she saw me enter with my shopping bag and offered to keep it for me at reception until I left, because food was not permitted in the library.

As I was packing up to leave later on, she called, 'Abbas?'

'Yes, madam?'

'Carol, please. How many times have I told you to call me Carol?'

'Sorry.' I blushed. 'Carol.'

'Where do you live?'

'Oh, you know, past King's,' I said, hoping she would accept a general answer, and when I saw that she would not, I continued, 'Wyld's Lane.'

'How are you getting there every night?'

'Oh, I walk.'

'Would you like a lift? You have shopping with you tonight, too.'

'You don't have to … it's probably out of your way,' I protested.

'Don't be silly,' she said, smiling at me. 'Let me just lock up first.'

I was relieved that I did not have to carry my shopping home or dodge the drunks and thugs on my street. Carol locked up and drove me down to Wyld's Lane. I could see that she was a little worried about her surroundings, but she did not say anything. I got out of her car, thanked her and went inside to my solitary meal on the floor, then retired to bed. I fell asleep thinking about how I had to impress Mr Samani so that I could keep my new job.

I woke up earlier than usual and was on Battenhall Road before 3.30 a.m., waiting for Mr Samani to come outside. Unlike Mr Patel, Mr Samani was not a morning person. His hair was dishevelled and he looked grumpy. His shirt was creased and half open. He grunted, handed me a sack of papers and a map with the relevant house numbers written on it and then turned to leave.

'Oh, and this will be your standard route,' he muttered. 'From tomorrow onwards your papers will be out the back. Just deliver them to the same houses. I will not be here.'

'No problem, sir.'

With that, he retired to his flat above the shop, no doubt to return to his warm bed. I began to jog my new route, delivering papers swiftly. The weather was extremely cold, so the steady jog felt good, and I finished my round in less than an hour. I jogged to Mr Patel's store, where he was up and hurrying about in his usual cheerful way.

'How did it go?'

'Great,' I said with a smile. 'Thank you again.'

'Good lad,' he said. 'You deserve it.'

He winked at me and I was off on my way. I finished Mr Patel's route swiftly, too, and was at school before six a.m, where I dashed for the shower. I was more lax about showering now, taking more time to enjoy the hot water since no one else was ever around at this time, but when I came out of the shower Mr Guest, my Physical Education teacher, was standing in the changing room, sweating profusely and wearing shorts, a vest and trainers.

I was terrified.

'I've been wondering who's been showering in the mornings.'

'Sorry, sir,' I said, my head down and soaking wet. 'I run before school, and it's easier if I run to school and shower here.'

'Oh, I don't mind,' he said, to my great surprise. 'I do the same. I'm training for the world canoeing championships, so I'm up early every day to train at the pool, and then I use the staff showers here. I was just shocked that someone else was up before me and wanted to come and see who it was!'

'Oh, well, sir, I just jog. Not quite at your level.'

'Good for you. Don't even worry about it, Abbas. Help yourself to the showers whenever you want. It's good to see someone use them. And I'm impressed that you run.'

'At prep school we had to do cross-country every day and I guess it's become a habit, sir.'

'Well, I like that,' he said with a chuckle. 'Now get dressed before you catch a cold.'

'Yes, sir.'

He left and I changed in a hurry. It felt like a close call, and I knew that I had to keep my guard up, because getting caught out was simply not an option. As much as I hated living alone, my visa was contingent upon my having an able and willing guardian, and I couldn't risk alerting anyone to the fact that Mehdi was neither. My entire education and all the hardships I had endured in Turkey and England would have been wasted if I were to be deported to Iran, where I no longer had a life ... or even the certainty of a father who loved me and who would be there for me.

Where was he?

I needed my father.

———

'Abs, do you want to come to my house this weekend?' Timmy asked casually at lunchtime one day.

'Er, sure,' I said, 'but I was going to do my laundry and—'

'What? You do your own laundry?' he asked, almost in shock.

'Yes,' I said, 'I do. So maybe if I do it Friday night, I could come on Saturday?'

'Or you can just bring it with you and my mum'll do it.'

'I don't think so, mate,' I said. 'That's not right.'

'No, come over Friday, and on Saturday we'll take care of it at my house.'

'Well ... okay then, if you're sure. What are your plans?' I asked.

'I dunno. Maybe a movie on Friday night. We've got to play that rugby match against Warwick on Saturday, remember – so after that we'll do something. Maybe go out for a curry with my parents or something.'

'Well, I may give the curry a miss, but the rest sounds good.'

'What? Don't you like Indian?'

'Love it, but ... but ... to be honest I'm a bit short of cash, mate.'

'Oh, don't worry about that. My parents will get it.'

'Timmy! I'm not letting your mother do my laundry and then have your parents buy me food.'

'Are you serious? If I came to your house, would I have to buy my own food?'

'No.'

'Well, that's that then.'

'Okay ... um, thank you.'

'Don't mention it. And you have to eat when you come over or my mum will get mad.'

'Not a problem!'

Before I knew it, it was Friday, and I was excited not to be spending another weekend in that miserable house eating cold beans. I got through my paper rounds quickly and was at school early already wishing the day would end so that I could go to Timmy's house. I had brought my laundry with me, and that was making me a little nervous. Why wouldn't someone at my own house do my laundry for me? I could see all kinds of questions being asked. The silver lining was that if Mrs Morris let me use her washing machine, it would be such a luxury to not have to wash my clothes by hand.

I was worried about my casual clothing, too. I could hardly get away with wearing my school pants, or even my old Aymestrey ones in case they were recognised as part of a school uniform. Besides them, I only had my tracksuit, which I was rapidly growing out of and which I had worn to death. I was not sure how I could go to tea in a threadbare tracksuit.

After school, I followed Timmy onto his bus and we made our way to his house. I had my plastic bag of dirty clothing and my newspaper sack with a few other clothes and toiletries in it. I still did not own a proper backpack.

Kevin was on the same bus as us, because he lived near Timmy.

'Nice bag, gypo,' he shouted across the bus. 'How's your transient lifestyle working out for you?'

I just sat there and took it while the kids all laughed. I slid down in my seat, hoping they might notice me less that way.

The bus stopped periodically, dropping off kids along the route. After about forty minutes, Timmy nudged me to indicate that our stop was coming up.

Kevin was still on the bus. As we walked by him to get off, he said, 'Hey, Abbas, my parents are looking for a new cleaner, but I'm not going to suggest you because I don't want our house blown up.'

Sure enough, there were roars of laughter from the ignorant mass of sheep-like boys around him. Kevin looked very happy with himself. The bus dropped us at the bottom of Timmy's street and I got off and looked back at him through the window, extending my middle finger to indicate what I thought of him. I wished that I could just fight him, but I had too much to lose.

Timmy lived in a quaint old village called Cropthorne. There was a pub on the corner of his street, and the beautiful country lane had magnificent houses on either side with manicured lawns and flourishing shrubs and flowers. Eventually we reached Timmy's driveway, which led to a lovely double-storey house. He walked me through the back door right into the laundry, where I could see dozens of shoes belonging to Timmy and his brother, who I had not yet met. It made me realise how tight my shoes were getting.

'Mum,' Timmy shouted, 'we're here.'

'In the living room,' came the response.

'Drop your clothes here, mate,' Timmy said.

The laundry led through to a homely open kitchen with a big wooden dining bench in the centre. Various counters lined the edges of the room, sporting a jumble of cookbooks, bowls of fruit, vegetables, papers and other odds and ends.

Timmy took three clementines and an apple from a fruit bowl.

'You want one?' he asked.

'No, I'm fine, thanks,' I said, feeling shy.

I watched Timmy devour the fruit and then go back for more. After he had eaten his fill, he opened the fridge door to see what else he could find. The fridge was packed full of food – a sight I hadn't seen in a long time. Timmy scoured it but nothing took his fancy. He then led me to the living room, where we found Mrs Morris watching television.

'Hello, boys,' she said with a smile. She looked a lot like Timmy: tall and thin, with short brown hair and distinguished features. 'You must be the famous Abbas.'

'Hello, Mrs Morris,' I said, extending my hand. 'Lovely to meet you.'

'I've heard so much about you.'

'All good, I hope!' I said. 'Thank you for having me over; I really appreciate it.'

'Oh, it's not a problem. Timmy said you needed to wash some stuff while you're here?'

'Yes, I'm sorry about that,' I apologised. 'If you just show me how your washing machine works, I'll take care of it.'

'Don't be silly. Timmy, you put the kettle on and I'll get the clothes started, and we'll have a cup of tea with some biscuits before our meal, while we wait for your dad and brother.'

'Thanks, Mum,' Timmy said.

'Thank you, Mrs Morris.'

'Call me Marilyn,' she said.

'Okay, Mrs Morris!' I grinned – I just couldn't bring myself to call her by her first name. She smiled back.

I met Timmy's brother, Richard, who was shyer than Timmy but equally polite. Timmy's dad was a man's man – tall, rugged, and with a great sense of humour. He was a sports enthusiast.

It was so nice to sit around the kitchen table and eat an amazing meal with good company. Tea was a lovely stew with lots of beef, and I felt so good tasting things other than bread and beans. Afterwards Timmy and I watched a movie before bed, which was a pull-out bed in Timmy's room. We talked about the game we were going to the following day, and silly things that thirteen-year-old boys talk about. Soon enough Timmy was asleep. The Morris family had made me feel really welcome, and I lay there smiling, happy that I was warm, safe and full.

The next day Timmy's dad took us to the game and watched from the sidelines, barracking noisily. Afterwards he analysed our victory, pointing out my best moves as well as Timmy's. He was a good man.

Excited by our victory, we went back to Timmy's house and showered. We were all set to go for the Indian meal when I remembered my dilemma. I slowly started to put on my tracksuit, feeling embarrassed. Just then Timmy walked into the room, one of his ever present smiles on his face.

'Are you going to get changed, mate?'

'Oh … yeah … you know, Timmy, I forgot my clothes,' I said apologetically.

'You plonker,' he said with a laugh. 'I told you we're going out.'

'I know, mate. Sorry. There's been so much going on.'

'I'm sure we can find you something,' he said kindly. He started to look through his drawers and eventually found me a pair of jeans. 'These are too big for me, so they'll fit you.'

I tried them on, and though they were a little long, they would work. Timmy also threw me a rugby shirt, which was an easier fit. I finished the look with my trainers.

The night was so much fun. The food was delicious, and Timmy's dad paid for everything. I was so happy and so grateful for this small break in my miserable routine. During tea, Mrs Morris made a point of telling me that I could visit anytime I wanted, which made me feel even better.

I was sad it was Sunday when I woke up. Timmy and I went downstairs to eat breakfast, and Mr and Mrs Morris were already at the table reading the Sunday paper with cups of tea in hand.

'So, what are your plans for the day, boys?' Mr Morris asked.

'Not much, just lounging around, I guess,' Timmy said with a yawn.

'Do the buses run on Sundays?' I asked.

'Not very frequently,' Mr Morris said. 'I can give you a lift. Where do you live?'

'In Worcester, near school, but you don't have to put yourself out,' I said. 'I can just wait.'

'Don't be silly, Abbas,' Mrs Morris piped up. 'Peter will give you a lift.'

'Thank you, but honestly, if it's too much trouble, just let me know.'

They just laughed.

A few hours later, Mrs Morris packed up all my clean clothes and a slice of cake for the road. I was excited about the cake; now I had dessert for the evening. Timmy came along with his dad for the ride, sitting in the front of the Volvo. I was not sure how I was going to deal with showing them where I lived.

Eventually we drew close to Wyld's Lane.

'You are going to be taking a left soon, Mr Morris,' I said quietly.

'Oh, okay then, Abbas,' he said, surprise evident in his voice. 'You know you can call me Pete,' he added with a smile.

'Yes, sir. I mean...turn left here, please!' I said as we approached Wyld's Lane.

As we turned, I saw the local thugs hanging out by the park. A few of them noticed me in the back of the car – the car driven by white people – and I could see the curiosity on their faces. As we approached my house I said, 'It's number eighty, on the right, coming up.'

Timmy turned to say goodbye, and I could see the shock on his face. Mr Morris's face was less expressive, but his demeanour had become solemn. I could just about see the light bulb going off in his head: *Boys who go to King's do not usually live in this area of Worcester.*

'You sure you're okay here, Abbas?' he asked.

'Yes, thank you, Mr Morris.'

'Is someone home?'

'I think so,' I lied. 'If not, they'll be right back.'

'You're welcome to check, and stay at ours if nobody's home, if you'd like. It's no bother,' he said, clearly really meaning it.

'I'm fine, really,' I protested. Deep down I very much wanted to go back with them. I hated having to lie, but I had little choice.

I got out of the car with my belongings and waved to Timmy and his father, then walked up the stairs and glanced back. Mr Morris was watching me like a hawk. I saw him say something to Timmy. I opened the door and waved again, then closed the door behind me and took a deep breath.

That night, as I ate my cold beans and bread, all I could think about was the previous night and what a marvellous time I'd had with the Morrises. I envied Timmy his family, but I was also happy for him – he was a good kid and a good friend, and he deserved that family. I just wished that I could be a part of it, too.

I sliced the piece of cake Mrs Morris had packed for me into two, so that I could save a piece for the following day, then devoured every little crumb of tonight's piece. It was delicious. Those few minutes made me smile. It was funny how small things were now so important to me; they had the ability to make me deeply happy.

I soon retired to the bedroom upstairs to wrap myself up and try to get through the cold night.

FOURTEEN

The autumn weather grew colder and colder, and when winter came it was a particularly cold one. I worked on my paper rounds and struggled to stay afloat through those long, difficult months. I was growing: I needed to buy clothes and bigger shoes as well as food and all the simple necessities that I had once taken for granted. I had acquired a few extra blankets as I'd earned more money, so for the most part I managed to stay warm at night. The most difficult thing was the loneliness of my secret, solitary life.

I saw Mehdi a few times. On one occasion he even gave me five pounds, which I thought must have been his conscience pricking him for a fraction of a second. He was not particularly pleasant that day, but he did not beat me and he wasn't unusually mean. He gave me the note and left the house as suddenly as he had arrived. I tried to see the upside – at least I didn't have to spend long periods of time with him.

Winter turned into spring. I had not seen Brian or Kate in this period, nor heard from my father, which made me feel very sad, like I had died to him along with my mother. I missed my Aymestrey friends and teachers, but did not go back to visit them – school kept me busy, and I was not keen to use up precious money on transport. As the time passed, my friendship with Timmy deepened, however, and I visited his home regularly on weekends. It became my safe place, providing solace from the harsher realities of my normal life. Mr and Mrs Morris must have known not all was as it should have been. Their response was to treat me with a type of kindness that I'd rarely seen: they never interfered or tried to pry into my life, but from a distance they were clearly watching out for me, and this gave me so much comfort and hope. It was to be critical in times to come.

It began to get slightly warmer as the summer term started, which was a great relief for me. One day – an average school day – I had been to cricket practice and then headed to the public library after a quick shower, wandering along the River Severn next to the cathedral and into the town centre in order to spend some time with Carol and do my homework. A little before the library closed, I set off home. I was particularly hungry and was looking forward to my solitary meal.

As I approached the house, I noticed that the door looked different. I ran up the stairs and saw that it had been bolted up. The bank had perhaps foreclosed on the house; I could not get inside. I looked up at the second storey to see if I could climb up the pipes to a window, and quickly realised I could not. There was not much inside, but those few clothes, food and blankets would still be costly to replace. And the house had provided a refuge; without it, I had no idea what I would do.

I had to think, but my mind was a blank. I felt an overwhelming sense of loneliness and insecurity. Luckily I had left my school uniform at school and was in my tracksuit. I had very little money on me and did not know what to do. I headed back towards the library and stood outside peering in through the windows. The library was closed and Carol was long gone, but the lights made it look so warm and comfortable inside.

I kept walking up the high street until it ran out. I could see a few drunks wandering about outside a pub and decided I would avoid it. The temperature had changed drastically since earlier that day and I was beginning to feel very cold. I still did not know what to do.

In the end I went inside a McDonald's and bought a coffee. It was not where I wanted to spend my money, but I needed to sit inside in the warmth for a few minutes and think things through.

I told myself to stay strong as I drank my coffee, but I could not come up with a plan. Eventually I decided to head back towards the school, hoping I could find some shelter there. I approached the shopping plaza near school, and although it was lit, I suddenly had an ominous feeling that sent shivers up and down my spine. The last time I had felt like this had been when I was attacked in Istanbul.

I passed the plaza successfully, then hesitated, suddenly unsure whether sheltering at school, where people knew me, was such a good idea after all. I walked for perhaps thirty seconds into the dark of the cathedral grounds before regretting my decision. As I turned around, my worst fears came true: two tramps towered over me, their eyes seeming to glow with an evil light. One was smiling and the other looked like he was going to kill me. I thought about running into the dark, but I was too scared – who knew what else I might find there?

I caught the unmistakeable smell of alcohol on their breath. The smiling one had a large belly and receding hairline. He wore a torn checked shirt and a combat jacket with jeans and black boots. The other was tall and thin, with short scruffy hair and heavy stubble on his mean-looking, pointy face. I decided to take my chances and make a dash for the darkness, but the thinner man grabbed me by the tracksuit.

'Come 'ere, you little runt,' he cried as he pulled me to him. 'I got business with you, sunshine.'

'F—in' right we do,' said the portly one with a sickening smile.

I kicked the fatter man in the shins then felt a heavy blow to the back of my head. I fell to the ground. The thinner man held something black in his hands, about the size of a ruler. Whatever it was had been heavy enough to almost knock me out. I was in shock and did not really know how badly I was hurt.

'Please let me go,' I begged.

'I don't f—in' think so,' said the thinner man as he straddled me. The fatter man pinioned my hands, but I struggled like an eel, kicking and twisting in his grasp. Adrenalin was pumping through my body, and I felt as if I was fighting for my life. The thinner man had his hands all over my face, and I was not sure if he was going to beat me or do something worse.

'Please let me go,' I begged, over and over.

'Shut the f— up,' the thinner man said and slapped me hard across the face. He tried to turn me over, but I kept squirming and struggling. This time he punched me in the face, and I was out to it. I woke up perhaps seconds later and could see the two men a few feet away from me.

'Did you have to knock him out, you prick?' said the fatter man.

'Shut the f— up. You can still have him.'

'Hardly bloody worth it in that state.'

I pretended to still be unconscious and thought fast while they talked. I had perhaps five feet on them, and I decided there was no time to hesitate. I leapt up and pelted back towards the road like my life depended on it. They immediately gave chase, but the lit road was not that far away, and a few drunks were crossing it as I approached. As soon as the two tramps saw the other people they gave up the chase.

I kept sprinting towards the town centre until I could go no further. When I stopped for breath I felt the pain for the first time. My head was pounding, and when I touched the back of my head and examined my hand I saw it was sticky with blood. My face was hurting, and I knew I'd have a bruise tomorrow. But I could not worry about school quite yet – I was still wondering how I would survive the rest of the night. I decided to walk to keep myself occupied and warm.

I was walking past a hospital when I realised that it was safe and warm there – and that I had a legitimate injury. I checked into the emergency room and sat there waiting to be called. I stared at my feet, feeling ashamed, tears rolling down my cheeks. I had done nothing wrong, but still I felt embarrassed, and dirty, as if the whole incident had been my fault. Nothing had actually happened, but it felt as if it had. I was tired and wanted a hot shower, but for now the warmth and safety of the ER was enough.

After three or four hours I was seen. They put a small patch on my head and checked that I was not concussed. They also iced my face. Eventually the young doctor, who had gathered that I had been attacked, asked, 'Do you want to file a police report?'

'No, thanks, I'm okay.'

'You sure?'

'Oh yeah, positive.'

I really did want those two put away for a long time, but I was too scared that I would be deported if I went to the police. This helplessness made me feel so insignificant and weak.

'You want to call your mum to come get you?' the doctor asked.

'She's on her way, actually.'

'Oh, okay then,' he retorted. 'You can wait here till she comes. I want to speak to her.'

As soon as he was out of sight, I left the ER in haste so that I wouldn't get caught out. It was really late, already close to the time when I'd have to do my first paper round. I really didn't feel like doing any work, but I had no choice if I wanted to keep my jobs.

I walked to Battenhall Road slowly, crying the entire time. I was so tired and felt so helpless. I just wanted a hug from my mother, but that would never be possible again. It had been almost three years since her death, but I missed her every day and right now I really needed her.

Tears kept rolling down my cheeks. I could no longer even imagine being looked after, protected, sheltered. Still, I longed to be able to talk to someone about all these horrible experiences. It felt as if bottling up my feelings was hurting me, and I did not know how much longer I could cope. I knew that I had to stay strong, and Mrs Griffiths' words about the hard path came back to me, but right now I was finding my path far too hard. I had been strong for so long and worked so diligently, with very little to show for it. What was the point in trying?

In a state of deep sadness I struggled through my paper rounds and arrived at school at six a.m. on the dot. I got my school uniform from my locker and went to the gym. Luckily Mr Guest had not appeared yet. I took my clothes off and stepped under the hot shower, letting the water heat me, then I slid to the floor and hugged my knees, crying uncontrollably. The bandage on my head came undone, and diluted blood dripped into the shower, reminding me of the events of the previous night. I was still in so much pain and shock over what had happened. My head felt as if it were going to burst, and I was feeling sick. Suddenly I ran out of the shower and vomited violently into the toilet until I had nothing left inside but yellow bile.

I re-entered the shower and began to wash myself over and over again, remembering being beaten in Istanbul too, as I tried to scrub away the touch of the two tramps from last night. How many more times would this happen?

I looked in the mirror and, sure enough, a huge bruise covered my left cheekbone. I could not continue to look at myself; I felt disgusted. The bruise reminded me of evil and hate and made me feel as if I were somehow disgusting, too.

A continuing feeling of nausea took my mind off my sadness as I dressed for school.

Timmy saw me in our first class together and immediately said, 'What the bloody hell happened to you?'

'Some kids jumped me near my house last night.'

'How many of them?'

'I dunno. The usual bastards who always call me a Paki and try to kick my head in every time I walk down Wyld's Lane.'

'Enough is enough, Abs,' he protested. 'You've gotta call the police and file a report.'

'No, Timmy,' I said. 'Please, mate, please, drop it.'

'But why? I don't get it. It's not right that—'

'Timmy.' I raised my voice. 'Just drop it.'

He could see I was upset. He raised his hands, gesturing that he was only trying to help.

'Sorry, mate,' I said. 'I didn't mean to—'

'Don't worry about it,' he said sadly. 'I get it, but if you change your mind ...'

'Thanks.'

I spent that entire morning at school fretting about what I would do during the coming night. I had to formulate a plan and snap out of my reverie. I simply could not wallow in sadness.

A faint smile lifted the corner of my mouth when I imagined the voice of my father saying, as he'd used to, 'Does Rocky cry? Does Rocky cry?'

It still worked, but mostly as a joke.

At lunchtime I was in the dining room watching Timmy eat when Joe came and joined us. He had a CD Discman with him.

'Have a look,' he said, smiling. 'I love this thing.'

'That's pretty cool,' Timmy said. 'When did you get it?'

'A couple of days ago,' Joe said. 'Now I'm trying to sell my little pocket radio. Anyone interested?'

'How much?' Timmy asked.

'I dunno – a few quid,' Joe responded, not really caring. 'A fiver?'

'I'll give you two,' I piped up.

'Five?' Joe responded.

'Three, and that's my final offer.'

Joe did not even think about it – he just gave me his pocket radio, along with its headphones. It was the size of a cassette tape and had both FM and AM bands.

'You just need some batteries now,' Joe said.

'I've got loads in my locker,' Timmy said. 'You want a few?'

'Sure, thanks,' I said.

The radio had used to keep me company during the blackouts in Iran. I also hated being so bored in the evenings. I thought a radio might help. Three pounds was a lot of money, but I hoped it would be worth it.

As I watched Timmy eat, I realised that I could no longer buy whole loaves of bread because I would not have anywhere to store it. I would have to buy something every night.

To my delight, Timmy did give me some batteries when he'd finished his lunch. After school I changed into my tracksuit, locked up most of my remaining money in my school locker and headed to the public library.

On the way, I thought about how cold the previous night had been, so I stopped by the thrift store and looked for a blanket. I found one for only a pound, bought it and put it in my sack, then went on my way to the library.

I saw Carol, who checked up on me as usual. She was always concerned about my welfare and frequently commented on how much weight I was losing. Tonight she was particularly upset to see the bruise on my face. On my way out she gave me a Mars Bar, my favourite chocolate bar, which made my day. I smiled and thanked her and set out into the night.

I had decided that I would stay away from the town centre, so I headed towards Battenhall and beyond, towards the countryside. There the houses were much larger, with extensive gardens and no drunks or tramps. I walked and walked into the night, until I saw a big house with a low fence and a shed. I looked out for a dog but couldn't see one. There were no lights on downstairs, so I jumped the low fence and ran to the shed. I opened the door to find a dark, damp space containing a mower and some gardening tools. I very carefully closed the door behind me and moved the tools aside. It was so dark that I realised I needed candles, but there was no doing anything about that now. I wrapped myself in my blanket and lay down. It was really uncomfortable but certainly better than the night before.

After about fifteen or twenty minutes my eyes adjusted to the dark and I could see fairly well. There were hoes, rakes, spades and forks, and a large bag of grass clippings. I shifted to lie against it and covered myself with my blanket once more, happy to have something soft and comfortable at my back. Then I turned on my radio, put the headphones over my head crookedly so that they only covered one ear and fiddled with the FM tuner until the reception cleared.

I'd tuned into Radio Wyvern, and John Taynton's *The Late Show* was on. I had such a grin on my face as I lay there on that sack of grass listening to John. It was cold and I was sleeping in a shed, but the company of that voice changed everything. I was no longer so bored, and had less opportunity to think about all my problems. My radio was now my most treasured possession.

I unwrapped the Mars Bar and slowly ate it as I listened

to my radio. Despite the cold and all my worries, I was content in the dark in an unknown person's shed. Before I knew it, I was asleep.

I continued to live in sheds in the countryside for the rest of the week, always on high alert. My diligence and paranoia about being caught kept me out of trouble. I had one golden rule: never stay in the same shed two nights in a row, nor in the same week if possible. That first week I stayed in a different shed every single night.

I woke early on Saturday and left that night's shed before it was light. However, I did not have a paper round on Saturdays, and I had nowhere to go until lunchtime, when my cricket team had a game scheduled at school. I made my way to school regardless, where I showered then started to walk around the playground to see what was happening. I saw Reverend Charles next to the school minibus with a few kids from different years.

'Morning, Reverend,' I said with a smile. 'How are you?'

'I'm well. It's quite a lovely morning,' he responded in his joyful way. 'What are you doing here so early?'

'Just woke up early, sir, so I came to school early.'

'Well, this is the community service club. If you want to lend a hand, it would be very much appreciated.'

Reverend Charles was a short, stocky bald man, always clean-shaven, who liked nothing better than to change into his running shorts and rugby shirt and run alongside the river. It was obvious by the way he carried himself that he was a holy man, and that his job meant everything to him.

'Sir, would I be back in time for my game at noon? I'm in the cricket team.'

'Of course. We do this from eight to eleven every Saturday morning.'

'Then put me to work, sir.'

That day we went to a few elderly people's homes, took their shopping lists and money and did their shopping for them. We also helped clean their homes and did random chores.

When we got back to school at eleven, Reverend Charles approached me.

'So, Abbas, what did you think? Enjoy it?'

'Yes, sir.' I realised as I spoke that it had been a great distraction – I had not thought about anything but helping people for those few hours.

'Good. If you're keen, we meet every Saturday, and I can guarantee to have you back at school in time for sport,' Reverend Charles said with a kind smile.

I continued to do community service every Saturday for the rest of my tenure at King's – anything from cleaning cathedral benches and stalls to helping the elderly to serving at soup kitchens. It gave me a place to be on Saturday mornings when I had nothing else to do, and some longed-for company.

———

For the next ten weeks I slept in sheds each night. I was about to complete fifth form, my final year at Aymestrey, and I turned fourteen during this period. I lost a lot of weight, my clothes were dirtier because I could only clean them at school and there was nowhere really to dry them, and I was always very tired. Doing my paper rounds so early each morning, putting up a front at school and sleeping rough was just too much. The constant fear of being caught, or beaten or assaulted in some new and horrible way, made sleeping harder and harder. I became not only physically exhausted and weak but mentally exhausted as well, and very stressed. It felt as if I was being pushed to my limit, and I was not sure what I had left or how long I could continue. But there seemed no way out – if I breathed a word about Mehdi's neglect, I would be deported. Everything I'd worked for, everything my mother had sacrificed, would then have been for nothing. I was trapped.

One morning I woke up in a shed and I could not get up. I felt weak and shivery; I was sweating and had a sore throat and a cracking headache. I could not risk missing work because I did not want to lose my jobs – I needed the money badly. I hobbled to my first paper round and did it in great distress. I then went to Wyld's Lane to see Mr Patel.

'Morning, Abbas,' Mr Patel said cheerfully.

'Morning,' I said, wiping the sweat off my brow.

'Are you okay?' he asked.

'Yes.'

'No, you're not,' he said as he felt my forehead. 'You are burning.'

'I'm fine,' I said. 'I can do it.'

'No way,' he protested. 'Go home.'

'Mr Patel,' I said sternly, 'please. I need this.'

'You're fine. You never miss work. Today is on me. You won't miss pay.'

'Mr Patel, I can't.'

'You can – now go home.'

'Thank you.'

I was so relieved, but there was nowhere I could go to rest and recover; I had to go to school. I sweated through the entire day, feeling sick as a dog. I really wanted some medication, but I could not afford any. The cough syrups and painkillers I needed would have used up half of my weekly salary, which I needed for food.

I had not been that sick for a very long time. I could barely walk; I vomited several times; my fever grew worse, and I had no energy. I dared not ask to see Matron for fear that she would phone Mehdi. It felt like the longest school day I'd ever endured.

After school I went to the gym, sat in the shower and turned on the cold water. I was so hot. It felt good, and I hoped that the cold shower would bring my temperature down. I sat there letting the cold water wash over me for what seemed like an hour. Eventually I dragged myself out and put on my tracksuit. I staggered outside again and headed to the school library. I went upstairs and sat at a table, put my head on my arms and tried to rest. I wished I could sleep, or that I had somewhere better to go. I stayed there until it closed, went to the public library until it closed too, then began a two-mile walk into the countryside, feeling utterly miserable.

It took every ounce of my willpower to walk up the hill into the Nunnery Wood area. I found a house where I had stayed before and jumped the fence without my usual check for observers. In the shed I lay on the floor with my blanket around me. At first the relief of being able to lie down felt good, but soon my fever intensified and I was hot, sweaty and very thirsty. I needed water but I did not have any.

I lay there listening to my radio in the cold shed in the absolute dark, trying to concentrate on John Taynton, to take my mind off my misery, but I was getting hotter and hotter and realised I was slightly delirious. I decided to leave the shed and look around.

There was a hose attached to a tap beside the house. It was risky, but I crept up to the tap and turned it on, then dragged the end of the hose behind the shed. I took off my tracksuit and showered myself in water, shaking in the dark. The cold water felt painful against my skin, but I forced myself to endure it for as long as possible. Then I had a long drink. That felt very good. It soothed my insides, which also seemed to be overheated, and quenched my thirst. I remembered how my mother had always used to give me cold showers or put my feet in cold water when I'd had fevers as a small child.

I felt cooler. I put the hose back and retired to the shed again. I was drenched, and it was a cold night. I had no towel to dry myself with, so I tried to use my T-shirt. Suddenly I found myself sweating and shivering all at the same time. I turned on my radio, but just then the batteries died.

I burst into tears. I could not catch a break. I was shivering all alone in a shed at night. Apart from the day I had learnt of my mother's death, this was the worst moment of my life. I had been feeling alone for so long, but never like this. A huge surge of emotion overcame me. I was crying and shaking, wondering why I had suffered so much. I was so tired; I could not carry on; I was emotionally and physically drained. Apart from the clothes on my back, and the small radio with no batteries, I had nothing to my name, and my life was not improving, however hard I tried to work and stay out of trouble. In fact, my life was getting worse.

I felt black depression swallowing me as I cried, and I wished that I had died rather than my mother. My life had become worthless to me; I had nothing to live for. I had tried the right path and done my best to survive. But that fight had taken me to a dark and painful place, and now I did not want any part in it.

Why had my parents forsaken me? And Brian and Kate? I had done everything everyone had asked of me, and perhaps even more. Life just was not fair.

Morbid thoughts filled my head, and that night I seriously contemplated suicide. I took out my penknife and opened the blade, holding it against my wrist and sobbing while I tried to prepare myself.

As I did, the thought of Mrs Griffiths came to me. I could hear her voice again in my mind, telling me to do everything for my mother. I thought about it and pretended I did not care. But I did care.

Tears were still streaming down my cheeks – it made me even sadder to think that I could not put myself out of my misery – but I put my knife down and decided to try to sweat out the fever.

I stared at the condensation on the small shed window, which seemed to be weeping with me. It was one of the longest nights of my life. I would sweat and then shiver. My bones ached, my skin was sore and the fatigue was unbearable.

The next day I woke up at two o'clock in the afternoon, having missed both my paper rounds and most of school. I still felt terrible and hot, but I was a little better than I had been yesterday.

It was daytime and I did not know what to do. I peeked out of the window and saw that no one was about. I quickly left the shed and managed to sneak back onto the street. I trudged to Wyld's Lane to see Mr Patel, but when I walked in and tried to speak, he took one look at me and said, 'Go back to bed.'

'But—'

'I knew you were ill. I called Samani. You're okay … actually, you look like death.'

I did not have the energy to argue. I just held my arms out in thanks and left. I walked to school and waited near the tuckshop for school to end and for Timmy to appear. Kevin walked by and saw me in my tracksuit.

'Hey, gypo, you may want to think about a shower and some new clothes. Mind you, you won't have to blow anyone up. You can poison them with your stink.' He thought he was hilarious.

Eventually Timmy appeared. 'Abs, where have you been?' he asked.

'Can I ask a favour?'

'What have you ... oh sure, what?' he asked inquisitively.

'Promise you won't ask any questions?'

'Sure.'

'Can I stay at your house for the weekend? I just need somewhere to rest. I feel like crap.'

'Yeah! In fact, I'm not taking the bus today, my mum's picking me up. I'll ask her. She loves you, so it shouldn't be a problem.'

Soon Mrs Morris arrived. Timmy ran to the car and Mrs Morris got out and came over.

'Abs, my dear, are you okay?'

'Yes, thanks, Mrs Morris. Sorry to be a bother.'

'Oh my God,' she exclaimed as she felt my forehead, 'you're burning up. Who's been looking after you?'

'Am I hot? I hadn't noticed.'

'Get in the car.'

We got in and I immediately felt safe. Within minutes, I was asleep.

I woke up as the car pulled into the driveway.

'Timmy, can I have a shower, mate?'

'Yeah, sure, of course.'

I went to the bathroom and took a long, relaxing shower, then went to Timmy's bedroom. He was doing his homework.

'Mate, can I sleep in the spare room?'

'Knock yourself out. Do you need anything?'

'If you could get me a drink of water, I'll owe you one.'

'Sure.'

I went to the next bedroom and lay on the bed. I was about to close my eyes when Mrs Morris arrived with medication and a jug of orange cordial.

'Take this, my dear.'

'Thank you,' I said. 'I'm so sorry to—'

'Shhh, just rest. It's fine.'

'Thank you.'

I immediately fell asleep. I had been so tired. Just being able to lie down and relax made me feel so much better. The emotional aspect of healing was harder than the physical – emotional fatigue had really taken me to my limit. I did not wake up until mid-morning the following day.

I stayed the entire weekend with the Morris family, and Mrs Morris took good care of me, feeding me light meals and giving me lots of liquids, so that by Sunday I was feeling much better. I tried to leave so that I could do my paper round on Monday morning, but Mrs Morris would have none of it. She insisted that I stay one more night and leave in the morning with Timmy.

I managed to get through the next week without much incident. It was the last week of the school year. I was not entirely well, but I had enough energy to do my paper rounds and go to school. All was well until Friday morning after rollcall. Mr Gardner had finished his announcements, but as we started to leave I heard him call my name.

'Yes, sir?'

'Can you come to my office for a second, please?'

'Yes, sir,' I said nervously. I had never been summoned there before. My heart was racing; I was not sure if I was in trouble or not. I went and stood outside his office until he walked up with a smile and opened the door for me.

'Come in.'

I followed him into his small office. There were papers all over his desk and books on his shelves.

'Sit down,' he said, still smiling.

'Thank you, sir,' I said quietly and sat.

'So,' he said after a pause, 'how are you?'

'Very well, sir, thank you.' I kept it short and to the point but polite.

'Are you?'

'Yes, thanks, sir.'

'Really? Everything is okay?'

'Yes, sir. Am I in trouble, sir?' I asked, becoming concerned. 'I am fairly sure my schoolwork is good.'

'It is, it is,' he said as he looked at me pensively, 'but something isn't adding up, Abbas.'

'Sorry, sir?'

'Come on, Abbas – you're keeping your head down, doing what you have to do to get by, but you aren't the boy I met at the beginning of the school year. I'm just concerned…'

My heart was pounding and I was beginning to shake. How much did Mr Gardner know?

'I am not sure in what way, sir. I am sorry if I have let you down.'

'No, it's not that. You're doing just fine, although I know you can do even better. It's more that you are a growing boy and yet you have lost weight. Your white shirts look grey, you always seem to need a haircut, but most importantly I can see you are unhappy. You always look either stressed or depressed – sometimes both.'

'Sorry, sir.' I was trying to hold it together.

'No, don't apologise, Abbas,' he said, smiling kindly. 'That is my point. You are too young to be carrying the weight of the world on your shoulders. You don't have to be sorry. You haven't done anything wrong.'

'Thank you, sir,' I said, struggling to hold back my tears. His words had touched me. 'I mean, I am sorry to give you concern.'

'Listen, where is your guardian? I think we should talk.'

'He is really busy with his new business…'

'He hasn't been to a single parents' evening this year. He needs to come and see me next week. I will come in to school on my holiday specially.'

'I don't know if he can make it at such short notice, sir.'

'I need to see him, Abbas. If you want to continue at school, he has to come and see me. I want to find out what is going on.'

'Yes, sir.'

'Okay, now you have a good last day at school, and know that you can tell me … whatever it is you need to talk about. You can always speak to me.'

'Thank you, sir.'

I was sure he meant what he was saying, but I could not risk it. If I told him about my situation, I knew he would have been obliged to tell someone.

I spent the rest of the day worrying, and not just about where I'd be sleeping that night. I knew I had no choice but to call Mehdi.

FIFTEEN

That Friday night I managed to find a shed that was actually quite comfortable, as the owners had stored the cushions for their garden furniture there. I'd got more batteries from Timmy at school earlier in the week and I lay in comfort listening to my radio, thinking that this was one of my better nights. But the thought of getting hold of Mehdi and speaking with him worried me.

I eventually fell asleep and woke with the dawn. I left the shed without being noticed and began my walk to school, enjoying the warmth and beauty of the sunrise.

I had a shower and presented myself nice and early for community service. We only had to walk to the cathedral that day, to polish the benches, which did not take long. I was back with close to two hours spare before my cricket match started.

I went to the phone boxes just outside the school. Mehdi had told me that he was running a new bar in Cheltenham called the Green Room, so I called directory inquiries and was given the number for the bar. When I called the number, a woman picked up. I asked for Mehdi and she asked me to wait.

'Hello?' It was Mehdi's voice, his tone upbeat.

'Hi, Mehdi,' I said. 'It's Abbas.'

'What do you want?' he snapped, his tone changing abruptly.'

'I don't want anything, but—'

'But what?'

'It's just that Mr Gardner, my housemaster, wants to speak to you.'

'About what? Doesn't he know how busy I am?' His voice was getting louder and angrier.

'I told him that, but he insisted that you see him next week. He said that if I want to carry on going to school, he needs to see you.'

'Why does he want to see me?'

'I'm not sure.'

'Don't f—ing lie to me,' he yelled.

'I'm not – I really don't know,' I protested.

'You must have an idea,' he pressed. 'Tell me what he wants.'

'He just said that he's worried about me.'

'He's what?' he screamed.

'He's…' – I hesitated, scared to say it again – 'worried.'

'Worried about what?'

'Me. I dunno, just me,' I responded desperately.

'What about you? Stop playing games and tell me.'

'I'm not playing games. I promise, I don't know. I'm not sure. He just suggested that he suspected my living situation.' My voice had dropped to a whisper. I was so scared.

'You f—ing snitched! Didn't you tell him you live in a

house? A perfectly good house, which is more than most people have?'

'I didn't tell him anything. And I don't live in a house. I haven't lived anywhere for three months. I haven't told a soul, so please stop shouting.' I was crying now. Why was he shouting at me? I had done nothing wrong and had maintained my silence for all these long months.

'What are you talking about? You have the house. And now you have the gall to tell me you don't have anywhere to live?'

'The house has been boarded up for three months. I can't get in,' I retorted.

'What the hell?' He was silent momentarily while he thought. 'Then where have you been staying?'

'Here and there.'

'Don't be cute, Abbas. You think you're smart, but you're not, you selfish little shit. I lose my house and you use it to snitch on me and make yourself look good.' I had never heard him this angry.

'You okay, baby?' a woman's voice sounded in the background.

'Shut up,' he snapped, before turning his attention back to me. 'You need to tell me exactly what you told these people.'

'Mehdi, please believe me. I did not tell anyone anything.'

'You are a f—ing liar,' he screamed. 'I gave you everything and every opportunity, and this is how you repay me?'

'Mehdi, please, I promise, I didn't tell anyone anything,' I pleaded.

'F— you and your lies, Abbas. I'll tell you one thing. You go to the house and stay there. I am driving there right now. When I see you, I'm going to put you six feet under, like that mother of yours.'

I snapped. He could do whatever else he wanted, but he could not talk about my mother.

'F— you,' I said, then, 'f— you,' even louder. 'F— you and everything that you do.' I was screaming.

'F— me?'

'Yes, f— you,' I shouted. 'I'm done with you.'

'You are done with me? You're done with me when I tell you you're done with me. I'm going to kill you, you lying bastard, and that's not an idle threat. I will kill you.'

'Well, that would be better than what you've done to me since I arrived in this country,' I screamed, tears rolling down my face. 'I'm not scared of you anymore.'

'You son—'

I slammed the receiver down then banged it repeatedly against the phone box as I screamed, 'Aaahhh.'

I had lost control. I hated him so much. Mehdi had taken me to places that I'd never thought I would go. I was hysterical, crying – angry and scared at the same time.

I immediately began to walk to Wyld's Lane, then broke into a jog, running as fast as I could. Cheltenham was a bit over an hour away from Worcester. I got to Mr Patel's shop and asked for a piece of paper and a pen. He handed them to me, and in my panic, I scribbled a note.

Dear Mehdi,
I have not snitched on you. You are wrong. I
appreciate the fact that you signed up as my
guardian, and I am sorry for all the trouble I
brought into your life. To tell the truth, you are
not a good man, but I do thank you for helping
me come here. You hurt everyone around you. I
may have deserved some hurt because you did not

choose for me to come into your life. But Kate and the other people you lie to and cheat on, they are good people.

I am leaving. I am running away and will not bother you again. Don't worry about me. I will contact you to let you know I am okay. I am sorry it all worked out like this, but I know I am a constant bother to you, and that will not continue. Good luck with your bar, and I hope you find what you are looking for.

Bye,
Abbas

I took the note to Mehdi's old house and pinned it to the door, then I slumped against it there for a moment, wondering desperately what I should do next.

I knew that I could not continue to go to school; there was a good chance I would be found out and deported. I was exhausted, and at my wits' end. I felt like a failure because I was giving up, but I could not and would not continue to live like this.

In a bit over an hour I was supposed to be playing cricket with my team, and I did not want to let down my friends and teammates, so I decided to formulate a plan after the game. Where I would go, I did not know yet – I was too upset to think straight – but I was running away; I was certain of that.

I walked to the cricket fields very slowly, tears leaking from my eyes. I felt beaten. A huge wave of guilt swept over me, because I related this failure to disappointing the memory of my mother.

Somewhere in the midst of this emotional turmoil,

though, was a feeling of relief, because I could stop living the way I had been living now – I could stop lying to everyone at school. I hated worrying about being caught out there all the time, and I was so tired…

On the way to the fields, I had an idea. I went to another telephone box and called Fereydoun and Nadine. I had nothing left to lose.

'Hello?' It was Fereydoun.

'Hi, Fereydoun? This is Abbas.'

'Hi, how are you?'

'Good, thanks…' As I said that, I burst into tears. I could no longer pretend.

'What's wrong?' he asked sympathetically. 'Are you okay?'

'No. Listen, I'm so sorry to call you,' I sobbed, 'and you can ignore me. You have no responsibility when it comes to me, but I have no one else to call. Mehdi told me he will kill me, because he thinks I told the school about how I am living. I promise you, I didn't do any such thing.'

'He wants to kill you?' Fereydoun sounded incredulous.

'Yes, he wants to kill me, and honestly I am done. I can't carry on living like this. I am tired, I am filthy, I have no money, I have no food, and I am homeless.'

'What?' he exclaimed.

'I am running away after I play cricket today. I will most likely be sent back to Iran, but I don't care anymore. I'm not sure if you can help me, and I don't expect you to. You owe me nothing, but you once said to call if ever I needed anything.'

'And I meant it.'

'But this is big, Fereydoun,' I said, still crying. 'I am not sure what you can do, but you are all I have left.'

'Listen, go to your game and don't do anything until I get there. I'll be around two hours. Stay put, okay?'

'You don't have to—'

'Stay put,' he ordered.

'Okay.'

'I'll see you soon.'

'Fereydoun?'

'Yes?'

'Thank you.'

'Don't mention it.'

I tried to dry my tears and put on a brave face as I went to the cricket game. We were fielding first, and I was in my favourite position at cover. I loved it because it kept me busy.

The usual parents were watching their children play. We were well into the game when I heard the screeching of brakes in the car park next to the field.

I didn't need to look up to know who it was; I just put my head down and began to sprint as fast as I could towards the river at the far end of the fields.

I ran and ran, but I could hear Mehdi's footfalls as he caught up with me. Before I knew it, he'd grabbed me by the collar and thrown me to the ground like a ragdoll then leapt on top of me. I tried to get up, but he held me by my neck with his left hand and punched me in the face. I heard my nose break. Blood poured out of my nostrils, but I did not feel it. The shock was overwhelming. I was sure he would kill me. Part of me did not care, and yet I was fighting back, swinging my fists, knowing that I was not even remotely hurting him.

He kept shouting, 'You ungrateful, selfish bastard.'

I kept trying to hit Mehdi, but he pinned my arms down with his knees and looked at me with such hate.

'I'm a bad person? I'm a bad person? I'll show you how bad I can be.'

He raised his fist, and I knew that when it fell I'd be seriously injured. Suddenly I felt calm. I would not show him fear.

'F— you,' I said, staring straight into his eyes.

At that moment, someone grabbed Mehdi's arm. People pulled him off me. He shook them off and stalked towards the car park.

'You okay?' one of the parents asked.

'Yeah,' I said, shaken and humiliated. 'I'll wash this off in a jiffy.'

Everyone was in shock as they watched me walk over to the pavilion. My eyes watered as the pain hit me. In the pavilion bathroom, I gingerly pushed toilet paper up my nostrils and washed my face. I took off my blood-splotched whites – I knew my game was over – then I came out and saw all the boys staring at me, even though they were meant to be playing cricket.

It was then that I saw Fereydoun. He was talking to Mehdi, who was waving his arms up and down in fury. I walked towards them but kept a distance of several yards between Mehdi and me.

'Mehdi,' Fereydoun said calmly, 'can I speak to Abbas alone?'

'Do what you like with him,' Mehdi spat.

Fereydoun walked over to me and looked at my face, then he put his arm around me and started to walk me to a bench behind the pavilion, out of sight of Mehdi.

'Why not just get in the car with me?' he said when we'd sat down together. 'You'll never have to see him again. You don't have to say another word to him.'

'Just like that?' I asked.

'That simple.'

'Really? I asked, looking for the catch.

'Really.'

Fereydoun smiled at me. I had nothing to think about.

'Okay, let's go.'

We walked over to the car and I got in, and Fereydoun just drove me away. I never saw Mehdi again, as Fereydoun had promised.

———

After I'd had my nose patched up a short while later, in the same ER but luckily not by the same doctor, Fereydoun drove me to his home.

On the way there, the only thing he said was, 'Listen, I want you to stay with us. But Nadine and Fiz are away this weekend. When she comes back, I'll ask her. If she and Fiz are okay with it, you stay with us. Is that okay?'

'Of course. Thank you so much. I meant what I said to you. You have no obligations to me; I did not expect this.'

I spent the weekend watching television and eating takeaway with Fereydoun. I relished the comforts of ordinary life. Fereydoun, being a quiet man, let me have my own space in between our meals and television shows.

As much as I was enjoying my time there, I was still nervous. I did not know how Nadine would react to any of this. My future was in her hands.

On Sunday morning I woke up very early, came downstairs and sat on the sofa. I did not turn on the television, I just sat. The only thought going through my head was that my future would be determined by lunchtime. I sat there in a state of reverie.

Eventually Fereydoun came downstairs, too.

'It'll be fine,' he said, 'you just wait. How's the nose?'

'Not so painful.'

'Listen, you told us you had an assisted place at your school. Is that still the case?'

'Yes.'

'Well, if you'd prefer not to leave your school, and if Nadine is okay with it, we could pay for the difference so that you can be a boarder and stay with your friends, and come to be with us on your holidays.'

I didn't know what more to say than thank you.

Eventually Nadine and Fiz arrived home. As soon as Fiz saw me he ran towards me.

'Why didn't anyone tell me Abbas was coming?' he shouted. Then, 'Hey, what happened to your face?'

'You should see the other guy,' I said, ruffling his hair.

'Hi, darling,' Nadine said with a huge smile. 'Come here.'

'Hello,' I said, standing up nervously and wondering how this would play out.

She gave me a big hug and kissed me gently on both cheeks, then held me at arm's length and studied my battered face. She glanced at Fereydoun, who shook his head slightly.

'Fiz, can you go to your room, please?' Fereydoun asked.

'What? Why? Can Abbas come?'

'In a few minutes.'

'Why?' Fiz protested.

'Go,' Fereydoun ordered.

Fiz stomped upstairs in a sulk.

I sat back down on the sofa as Fereydoun pulled Nadine into another room. I could not hear their conversation, but clearly it was about me, and it seemed to go on for a long time. Eventually Nadine returned and sat next to me.

'Sweetheart, of course you can stay with us. Was there ever a doubt?'

'I don't know,' I said. I started to cry, not knowing how to thank her. I was overwhelmed. She hugged me close and I just wept silently. I had no words.

That night Nadine told me that she had spoken to Mehdi and he had agreed with the plan. Fereydoun and Nadine would apply to be my new guardians, and I would go back to King's as a boarder, starting when the new school year began in September. I would move from Creighton to Choir House, which was for boarders rather than day boys.

She also told me that Mehdi had made some arrangement with the bank so that they could open the house the next day and get the last of my property out of it. There were only a few possessions that I wanted.

Of course Nadine and Fereydoun both asked about what had happened to me after the house had been boarded up, but I found that I was not ready to speak to them about it yet, and so they did not find out the full truth until years later.

Nadine took me to Worcester on the Monday; Fereydoun had to work. We stopped at a few shops along the way, and she bought me an entirely new wardrobe of clothes. I'd had none worth mentioning prior to that. Besides those stops, we spent the rest of the journey in silence.

Eventually we arrived at Wyld's Lane. Sure enough, the wood that had covered the door had been taken away and a key left for us. I could see the look on Nadine's face as she glanced up and down the road.

Things in the house were exactly the way I had left them. Nadine strolled around and took in the conditions in which I had been living. Mould was now visible on most of the walls, and the house echoed.

Nadine still did not say anything. She walked upstairs to see the blankets on the floor, my makeshift bed. A few empty cans of baked beans with mould growing out of them were scattered about in the kitchen, and the loaf of bread I had left behind was completely blue with mould. Little bits of candle wax were all over the floor.

'Did Mehdi beat us here and take his furniture?' Nadine said.

'No.'

'It was like this when you lived here?' she asked. I felt like she knew the answer but wanted to hear me say something different.

'Yes.'

She came over to me and held me. Suddenly I felt her tears on my face, and that made me cry, too. She held me for a long time.

'It'll be okay now, Abs,' she said. 'It'll be okay.'

AFTERWORD

Dear Reader,

My first book, *On Two Feet and Wings*, tells the story of how my parents sent me to Istanbul, Turkey, to save me from being conscripted into the Iranian army as a nine-year-old. I survived for almost three months alone in Istanbul, waiting for a visa to what I'd imagined would be a safe life in England.

I'd thought that after having written *On Two Feet and Wings*, writing this story would be easier. I was wrong! This is a darker book, and I often found myself remembering bits of my past that I had perhaps subconsciously decided to forget. Bringing those experiences back up was at times very sad for me.

I am happy to have done it now, though. I am happy because I hope it will help to show others that even in your darkest hour, when you may think life cannot be any harder, you *can* reach a little deeper to find one more ounce of hope and courage – so believe in yourself and don't give up. If life seems hard, it probably means you are doing something worthwhile – and the experiences that reduce you to your weakest self sometimes lead to the greatest victories!

Abbas Kazerooni, California 2015

ACKNOWLEDGEMENTS

I would like to thank my wonderful and most incredible Australian Allen & Unwin team. I would most like to thank Nan McNab, Elise Jones and Erica Wagner for giving me the opportunity to continue my story in this sequel in Australia and for doing such a wonderful job of editing the book. Thank you ALL for the incredible job that you have done. It is rare to find editors who care about the author's voice in the way that you all have.

ABOUT THE AUTHOR

Abbas Kazerooni is a lawyer in California, USA. He is also a professional actor, writer and producer. Shows he has acted in include *Sleuth* on the London stage (lead role); the BBC's *The Land of the Green Ginger* (lead role); HBO's *The Hamburg Cell*; and the independent feature film *Universal Senses*. *On Two Feet and Wings* was his first book.